FIVE

BY

FIVE

FIVE
BY
FIVE

Aaron Allston
Kevin J. Anderson
Loren L. Coleman
B.V. Larson
Michael A. Stackpole

Edited by Kevin J. Anderson

WordFire Press
Colorado Springs, Colorado

Published by
WordFire Press, an imprint of
WordFire Inc
PO Box 1840
Monument CO 80132

ISBN: 978-1-61475-057-4

WordFire Press Trade Paperback Edition: March 2013
Printed in the USA
www.wordfire.com

CONTENTS

BIG PLUSH

An "Action Figures" Story

Aaron Allston

— 1 —

Doc

His booted foot, as long as I am tall, came down on me, grinding me into the black earth. All the air went out of me.

My body held together, though. It was made of hardier stuff than human skin and bone. I didn't black out.

The giant's boot covered me from my neck to below my feet, but my head was exposed and I could look up at him. One standard-issue human male, mid-twenties, dressed in camouflage uniform and green-black body armor, glaring down at me, forest canopy over his head.

He had no rifle, but reached for his hip holster.

I knew what was coming. He'd raise his foot and, before I could pry myself from the soil, he'd shoot me. I'd be as dead as my co-conspirators intended me to be.

It was not the way I wanted to spend my day.

* * *

I probably ought to turn the calendar back to explain how me getting stepped on came about.

Picture a living room, sort of triangular. The longest section of sky-blue wall, decorated with imbedded lighting and flexmonitors showing images of Chiron's forests, oceans, and mountains, is slightly curved because the other side of it is the exterior of a three-story, old-style habitat dome. The other two walls meet at a right angle. There's white carpet on the floor, the expensive self-cleaning kind, and comfortable puffy furniture everywhere. That's where I was five weeks before I got stepped on.

For an hour I'd been watching another giant, his head as tall as my whole body, as he napped on his recliner. I sat on the chair arm and waited for him to wake up. I didn't think he was going to die that day, but you never know what a sudden start might do to someone so old, so I didn't wake him.

His name was Dr. Bowen Chiang—Doc to me and most people who knew him. At this point he was about two hundred years old, and looking it. His white hair was so sparse it was almost gone and his skin was thin and translucent. He was skinny like so many old humans. He always wore pajamas those days because he was wealthy and eccentric and retired. The ones he had on now were jade-green silk.

I looked like him, too. Not the way he was then, but the way he'd been when he was thirty, when he first left on his emigration to Chiron. I had the tint to my skin and slant to my eyes that used to say "Chinese" to people who worried about that sort of thing, and my hair was thick and black, worn short. Of average height and build for a 'ganger male, I was, by human standards, handsome, with a face that Doc said belonged on the young bad-guy lieutenant in a martial-arts immersive. Doc told me these looks had served him well when he'd lived in a place called Singapore, designing house-cleaning robots and chasing women, before he got married.

You've probably never heard of Doc Chiang by that name, but you know him by another. When Chiron was finally terraformed, opening for colonists, he was on the first colony ship headed this way from Earth. His passage came at a reduced rate because he served as a programmer and systems maintenance engineer during the transit. And during those twenty long years, he never went into coldsleep.

Instead, he invented. By the time they made orbit above Chiron, he'd developed the first-generation Dollgangers.

There's been a lot of misinformation circulated about 'gangers. Let me set matters straight.

Start with a human-like skeleton made of sturdy metal composites. It stands anywhere from 175 to 250 mm tall. (I'm 225 mm, about average for an adult male.) Inside the skull, bones, and ribcage is machinery—a computer system, a plant producing nanite crawlers that diagnose and repair damage, reservoirs of materials for the nanites to use, communications gear ranging from broadband radio to microwave transmitters to laser, extensible microwires for direct data upload/download, voice synthesizer, sensors where the corresponding human organs would be, battery arrays…

Over all that is a musculature of hard-wearing memory polymers attached at innumerable points to the skeleton, and over that a realistic-feeling skin laced with a sophisticated neural net allowing for sensations like pain and pleasure. Throughout the whole body runs a peristalsis-based circulatory system that sends the nanites wherever they need to go.

And that's only the start. The skin, the facial features, are shaped to individual appearances, making each of us distinctive. We get realistic hair that, supplied and reinforced by the nanites, can grow. Realistic human eyes and skin colors. Fingernails and toenails. Functional genitalia—'gangers are anatomically correct.

But what made us a financial success and first made Chiron a profit-generating world was Doc Chiang's last innovation before the suits took control of the technology. That innovation was the personality template.

Dollganger programming starts with an unbelievably complex personality system derived from a real human. It might be calculated from a lengthy series of tests or reconstructed from analyses of archival recordings and guesswork. Then, add learning capacity, abstract reasoning, subconscious motivations, complex emotions. The coding is so complex it has to be designed in large part by other machines, and it's so intricate that it can't be overridden just by introducing patches of new code.

Though we're individuals, we have a lot of personality traits in common—cheerfulness, helpfulness, obedience. At least when we're young.

So the success of the Dollgangers was because each little guy or gal could be made in the likeness of someone specific—of the buyer, of a famous performer, of a planet's most glamorous model, of an unobtainable object of desire, of a long-dead son or daughter. Oh, yeah, and because we cost a fortune and some people would mortgage their whole futures just to have one of us.

There was just about no task we weren't put to. Quality assurance on assembly lines making expensive components. Entertainments. Exploration, whether cave strata or new wormhole routes—put us in a miniature spacecraft with a Q-drive and no life support and we'd navigate wormholes too small for human ships and come back with star maps crucial to space exploitation corporations.

And then there was the sex trade. I don't know the name of the bastard genius who invented the "gang-bangers," or Dollganger remotes. They weren't really 'gangers. They looked like us, but they were just sensor platforms, mindless, linked wirelessly to full-immersion body suits and helmets worn by meat people. A human could put on one of those rigs and link up with a gang-banger. Then everything that the remote experienced was felt by its human operator. Gang-bangers did a lot of things, but mostly they had sex with 'gangers. You want a night with supermodel Sasu of Earth or Derek Ayala, Sexiest Man on Arkon? Well, you couldn't get the real ones, but you could rent a gang-banger and some time with the 'ganger replica of one of those celebrities.

Which was fine in the early days. We were made to serve, to please. And we couldn't say no anyway. We were property. But over the years, the fact that all the emotional fulfillment was in one direction only began to make a difference.

And that's what the meat people never really grasped. Technically, yes, we were robots. But the War of Independence didn't come about because we were infected with bad code, as governments and news media always imply. It came about because we're living, feeling creatures.

Anyway, Doc. That's what Doc invented. He was the Dollmaker of Chiron, and it's by that nickname most everybody remembers him.

And here I was, perched on his chair arm, watching him sleep, watching him die.

Finally Doc's breathing changed. His eyes opened. He glanced over at me and smiled. He fumbled for his wire-rimmed glasses and put them on. "Bow. It's good to see you up and around." Unlike mine, his voice still carried traces of a Cantonese accent; he'd learned English and other languages well after reaching adolescence.

I cranked my volume levels so he could hear me speak. "Yeah, about that. My system clock and my mental processes clock are offset by nearly twelve hours. There's a big gap between my last memory and when I woke up in my charger-bed. Something happened to me."

He nodded, the movement languid. "What do you remember?"

"The *Rockrunner* shuttle. The heat shields."

* * *

In those days, Doc lived mostly off his patent royalties, much reduced as patent after patent lapsed. They maintained his home and kept him in essentials, but didn't allow for luxuries. Luxuries were my department. He rented me out to employers as a hazardous-environment systems maintenance guy, a vehicle specialist, a high-end mechanic. As old and experienced as I was, I earned good money for Doc.

I'd been just about done with one such contract when my memory skip occurred. *Rockrunner* was a metal hauler that made regular runs out to the system's metal-rich mining moons. We'd come back with a load and the command crew was getting ready for the return to planetside. But the mission commander saw odd readings on the shuttle's heat-shield diagnostics.

It was my job to find and fix the problem, of course. In a little full-coverage insulation suit, all crinkly silver, with magnetic boots and a clear bubble helmet, I went extravehicular on the shuttle's surface to look at the situation.

First I took in the view, of course. Dollgangers do have an aesthetic sense. From high Chiron orbit, I could see the planet of my manufacture dominate the sky. Two-thirds water, the land mass temperate zones full of forests, a hurricane pattern forming in the equatorial portion of the Ephialtes Ocean. The planet was half in daylight, with nighttime at about the midpoint of the continent facing me and racing westward. It was, well, gorgeous.

The damage to the heat shields wasn't gorgeous, but it also wasn't too bad. It looked like debris of some sort had scored a couple of forward belly shields. It would take a little work to fix—delaminate the damaged shields, remove them to the shuttle bay, put in a couple of fresh ones, laminate them in place.

I directed a microwave burst toward the cockpit to let the meat crew know the situation. They told me that Punch would assist me with repairs. Five minutes later, he was out there beside me in an identical insulation suit.

I'd known Punch for all my life. He'd been fabbed and awakened a week before I was. Property of *Rockrunner*'s owner partnership, he was the freighter's cockpit infielder, capable of acting as comm officer, navigator, or even co-pilot. He had a long, pointed, saturnine face that showed a lot of teeth when he smiled.

He wasn't smiling today. He was unusually quiet during the repairs. When we were laminating the second of the replacement shields, I bumped helmets with him and held the contact.

I adjusted my vocal tuners to make it easier to hear across the weird medium of plastic bowls. Talking this way, we wouldn't broadcast. "Let's hear it, Punch."

He shook his head. "I'll tell you when we're done. I want to talk to you. When it won't be conspicuous."

"All r—"

And that's where my memory ended, right there on that letter "R."

Eleven hours, thirty-nine minutes, forty-seven point four seconds later, I rebooted, woke up, and found myself in my own charger-bed in Doc's dome just outside Zhou City, with no idea what had happened.

* * *

I told Doc all this, except the part about Punch wanting to talk to me.

He nodded. "Bow, you got flash-fried yesterday."

I frowned. Coronal mass ejection, outside a planetary atmosphere, can be pretty dangerous to meat people, but most times it doesn't do any damage to a Dollganger. When it affects us at all, the damage is usually limited to a reboot. To us, it's like fainting, then coming to a minute later.

The sympathy on Doc's face didn't relent as he continued. "A bad one. The pulse put you down and prevented a normal restart."

"And Punch?"

He didn't answer immediately. I had a sinking feeling in my gut.

"They... didn't find Punch. At best guess, he lost brain functions and his transponder went offline. He probably drifted away from the shuttle."

"His magnetic boots—"

"He must have kicked himself free of the hull in a muscular spasm. They think his orbit decayed and he went through reentry."

I sat down. I couldn't say anything.

Okay, yeah. People praise the programming of the Dollgangers for the way it simulates human emotions. I can tell you, there's nothing simulated about it, and I was floored.

Punch wasn't really a close friend. We didn't pal around on our time off. But he was cheerful, reliable, outspoken, funny.

And now he was dust in the high atmosphere, and I was lucky not to be there beside him.

"I'm sorry, Bow." Doc's voice made it clear that he really was. "Look, I don't need to line up anything for you in the next few days. Take some time off."

— 2 —

Lina

In something like a state of shock, I drove my six-wheeled buggy to the west end of Zhou City and beyond.

In the 'ganger lane of the westbound road, just outside the city limits, where landscaped human neighborhoods gave way to dense, two-century-old forest, a dog spotted me and gave chase. It was a good-sized animal, a floppy-eared tan hound.

Dogs seldom mess with 'gangers, but when they do, they can inflict a lot of damage. This one seemed content to chase, wag, and bark, but it was fast enough to gain on my buggy. So before it got too close I hit a dashboard control. This caused a cloud of lemon-scented stink to jet out of the buggy's rear end. The dog ran into it, then ran off, offended but unhurt.

I turned off the human highway and onto the dirt road leading to Atlas Hill. My buggy's motor strained as I took the road up to the top. At the hill's summit, the road leveled off and entered the broad dirt lot surrounding the squat gray building that was the entrance to the Warrens.

I parked as close to the entrance as spaces allowed; there were plenty of other 'ganger transports, especially buggies, parked already. Then I wandered through the vast, human-scale doorway in front and to the first of the ramps leading down.

Meat people had their own ideas about what life should be like for Dollgangers. In their vision, on the downtime hours we needed for recharging, maintenance, and (they eventually discovered) socializing and creative expression, we'd go to the dorms set up for us by our corporate owners or the 'ganger-houses bought for us by individual owners. I had one of those dwellings, a Dollganger-scaled dome that was a miniature replica of Doc's house; it occupied a small ground-floor back room in his dome. Dorms and dollhouses were the only structures built for us.

But 'gangers, like meat people, have a need to spend time in environments of our own making. So we built the Warrens.

It had been one of the habitats built for human bioengineers during the transitional years when Chiron was undergoing the last stages of terraforming. They'd used explosives, cutters, and tunnelers to carve burrows throughout a hard rock hill. They'd lived in its tunnels and squared-off caves for years, then had stripped out most of the equipment and abandoned the site the instant the Harringen Corporation began landing prefabs in what was to become Zhou City. A century ago, 'gangers found the place and begun building their own environment inside.

There were apartment blocks and individual homes, some of them with close-cropped lichen lawns. You could find works of art—murals on the walls, sculptures, motorized mobiles, lightshows in constant motion in black-walled chambers. There were businesses: bars and restaurants, dance halls, ball fields, theaters, repair shops.

Twenty-story skyscrapers engineered from resin-saturated cardboard over foam-steel scrap skeletons dominated the main atrium. A stadium occupied what had once been a gymnasium. Housing sprawled through the innumerable former laboratories and dorms. Buildings made from scrap sometimes collapsed or their inhabitants, tiring of unlovely angles and sagging floors, would dismantle them and replace them with something new. It was a one-eighth scale city undergoing constant renovation.

I once had a home in the Warrens, but it kept being dismantled or burned out whenever I was away, so I gave it up. Dollgangers of my sort, the ones who get on really well with their owners and got special privileges—plushes, we were called— weren't too popular with those who didn't, and there were places in the Warrens where I just didn't go. Even now, as I walked, distracted, down Royal Road between the open-air Top Shelf Club, which had once been a set of heavy-duty warehouse shelves, and the monolithic black Simulator Palace, I heard

Bluetop, a Zhou City waterworks engineer, call out, "Hey, Big Plush, kissed any new asses lately?"

I ignored him, kept my eyes mostly on the gray tunnel ceiling ten stories up. And in a few minutes I reached the King's Palace.

The King was even older than I was. He claimed to be the first 'ganger replica of a historic figure, and nobody had evidence otherwise. His movement algorithms reflected his antiquity. He was full of limb twitches and facial tics that were the result of old, never-optimized code. He wore his rhinestone-studded jumpsuits, he served drinks and sang, he sneered at his customers but didn't mean it. Given his freedom by the terms of his owner's will when that grand old dame died half a century ago, he built his bar, with game rooms to the side, rental bedrooms above, neon everywhere, to look like a casino from one of Earth's great gambling centers of centuries ago.

Now I sat at the King's bar and nursed a drink. Dollgangers don't need to eat or drink much, just a few lubes and materials saturations for our nanoplants to use for maintenance, but we have taste sensors, so our food and drink makers are all about creating taste combinations that delight, surprise, offend, or remind. My choice today was a Greasepaint Surprise, a thick, chalk-white concoction that tasted as good as it sounded. But it was Punch's favorite, so I drank it in his memory.

There were a few other bar patrons at this hour. They tended to ignore me. The King returned from serving one of them and plunked his elbows down on the bar before me. "He'll be missed. Punch."

I snorted. "Will *you* miss him, King?"

He thought about that and adjusted his tinted, for-cosmetic-purpose-only glasses. "No, I surely won't. I barely knew him. But *you* will. So he'll be missed. The logic of my statement is irrefutable, thankyouverymuch."

The stool next to me creaked as someone settled onto it. I glanced over and my heart skipped a beat.

Okay, sure. Dollgangers have no hearts, so there's nothing to skip. But the coding at the core of our individual behavior is inherited from human emotions, including physical reactions to those feelings. So seeing a gorgeous female does to me what it does to a straight human male.

Too bad it was Lina.

That's not her full name. A Shavery Corporation safety engineer, named by a middle manager who should have been drowned at birth, she bore the unfortunate moniker of Thumbelina 1109-X-Ray-Baker. But to herself, and to all of us, she was Lina, and she'd give you hell if you used the full version of her first name.

I don't know who her creators had modeled her on, but they'd chosen well. She was small and lean, with coloration Doc referred to as Mediterranean. She had long, straight dark-brown hair and a face that looked like it belonged in old immersives from back when they were called movies. Her human original had apparently been a dancer and her movements were graceful, fascinating. Today, she'd already changed out of the lime-green Shavery Corporation jumpsuit that was the duty uniform for their 'gangers, and she wore a burgundy skirt and white peasant blouse; she was barefoot, as was usual in her off-duty hours. On her right cheek was the small image of a rose—not a tattoo, because Shavery would never have allowed that, but paint that she'd wash off before reporting for her next shift.

Yeah, Lina was hot, and that means the same thing to 'gangers that it does to meat people.

On the other hand, the nicest thing she'd ever brought herself to call me was Big Plush.

But this time Lina looked at me like she suddenly gave a damn. "Bow, are you all right?"

"You heard about Punch, then."

"Yeah."

"I'm coping." I tilted my glass at her. "Even though he had the worst taste in drinks."

"Have you had any weird thoughts or dreams since it happened?"

I shook my head. "That's a strange question."

"Any hint that maybe you've had your transponder modded, or had a new one installed?"

That caused me to set my glass down. "Now you're talking paranoid."

"I don't think I am. Bow, we need to get you checked out. Go ahead and settle up."

The word "we" raised some flags in my mind. She could have just meant herself and me, but Lina's dislike of me wasn't just an individual antipathy. There was a whole population of 'gangers who constantly talked about freedom from the meat people. She was one of them.

Her interest made me curious. I glanced past the King at his scanner, the gleaming four-sided black post rising behind the bar. In my mind's eye, I called up my tab, paid it with Warrens credit, and added an okay tip.

The King frowned. "You could do better than that."

I frowned back. "You could have pretended to like Punch."

— 3 —

BeeBee

Lina took me to BeeBee's BodyWerks.

I'd heard about the place over the years but never had an idea where it was. It turned out to be several levels down in a deep chamber where the terraformers had set up their original transformers, converters, pumping stations, and other infrastructure machinery.

I'd been on the crew that repaired and restored the pumping station. Now, to my surprise, as Lina and I turned the final corner bringing us behind the floor-to-ceiling block of machinery and were out of sight of other 'gangers, a floor-level back panel of the station housing slid aside, revealing a 'ganger-scale portal. Lina preceded me in and the panel slid shut behind us. Inside, our ears were hammered by the rhythmic clanking of the old machinery.

Since I'd last seen the station interior, maybe fifty years previously, it had clearly been worked on. Some of its old-style systems had been replaced with more modern solid-state gear, opening up a lot of room in the huge casing. Dollganger-scale rooms, stairs, and elevators, all painted black with glossy chrome and silver appointments, had been installed.

Years back, after decades of serving the Chiron Defense Force as a demolitions expert, after being blown up and fully restored three times, BeeBee had burned out her transponder and disappeared, living as a fugitive in the Warrens. She traded her mechanical expertise for supplies, equipment, and favors. I'd run into her a number of times, occasions when she let me know just what she thought of plushes, then scrammed in case I called in her owners. I didn't, but plushes were always suspected of ratting out 'gangers who broke the rules.

Lina and I climbed several flights of stairs, up to a broad, low-ceilinged chamber where the sound of water pumping was much reduced. There, against one black wall, sat a scratch-built charging and maintenance bed. It was a chrome-plated steel tubing frame with electronic gear, some of it naked circuitry, laced all through the framework. The bed surface itself was a 'ganger-scale mattress unattractively wrapped in clear plastic. On the opposite wall was a black desk which looked like it had been modded from a human-scale ammo case, It supported a bank of monitors. BeeBee sat in a fake-leather office chair there.

She looked as unhappy as if she'd just been drinking a Greasepaint Surprise. She barely glanced at me, but gave Lina a full-bore "You had to do it" look.

BeeBee, like Lina, was nice to look at. So many 'gangers are, regardless of whether their personalities matched. BeeBee was tall, facial features that were all dewy-eyed ingenue, body that filled out her black jumpsuit in all the right ways. Ages ago, she had cut her original long blond hair into a bob and dyed it black, and she wore big reflective-lens sunglasses that hid her eyes.

Shaking her head, she turned back to her monitor screens. "On the dissecting table, plush."

I stretched out on the mattress. "Good to see you, too, Boom-Boom."

Her shoulders rose a little. She didn't much care for that nickname or the others I'd coined for her, including Ball-Buster and Ballistic Barbie. No one knew what her original name had been.

Lina helped pull the direct-link gloves onto my hands. Looking like human-style leather work gloves, they had braided cables of transparent data lines leading from the cuffs into the machinery of the bed. As soon as I had them on, I felt probes extrude from the inner fingertips and creep under my fingernails, where they jacked in.

I suppressed an expression of distaste. Direct links are damned intrusive, pleasant only during sex.

Screens lit up in front of BeeBee, showing graphical schematics and scrolling screens of data. I was surprised she wasn't just receiving all that stuff wirelessly, but then it made sense—she probably limited radio traffic in her shop to keep sensor-bots, which sometimes entered the Warrens, from detecting her.

Looking at the data, she shook her head. "No overt sign of recent mods. Let's see what the tests tell us." She typed a quick command on a virtual on-screen keypad.

A pop-up authorization box appeared in my vision, requesting access to my memories, permission to alter data, permission to thrash my hardware. Grudgingly, I approved the first and third choices.

Now, imagine suddenly being plunged back into previous events of your life, immersively, with those events sometimes stuttering, skipping, time flowing forward and backward, images and sounds overlapping. Imagine your limbs twitching uncontrollably, sometimes in sequence, sometimes randomly or all at once. Imagine the sensation of your internal fluid pressure rising to the point that you're certain you're going to pop, then dropping until you almost black out.

Imagine that going on for half an hour and it feeling like two days.

When it was done, I was happy to yank the gloves off and clamber, still twitching, free from that device of torture. I leaned against its metal headboard while BeeBee clucked over the data.

Then she looked up at Lina. "It was not a natural power-down. I'm sure he tracked for an hour or more after the break in his memory … and then he was zapped."

I glared at her. "I'm right here."

She glanced at me over the top of her glasses. I could see her weird red pupils, mods she'd acquired to replace her original sky-blues. "Quiet, plush. Free people are talking." She returned her attention to Lina. "But there's no sign of new programming or hardware. His one transponder is stock, factory issue. Ancient."

Lina arched an eyebrow at BeeBee. "And?"

"And, nothing. I still say no. For the record."

"Punch trusted him."

BeeBee gave her a you're-dumber-than-a-motorized-wheelbarrow look. "And now he's dead."

"Sorry, BeeBee. It's my call." Lina turned her attention back to me. "I have a recording I want you to see." She held up a hand toward mine, fingers outstretched.

I hesitated. A really good technician—like me, like BeeBee—could potentially disguise harmful code as innocuous data. Still, dammit, I wanted all the facts. I brought my right hand up to her left, fingertips to fingertips.

Probes stretched from under two of my fingernails and slid under her corresponding nails; probes of two of hers slid under mine. I detected an audio/video file coming in and authorized it being saved. My internals found no malicious code in the file. A moment later, Lina pulled her hand away.

I activated the file. It showed Punch in the purple jumpsuit he'd been wearing the day we repaired the shuttle. Behind him was a gray wall marked with stray blotches of black paint and what looked like insect droppings. This was probably the interior of a ship's compartment wall on *Rockrunner*. Every 'ganger had hidey-holes at his place of work.

Looking more serious than usual, Punch spoke. "Today I'm going to talk with Bow. If something goes wrong, I'll fry myself before I let them have any of my data. But I don't think that's going to happen."

There was a skip, and there he was again, same clothes but more rumpled. He looked a little relieved. "Talked to Bow. He didn't commit, but it's clear that it's weighing on him. I give it better than fifty-fifty."

Then the recording ended.

I checked the time stamps. The first segment was recorded hours before he and I repaired the shuttle. The second was about an hour after my memory of the repair job terminated—a time when I was supposed to be unconscious and Punch drifting down toward his final incineration.

What the hell had Punch told me?

BeeBee doubtless thought that I'd turned him in. But she had to know I didn't remember any such event. Was I guilty of betraying Punch but innocent by reason of amnesia? Not even I knew.

Lina, regardless of her distaste for me, had to believe I was innocent. Otherwise she wouldn't have made contact, exposing both herself and BeeBee to betrayal.

I looked between them. "What did Punch tell me?"

Lina jerked her head toward the exit. "Let's take a walk."

* * *

Lina and I walked the High Road.

The Warrens constituted a city built by anarchic cooperation, with anyone contributing anything he wanted. Some of the stuff was pretty strange. Sculptures welded together from discarded human-sized appliances, amusement park rides cobbled together from radio-controlled toys, dance floors fashioned from tough old monitor faces. The High Road was an engineering impossibility, miraculous because it was still up—an elevated walkway, rising in places to eight meters above the city floor, welded from scrap by geniuses and idiots. It swayed under the weight of pedestrians and was sometimes the target of medieval-style siege engines. But since so few 'gangers actually wanted to risk injury on its dangerous heights, it was pretty private, and Lina and I could walk its length, gripping the uneven rails to either side, without bumping into anyone else.

We had stopped midway along the walkway three meters above the summit of Lemuel's Needle, a wire-frame Egyptian-style obelisk made of struts and cables, its interior open for all to see. At its summit, an amorous pair of guys, when not grazing on each other's necks, waved up at us. Lina watched them without really noticing them. ""It was top secret. But a replacement-parts order that went off-course tipped us off."

"To what?" I figured that if the rail gave way at this exact moment, I'd plummet and smash into the top of the Needle, flattening the two lovers. I wondered how much of the Needle the impact would collapse.

"A ComFab. A compact nanotech fabrication unit, Bow. Set up for 'gangers. We know where and when it's going to be ready for delivery."

A chill gripped me. It was like discovering that I'd walked up to the edge of a thousand-meter clifftop without noticing, and one more step would send me on a long, fatal fall. I turned so that I was facing her square on, not just looking at her. The walkway swayed under my feet.

Understand, 'gangers have always considered ourselves as living beings, a species. But we don't reproduce. There were no 'ganger babies or children. Creation of new 'gangers took place in automated fabrication units. The units of a century and a half back were full-sized factories, but modern nanotech-based fabbers could fit on a full-sized hauler trailer.

All fabbers were in the hands of humans, of course. They cost as much as a continent on a newly-terraformed colony world. One of them could jump-start a whole planetary economy.

And valid or not, one of the stated reasons the meats didn't class us as a true life form was that we couldn't reproduce without their help. The unstated reason behind the reason was that we were far too valuable to be allowed to "breed in the wild."

But if a fabber set up for Dollganger production fell into our hands…

Lina looked up at me as solemnly as if she'd been telling me about meeting the human God.

It took me a moment to find my voice. "You're going to steal it."

"We sure as hell are. And we need you, Bow." Lina's voice was barely loud enough for me to hear. And neither of us was transmitting wirelessly for clarity; we didn't want any part of this conversation to be overheard. "To do this, we need vehicles. Megas. Weapons. On all of Chiron, you're the 'ganger with the most access, the most experience with these things."

"Dammit, Lina, there are only two ways for this to end. Fail, and the humans wipe out all the participants and probably a lot of innocent 'gangers as well. Succeed, and we have to hide for years while the humans try to find and exterminate us ... and they'll still wipe out 'gangers who had nothing to do with the operation."

She nodded. "Either one is better than what we have now."

"You're not speaking for all of us. You're not speaking for me."

"I know." An expression crossed her face, anger at odds with the flower on her cheek, doubtless some bitter recrimination of the plushes. But she held it in check, unwilling to insult someone whose help she needed.

I looked out over the old atrium, at the 'ganger city of discarded scrap shaped to our tastes. The atrium walls were covered in mirrored polymers, giving the place an illusion of greater size and allowing me to look at my own reflection an apparent hundred meters away.

I liked my life the way it was. I felt no need to be involved in the insanity Lina was proposing.

But then I looked at her, at the yearning on her face, and I hesitated. If I said no, I was deciding to keep her and others like her as they were. People of no consequence who could be endangered, used up, even murdered by their owners with no consequence except financial loss.

I looked down at the two lovers. Arms around each other, they now descended the internal stairs of the Needle. They'd forgotten all about us.

I returned my attention to Lina. "I have to think about this."

— **4** —

Stand-Ups

I sat on Doc's recliner arm and watched him sleep.

He had always treated me well, with fairness and affection.

Except ... the scrubbing of part of my memory had to have been done with his permission. Maybe he'd done it himself. He certainly had the skills.

Why had he done that?

To protect me, obviously. I had to assume Punch had slipped up, been detected, been pursued. He'd fried out his own mind rather than be captured—otherwise Lina and BeeBee would have already been picked up. And he hadn't told me about the ComFab, had probably just hinted that a group needed my help on some crazy independence-related plan.

Then, because I'd been in protracted contact with Punch, I'd been zapped and examined. The authorities had found that I hadn't agreed to help Punch. They'd returned me to Doc. Doc had purged the Punch conversation from my memory so I wouldn't follow up on it.

But whatever his good intentions, Doc had messed with my memory, something he'd promised he would never do. He'd betrayed that promise.

I watched him breathe, and wondered how much longer he'd live. A world without Doc seemed like an unlovely and spooky place.

If I helped Lina and BeeBee, I'd have to leave Doc forever. I wouldn't be with him as he got older and more frail. I wouldn't be there as his need for my help increased.

I'd be betraying *him*.

Doc or the 'gangers. My maker or my kind. Someone who loved me or a group of revolutionaries who hated me.

The past or the future.

Some 'gangers can cry. I'm not one of them, no microtube tear ducts or tear fluid reservoirs in me, but I felt a burning in my eyes that meant I needed to.

* * *

The next day I became a member of the Stand-Ups. Yeah, the original Stand-Up Gang of Chiron, the instigators of the War of Independence.

There was BeeBee, in charge of internal security. I knew she'd be good at it, like a cat is good at convincing mice to stay still.

There was Richter, skinny and pointy-jawed and cerebral. Richter was the overall leader of the Stand-Ups, in charge of planning and coordinating.

There was Memnon, whose career as an entertainer—you'll remember the Krazy Keys, the troupe who played full-sized keyboards by dancing on them—seemed to have nothing to do with his Stand-Ups role as field commander.

Lina, youngest member of the conspiracy, was in charge of personnel, both recruitment and management.

And then there was me, the oldest, in charge of materiel—defining, obtaining, modifying, accounting for them. In a world where every pot and pan has its own transponder and its current location was tracked by computer, having the right materiel to do this job was a monumental task. It was true, there weren't that many 'gangers in all human-occupied space who could pull it off, and I was probably the only one on Chiron.

Looking at the other Stand-Ups, I felt dismay. I had respect for all of them, but where were the big guns of the 'ganger independence movement? Where was Petal, whose rich, soul-filling voice we first heard in the broadcasts after the Settlers' Day disaster all those years ago? Where was Pothole Charlie, who had led so many wormhole mapping expeditions and brought his people back alive?

Actually, I was kind of relieved not to see Pothole Charlie. He had coined the term "plush," had been the first to call me Big

Plush, hated me worse than anyone, all because of my affection for a human. He would have made life hell for me if he were one of the Stand-Ups.

In a tiny cave scores of meters under the Warrens, with a battery-pack LED fixed overhead for light, we sat around a 'ganger-scale card table and plotted the future of our race.

Richter got right to it. "We don't know how to fight, and we're going to have to."

Memnon smiled, his teeth gleaming white in his ebon-colored face. "Movement is movement. Kinetics are kinetics. I can teach our soldiers to *move*."

BeeBee gave him a red-eyed look over the tops of her sunglasses. "Can you teach them to put a bullet in the brain of a meat soldier? Without hesitating, without flinching? That's what we need."

Memnon shut up. We all shut up.

Dollgangers don't fight. Well, we do, among ourselves, for the same reasons that meat people do in social situations, but we're no good at it. And we don't wage war. Age-old programming and cultural inhibitions make it nearly impossible for us to initiate violence directly against meat people.

Then I realized that I had the answer. A partial answer. "According to something Doc Chiang told me before any of you were fabbed, our deep-down proscription against violence is an enhancement of a natural human inclination against deadly force. Yeah, like all animals, the meats engage in dominance behavior, but it's supposed to end when one side surrenders or slinks away. They have a built-in resistance to killing … which their leaders learned to overcome when warfare became scientific, back on Earth. One of the secrets was conditioning."

They looked at each other, blank.

I sighed. "I'll misappropriate us some interactive shooter immersives. But we'll need crack programmers and artists to re-render the content, make the targets explicitly human, make the violence extremely realistic. Those of us who can stand it will go through these immersives over and over again until it starts to get easy." The thought actually made me a little sick, but I tried to hide the fact. "That's one step. Here's another. We'll be doing most of our fighting from inside megas. It might be best to run the megas only on instruments and cameras—and to have filters for the camera images to make them, I don't know, more stylized. Less horrible."

"That ... might work." There was grudging acceptance in BeeBee's voice.

Richter smiled. "All right. Memnon, that's now your department. Next item on the agenda. We're all now in resource-gathering mode. Maximum security on all communications ..."

* * *

So in chronicles of the revolution, my entry will talk about Bow, who conceived the conditioning the 'gangers used to make themselves killers. Hooray, me.

But what I mostly did for the operation was steal and modify vehicles.

I told Doc that I'd like to do some groundside work. Luck was with me and I was able to accept a contract with Harringen, the manufacturer of the ComFab, in their transportation and motor pool division. I volunteered for "reclamation projects"— vehicles and machinery too badly worn or damaged for the rank-and-file mechanics to want to mess with.

Well, I messed with it. I repaired some vehicles but only put about half back in service, storing the rest with notations that they were waiting for back-ordered parts. I also sabotaged perfectly good equipment and did the same with it.

I stole a lot of megas. Megas are in service only where Dollgangers are found, so you may not be familiar with them.

They're vehicles, robots without self-direction, shaped roughly like humans but massive and distorted. Some are only a meter tall, some as tall as three meters. They have 'ganger-sized cockpits in their chests or heads. Arms and sometimes legs are articulated, and on many models there are treads where human feet would be.

There are lots of different kinds. Mostly I concentrated on forklift megas, medium-tall vehicles with upper arms that could elongate, lower arms optimized for lifting cargo. Forklift megas are very tough.

I also needed, and found, a piloting mega. This type of machine is no bigger than a normal human man and has especially good articulation of limbs and hands. It can occupy the cockpit of a human-scale vehicle and pilot it. On Chiron, I had more experience with piloting megas than any other 'ganger.

Most megas were painted in eye-hurting alternating yellow and orange stripes and had a rotating yellow light on top, which made them really ugly but easy to see. I repainted the ones I stole, giving them a forest camouflage pattern in greens and browns. I got rid of their rotating lights and transponders.

I also stole small ground haulers and trailers. The Stand-Ups supplied me with a crew of workers; I cleared all security measures out of an entry route involving drain pipes and air ducts so they could sneak into my warehouse to work.

Then there were the weapons. My crew built a few different varieties that could be fitted onto megas or haulers.

Most common were the railguns. Take parallel lengths of conductive railing and a power source, assembling them as an electromagnet. That assembly goes on the mega's arm. On the corresponding shoulder is a magazine holding short lathed sections of steel cylinder or similar-shaped projectiles consisting of ferrous junk—ball bearings, bolts, nuts, broken pieces of tools, filings—in a ceramic casing. A feeder from the magazine drops the projectile to the near end of the weapon. Point the weapon, activate it, and the magnetics accelerate the payload to several times the speed of sound. Nothing short of heavy armor or military-grade shielding can stand up to that. Of course, you can't have anyone, human or 'ganger, standing close to the weapon when it goes off, because the heat it generates fries people dead—and invites retaliation from heat-seeking missiles. And insulating the mega against damage from the magnetic pulse is an issue.

BeeBee and her people made explosives charges—lots of plastic explosives and a few small fuel-air payloads. Compressed-air underlugs affixed to mega arms were easy rigs for us.

And we had the simple, one-shot horrors we called claymore cannons or shotgun cannons. On a trailer bed, mount a durable metal tube and gearing for aiming it. Pack the bottom of the tube with an explosives charge and pack a mass of scrap metal on top of that. Then fill the trailer with more of those cannons, a half-dozen or twenty.

We had plate-metal shields and other weapons, too, everything so low-tech that it was ridiculous by modern warfare standards—ridiculous, but canny. Dollgangers are great at setting up communication networks in a work environment, meaning that we can feed each other sensor data, do distributed processing on range-and-elevation calculations, and so on. Having no radar-based weapon systems meant we couldn't alert a target with a radar lock. Ditto laser painting.

Then there was Scarecrow. He started out as a thoroughly trashed emergency-response training robot. Once upon a time, covered in simulated skin, he'd run around on fire or with simulated shrapnel wounds pouring out simulated blood so human emergency responder trainees could tackle him, put him out, patch him up, resuscitate him. When he came to us, his top half had been crushed in an accident with a tracked vehicle. We pried and hammered his upper proportions back into shape, replaced his cables and servos, installed a 'ganger-sized pilot's chair and controls in the chest, dressed him in human clothes neck to foot, and fabbed up a realistic-looking head. He wouldn't stand close inspection, but from a distance of five meters or more he looked pretty human.

* * *

Whenever the subject of all this preparation comes up, people, both meat and 'ganger, inevitably ask, "Why did you gear up for war? Why didn't you just arrange the theft of the ComFab? When the first human died, it was sure to make them hate you."

Yeah, but. Our goal wasn't just to steal the ComFab. It was to say, "We are a life form." It was especially to make it clear, "You can no longer kill us without suffering the consequence.

Your lives are not more valuable than ours." We had to make it understood that, like most species, we would fight to live.

If attacked, we had to kill, and we knew it.

* * *

Back in the Warrens and elsewhere, the other Stand-Ups recruited, trained, planned. I didn't see them much, though I did go into the Warrens every other day for training on the shooter immersives. In a simulator theater, I'd sit in a reclining chair and slide my hands into the gloves, then I'd be plunged into what increasingly was a vision of Hell.

Around me would be heavy forest. I'd be in one of our megas, a railgun fitted to the arm. And meat men and women would attack me, sometimes shooting from a distance, sometimes rushing forward to bring short-range weapons like grenades to bear.

And I'd kill them.

Dollgangers don't throw up. The materials we consume go into our nanoplant reservoirs as soon as we internalize them. But the urge, inherited from humans, can hit us at appropriate times, and during these immersives it hit me again and again.

But as the weeks passed, the urge came less and less frequently. I didn't want it to fade, but I needed it to.

— 5 —

ComFab

The plan for the capture of the ComFab looked pretty straightforward.

Things would start the night before the main part of the operation got underway. We had maneuvered to get Tink, a member of BeeBee's crew, assigned as backup mechanic on a routine shuttle op for communications satellite maintenance. While she and her crew were in orbit, code she'd planted in the shuttle computer would simulate receipt of error-condition alerts from the observation and mapping satellites that offered Chiron's government most of its orbital visual imagery. In repairing these nonexistent issues, Tink would actually plant small explosives packages on the two satellites.

If all went according to schedule, Tink would be back on the ground and in hiding before the main operation began. If she weren't, she'd still be in orbit, probably suspected of involvement with the operation. She'd probably choose to fry out her own volatiles, like Punch had, rather than suffer whatever revenge the meats chose for her. I really hoped it didn't come to that.

Skip ahead to the Harringen Corporation main plant on the north side of Zhou City, a couple of hours after noon. A hauler would drag a wheeled trailer out of one of the high-security assembly areas into the middle of Loading Bay 16, an open-air area where big loads were routinely prepped for transport. This particular trailer would have a generic cargo container, twenty meters by five by three, atop it.

And by "generic," I'm not exaggerating. These containers are ubiquitous, used on every human-occupied world. They're made up of a metal framework onto which sides, flooring, and roof of metal sheeting can be temporarily or permanently affixed. Numbers and symbols, some of them ancient or meaningless, are painted on the sides. Some of these containers have been to more worlds than any human pilot. In some places, poverty-stricken humans live in abandoned containers. Businesses and apartment blocks in the Warrens were constructed with them.

In the middle of the bay, meters away from any other trailer waiting there, innocuously guarded by disguised Harringen Security personnel, this container would sit for a few minutes until Chiron Defense Force personnel arrived from General Millfield Base to take charge of it. They'd take it to the Zhou City spaceport, where its contents, the ComFab, would be prepared for eventual transportation to the newly-established business colony on Cardiff's Giant.

That was their plan, anyway. Ours was different.

Soon after the trailer and container were in place, explosive charges planted around the bay would detonate, filling the area with thick smoke—smoke impervious to security cameras but not to the imaging radar units the 'gangers would be using. Dollgangers would climb to the top of the container and wait.

Then I, in my piloting mega, operating the heavy chopper-hauler I had misappropriated, would fly in and drop cables. The 'gangers below would hook us up to the container. We'd fly off, keeping below radar.

That's when our alerts would go out—flash traffic informing all the 'gangers in wireless range of what we'd done. The implicit message would be, "Hide if you want to live. Best of luck."

Another radio signal, this one sent into the planetary communications grid, would trigger the explosives charges on the observation and mapping satellites. The government would lose its eyes in the sky and not be able to follow our escape.

There were more details, mostly dealing with possible pursuit by the humans, but that was the plan as most of its participants knew it.

* * *

And that brings us up to a week before the operation.

The sun was setting, but it had been a very pretty day, and when my buggy came within sight of Doc's dome, I saw him out on the raised wooden deck in front, sitting on one of the deck chairs, a pitcher of lemonade on the table beside him, a broad white parasol above him. I finished the drive up, left the buggy, and bounded up the deck steps, then leaped up onto the chair next to his.

He didn't say anything. He just watched the sunset, a slight smile on his face.

I leaned back against the plastic chair arm. "You did good, Doc."

He spared me a look. "When?"

I gestured out at Zhou City, the great sprawl of it, now colored a monochrome orange-gold by the sunset. "Dollgangers made Chiron's economy. Without them, most people here would be struggling farmers. A few researchers hoping that some of the plants they were developing would turn into useful medicines.

Without you, Chiron would be nothing. They should have named the capital Chiang City."

He gestured at me as if shooting away flies. "It was named before I got here. And I don't need a whole city named after me. Maybe a new flavor of ice cream."

"I'll get to work on that."

"But, yes. I wish Kim had lived to see this. She would be proud. And little Rhona."

In all the time I'd been with Doc, he'd seldom spoken about his wife and daughter. They'd died in one of the superflu epidemics on Earth, just two years before Doc emigrated. The stills and videos that decorated the little room dedicated to their memory, even the passwords he used to protect his most secure files, reflected the way they continued to be with him.

"Doc, I probably shouldn't say this. But you should have married again. Had more children."

The sun by now had dripped to the horizon. Light shone straight into Doc's face, turning his skin and the dome behind us a brilliant orange. He closed his eyes against the light, comfortable. "I did have more children, Bow. That story is not yet completely told. And the only lesson I've learned from it so far is that some children take longer to mature than others."

While I puzzled over his meaning, his breathing became deeper, more regular, as he drifted off into a nap.

* * *

Having a life-changing realization is startling enough. Having two back-to-back can floor you. But at least they keep meetings interesting.

My first realization came the next evening, at the gathering of the Stand-Up Gang, even before Richter started into his agenda. Looking around at the faces of everyone present, I suddenly understood what Doc had meant. I felt dizzy, as if my internal gyros had just gone barmy.

I took a few moments to get myself under control. Richter was still in his opening remarks, introducing a new Stand-Up department head, Malibu. "He'll be in charge of community planning for the Nest, the habitat that will house the ComFab."

Malibu, who was as bronzed and handsome as his name suggested, took over. "Obviously, security is of paramount concern. The population of the Nest will be the minimum necessary to operate and protect the ComFab. Deadwood will be trimmed away without sentiment. Traffic into and out of the Nest will be minimal. Many of our members will inhabit a different community, code-named Swift, that will, potentially, serve as a decoy—if humans attack Swift, we'll know that the Nest is possibly on the verge of being discovered."

That's about the point I tuned out. The words "Deadwood will be trimmed away without sentiment" triggered my second life-changing realization.

I'd heard those words on many occasions over the years, but not from Malibu. From Pothole Charlie. Charlie was a great planner but not much of a public speaker, and I'd never heard anyone but good friends of his repeat his phrasing. So far as I knew, Malibu wasn't in his circle of intimates.

So far as I knew.

When the meeting was done, Lina, this time in a peasant blouse and a skirt of broad horizontal stripes in warm colors, a panda painted in the hollow of her neck, sidled up to me. "Care for a walk?" She affected cheerfulness, but in her eyes was the slightly haunted look I was seeing a lot with the 'gangers who were experiencing combat training, myself included.

"Sure." I know I sounded vague. "Might as well."

We ascended to Finest Kind Park. I'd helped build it long ago. It was a patch of green belt kept that way by full-spectrum overhead lights. A stream, a flow of water diverted from the humans' nearest water treatment plant, pure and clean, ran through the park. On a stony bank, Lina sat and dangled her bare feet into the water. "Come on, give it a try."

I sat on a low concrete fence, scavenged curb from a human street. "No."

She affected unconcern. "You got kind of wide-eyed during the meeting. I was wondering if anything was wrong."

I shrugged. "Depends on your definition of 'wrong.' I'd say everything is going according to plan. Not necessarily my plan."

"Whose?"

"Doc's. And yours."

She frowned. "I don't understand."

I sighed and looked out to where the water ran over an uneven portion of culvert and pebbles. There it broke and tumble, a pretty display, almost natural. "I thought I knew why Doc scrubbed my memory after the shuttle repair—to protect me—but at the start of the meeting, I realized I was wrong, I figured it out."

"Why did he do it?"

"To shove a wedge between us. To make me think. To make it impossible for me to ask him for advice. Lina, he figured out that Punch was with the independence movement and he hoped I'd join it."

"Then why didn't he just tell you to?"

"Because he wants me to be free. He can never admit it to the other meats, but he wants ... all his descendants to be free." I gave Lina a somber look. "But he can't help. He'd be imprisoned. Maybe executed. He's an old, old man, and he wants whatever time he has left."

She looked down into the water, to where little black fish were now congregating to nibble at her toes. "And that's what took you by surprise at the meeting."

"That was just the first thing. The second was the realization that Doc is going to outlive me. The realization that you plan to kill me."

Her head whipped around and she looked at me again, unable to conceal her surprise. She shook her head, denying it.

"Oh, please, Lina. It took me a while, in the absence of sufficient data, but today I got it. The Stand-Up Gang. I thought the name was because we were representing ourselves as 'stand-up guys.' But it's not. We're cardboard stand-ups, concealing the existence of the real planners of this operation. We're here to be knocked down—destroyed—if the operation is a failure. Pothole

Charlie and maybe some of his close friends are actually in charge."

"I don't ... I don't ..."

"When Malibu began using Pothole Charlie's pet phrases, it became clear that Malibu had been training with him. Malibu's just not as good at hiding it as the rest of you. And like Swift is going to be the decoy for the Nest, the Stand-Ups are decoys, there to be killed in case I betray you."

When she spoke again, her voice was a whisper. "What are you going to do, Bow?"

"I'm going to keep my mouth shut, and do my part in this operation, and I guess I'll die when you kill me."

She stood up, her feet dripping. She moved to stand over me. "I don't *understand.*"

"Don't you?" I gave her what I knew was a bleak look. "I could live among the meats forever. I'd be happy. That was my choice. But I want the operation to succeed. Because if I hadn't had my choice, I'd have been in hell all these years. Which is obviously where you are. You and everyone else who's willing to die to pull this off. The ComFab offers you that choice." I looked back into the water. "But I know, because I know *him,* that Pothole Charlie can't accept a 'ganger civilization that has me in it. Do you think the Stand-Ups can be persuaded not to kill me? With him in charge?"

She took a while considering how to answer. "No."

"That's what I thought." It was one thing to have grasped it intellectually. Learning I was right from the lips of one of the people planning my death made it real. I felt as though my muscles had suddenly degraded past the point of functionality. "It wouldn't be so hard, except for the last few weeks thinking that I was actually one of you. The most disliked one, but a member. Realizing I was still Big Plush, that's ... hard."

"Bow ..."

"Quiet. No, I'll do my job, but I want something from you. From you specifically."

Her face went blank, but she gulped. That's another physical reflex handed down in our deep coding. She squared her shoulders and looked me in the eye. "What?"

I don't know what she thought I was going to demand. A night of sex, maybe, or servile behavior. But I just stood up and leaned in close. "I want you to stop pretending to be my friend."

Her lower lip quivered. But all she said was, "All right."

— 6 —

Elzoc

Things actually became easier for me after that. I didn't want to die, but knowing I was going to, the assurance of it, took a lot of strain off me.

Lina kept her distance, dealing with me only when our respective duties demanded. I was certain she hadn't told the other Stand-Ups what I'd told her; their behavior toward me didn't change. I actually began to appreciate BeeBee, whose stance toward me had remained hostile but honest throughout the whole operation.

As the operation day neared, I knew I'd be doing some difficult climbing—on factory walls and megas at least. So I asked BeeBee for a set of multi-mode climbing gear, the same sort she had used when she was with her military demolitions team. She delivered it within a day, no questions asked.

Despite my newfound peace of mind, I made my murder as difficult as I could for my killers. I meticulously checked and re-checked my piloting mega, my climbing gear, the chopper-hauler I'd be flying. I found no sabotage.

The night before the operation, on my way home from Harringen, I stopped in at a pastry shop and picked up something I'd ordered—it was sometimes useful to be entrusted with a portion of the household account. With the strawberry cream cake, Doc's favorite, strapped to the back of my buggy, I crept home at a human walking pace but got the cake there intact.

After Doc's dinner, I brought the cake out and sat down with him for a game or two of Elzoc.

Do humans still play Elzoc? Doc's dedicated tablet for the game was a century old at that time and I don't recall ever seeing another human play it. Elzoc used a square-grid board, user-selectable in size. Each square represented a type of terrain that facilitated or slowed unit movement. Each player had a force of mixed military units—armored cavalry, infantry, artillery, air support, supply, command posts, and so on. Each piece exerted a certain amount of control against adjacent and diagonal squares, and enough pieces acting in concert could slow an enemy piece's movement to nothing. Plus most of them could project force at a distance—close for infantry, far for air support or heavy artillery, for example.

We hadn't played in a while. I creamed Doc in the first game that night, and he hit the reset button for another scenario, randomly picked by the tablet.

He gave me a cheerful look. "You're thinking more tactically."

"Am I? I guess I have to. Coordinating all those motor pool assignments."

"Ah, yes, motor pool." He touched each of his pieces in turn, sliding them to different squares on the board. No piece actually moved until the last one had been repositioned, then they all appeared on their new squares at once. I saw he was putting together three blocks of firepower, each almost at optimal distance to unload their destructive power on my main concentration of armored cavalry.

He watched me considering my moves. "Bow, did you ever think you might be destined for greater things than a motor pool?"

I blithely left the formation he was targeting where it was. I amped up its defensive power at the expense of offense. I also scattered other pieces in a loose formation off at an angle from his forces. "I'm a Dollganger, Doc. For me to be destined for bigger things, *you* would have had to promote that destiny."

"I suppose that's true." He set all his pieces into motion, moving them to optimal firing range. Then he unloaded their firepower. My armored cav formation took a pounding. In spite of their increased defensive capability. Piece after piece vanished from the board, about half the formation.

I responded. The remaining armored cav marched doggedly on the enemy infantry. I also sent all my remaining pieces into coordinated motion. Suddenly his forces were faced off individually with fast-moving air support pieces that couldn't really hurt them but could lock them in place while other pieces obliterated the tail end of his supply line.

He stared at the damage I had wrought, which was minimal, and calculated the damage that was to come, which would be impressive. "I should resign now."

"And deny me the pleasure of driving you from the board? No fair, Doc."

"You're right. You deserve the endgame. We both do." He smiled at me.

I smiled back. It was clear to me that he had a sense of what I was up to with the 'gangers.

And the fact that after I left the house tomorrow morning, however things played out, I would never see him again raised a lump in my throat. But at least my last memory of him would be of Doc smiling, his favorite game in front of him, his favorite cake at hand, his closest surviving descendant planning for something grander than a future of motor pool duty.

* * *

And then there we were, the day of the operation.

Before I reached Harringen that morning, I received a brief, coded message confirming that Tink was in orbit and her part of the operation was well underway.

At the motor pool, I told the human manager on duty, Fil, that I had the case load well in hand. As I knew he would, he took this as an excuse to goof off. He left to find a place to nap. I did some scrambling of security codes so I could lock him out at a moment's notice.

BeeBee arrived an hour after noon. I'd told her which tool compartment of which personal transport to hide in, and when it stopped in for a battery recharge, she popped out of the compartment and sneaked straight into Fil's office.

I suppressed the urge to laugh. She had on a blue Harringen jumpsuit and a big-hair blond wig whose bangs drooped over her eyes and hid their color. There was a pink scarf around her throat.

She saw my struggle and her expression reverted to its familiar, comforting hostility. "Don't laugh."

"Whatever you say." I sent a radio command to slide the office door shut and lock it. "Come on up."

Hefting her backpack, which was as pink as her scarf, she bounded up to the chair. "Tink has reported in. She's on the ground and headed for cover."

I breathed a sigh of relief.

BeeBee made it to the desktop without effort. She shucked her wig and scarf, then unsealed her backpack and began pulling out gear—her sunglasses, which she put on, then climbing gear, a 'ganger surgical probe, skin fuser. "Shirt off, plush."

I shucked my jumpsuit down to the waist.

With what was probably unnecessary roughness, BeeBee inserted the probe in my left side, down where floating ribs would be on a human. I felt sharp stings as the probe went through my neural net and more as she dug around with it. But she found what she was looking for. She tugged, and my transponder, a little silver cylinder, emerged from the incision, still trailing its combined power/data/antenna cable. In moments, BeeBee attached the transponder to an external battery, then snipped it free of my body. Her last step was to insert some fuser paste in the incision to speed the repairs my body would make to that little injury.

"All done. You were a good boy. You didn't cry." She handed me the transponder. "Consider yourself free."

I dropped it over the edge of the desk into a wastecan. I wriggled back into the top of my jumpsuit and sealed it.

From a satchel atop the desk, I extracted my climbing rig and donned it. Special boots, knee pads, broad strap-on cuffs for the wrists, all in black. BeeBee got to work putting on a similar set.

I used the rig to clamber down the side of the wooden desk rather than bounding down to the chair and then the floor as was my habit. The rig handled the climb as well as it had during my previous tests.

Multi-mode climbing gear is pretty useful. The cuffs, pads, and boots extrude gripping extensions suited to the climbing environment, any of three different types: magnetic couplers for ship's hulls and other ferrous surfaces, tufts of "gecko monofilaments" for other sheer surfaces like glass or stone, and sharp claw-and-hook assemblies for organic surfaces like trees. The gear responds to 'ganger radio or microwave pulses.

When BeeBee joined me on the floor, I issued wireless commands setting in motion the last elements of our part of the operation. I opened a series of drainage flues between the Harringen's exterior, Loading Bay 4, where my stolen vehicles waited, and Loading Bay 16, where the ComFab would be. I broadcast the go-ahead to 'gangers waiting outside Harringen. I uploaded all Fil's personal and biometric data to Harringen Security, identifying him as an industrial spy. He'd be grabbed the first time any device scanned his ID, and until Security confirmed his true identity they wouldn't believe a thing he said.

Then BeeBee and I left the motor pool operations center. Its door slid shut behind us with an authoritative thump, leaving us out in the sunlight.

We went over the concrete wall separating the motor pool service yard from Bay 4. As we arrived, our crews were in the process of trickling in from outside. Many of the 'gangers were already in the cockpits of their megas or other vehicles. Some of those megas waited at the big doors leading into the access tunnels that would take them to Bay 16. Others rolled up the ramp into the main compartment of the chopper-hauler, the biggest vehicle I had misappropriated.

In ten minutes, I was in my piloting mega in the chopper-hauler's cockpit, doing my pre-flight checklist. BeeBee, in her own forklift mega, took up position in the crowded main compartment and began receiving feeds from the engines.

Helicopters are ancient technology. The originals were prone to breakdowns and were comparatively dangerous to fly, but very, very useful. Their modern descendants, built with improved materials and engineering, are more rugged, so sturdy and dependable that humans considered them dull. The one I'd benched for imaginary engine problems was a two-rotor freight hauler, painted in Harringen blue, the corporation's interlocked-gears symbol in white on both sides.

I set up one of the cockpit monitors to receive a feed showing Bay 16.

The ComFab cargo container was already in position. Harringen Security operatives wearing innocuous worker clothes stood around like they were goofing off. I felt my nonexistent heart pound in my chest.

If I or any of the other Stand-Ups issued the scrub command right now, we could erase all sign that we'd had an operation in progress. We could all go home and pretend it never happened.

I toggled the chopper intercom. "Pilot to crew. Prepare to lift." And I brought the rotors up to speed.

* * *

As soon as we lifted, Richter, from his observation post within Bay 16, triggered the explosions. I saw the results on my monitor.

From positions all over Bay 16, devices—designed by BeeBee and planted by members of my crew, looking like lunch pails and discarded monitoring tablets—detonated. I heard the dull "crump" noise as they blew. In moments, Bay 16 was full from wall to wall, ground to wall-top with roiling black smoke. Some of the smoke rose above the wall-tops, was grabbed by breezes, and began flowing southward like a transparent serpent crawling toward Zhou City.

Shrill alarms sounded. People shouted. Sudden squawk traffic erupted over the radio.

Methodically, I took the chopper up a few meters above the wall tops and the corrugated-metal building roofs, then eased forward until Bay 16 was in sight ahead. As the chopper neared the bay, wash from my rotors stirred the smoke, making an evil-looking rough sea of the surface. As I moved over the bay, the rotor wash blew the smoke all over the place; it rose in plumes, poured out of the bay in waves, obscured the sky.

But below me I could see the ComFab container. Atop it were 'gangers, Richter's crew. I positioned the chopper directly above the container. BeeBee operated the winches to lower cables. On my monitor, I could see the rotor wash hammering the 'gangers below, nearly blowing some of them off the container roof as they hooked the cables to the container's frame.

No, the security humans weren't gone. They were meters away, choking and vomiting, many of them feeling their way along the walls, some shouting into their hand and lapel radios.

Blind, of course, tears streaming from their suddenly puffy eyes. There was stuff in that smoke that smelled bad to 'gangers but inflamed meat people's mucous membranes like nobody's business. A couple of the meats produced sidearms and took bat-blind shots in the direction of the chopper-hauler, but they were shouted down by more sensible but equally blind superiors.

You've probably seen the recordings from that day. With speed and discipline, the 'gangers finished hooking our cables to the cargo container. I eased the chopper-hauler up into the air, checking the demands made by its weight on my rotors. They took the load exactly as I knew they would. And with care suited to carrying the most precious object in all the universe, I turned us northward and headed out over the forest.

* * *

We were only twenty kilometers north, still being seen and reported by meats in their cabins and logging camps, when BeeBee reported two blips incoming from General Millfield Base. The speed of the blips made it a near-certainty that they were weapons platforms.

A chopper-hauler full of forklift megas with low-tech weapons is no match for a weapons platform. Picture a circular plate of ducted-fan motivators; at its center is a spherical fuselage packed with weapon systems. Real ones like rockets and autocannons. These craft would be on us in moments. Because of the value of our cargo, they might not shoot us, but they could easily force us down.

Except ... their commander and pilots were too eager, too confident. They came on in a straight line directly from the base.

And they flew over Intercept Point Alpha, a broad field north of Zhou City. Where we had claymore cannon trailers set up.

Our gunners plotted the weapons platforms' locations and courses by eye, cranked those cannon barrels around to aim them, and triggered the cannons in sequence, filling the sky with shrapnel.

We have recordings of that, too. Both vehicles began issuing smoke and plummeted. The pilot of one ejected. The other pilot tried to hold it together for a landing. She did okay, scoring a trench in the big field, not rolling her platform, leaving it repairable. The news media later said she had shrapnel damage to both legs and her pelvis, but she lived.

All I knew at the time was that the weapons platforms dropped off our passive radar. I changed course and struck off northwest.

– 7 –

Chopper

We were a hundred and sixty klicks out from Zhou City when the chopper's diagnostic readouts began lighting up red. I glanced at them, toggled my intercom. "What is it, BeeBee?"

BeeBee offered a couple of swear words I'd only ever heard humans use. Then: "Angle of attack's not ... right. We're losing lift."

"Did we take a hit when those idiots were shooting in the bay?"

"That's probably it."

"Can you fix it in flight?"

"Hell, no."

"Can you fix it *fast* on the ground?"

"… Probably."

"Great."

At this point, we had the meats blind with their mapping satellites down, but it was only a matter of time before they got some sort of observation craft launched. Enough time on the ground and we'd be spotted.

I saw a clearing big enough for our needs and descended. Gentle as a kiss, I lowered the cargo container to the irregular clearing floor and waited while the 'ganger crew detached the cables, then I sideslipped thirty meters and set the chopper down.

And while BeeBee got to work on the engine, we waited.

* * *

Twenty minutes passed, then the situation was resolved. But not with the announcement that repairs were done.

Richter sent us a wireless burst. "Incoming weapons platforms and something big, maybe another chopper-hauler. Get clear. I say again, get clear."

Yeah, I got clear. I threw open the pilot's hatch and leaped free. Understand, megas aren't all that well-suited for leaping and landing, but I managed to keep mine on both legs, with yellow flashes but no red lighting up my diagnostics, when I hit the ground. I straightened and ran toward the cargo container. Behind me, the chopper's side door rolled open and the megas, vehicles, and individual 'gangers inside came roiling out like upset wasps.

Just in time, too. There was a noise like distant drums being beaten by overcaffeinated musicians and then two more weapons platforms roared into view over the clearing edge. The lead one flashed by harmlessly, but the second platform opened fire, putting a burst of high explosive armor-piercing rounds into the chopper.

I saw the armor all along the starboard side pucker and disintegrate, saw sparks erupt from the forward engine as it ceased to be recognizable as machinery. One of the forward rotor vanes snapped off entirely.

The chopper was dead. I gulped.

Memnon, in one of the forklift megas, traversed to track the weapons platforms on their outbound path. He aimed and the globe-launcher affixed to his arm triggered with a loud "chuff" noise. I saw the black globe arc up after the weapons platforms, gaining on them, dropping toward them from above—then it detonated.

One of BeeBee's fuel-air bombs. That whole quadrant of sky filled with fire. A shockwave of noise and pressure hit us, knocking ranks of 'gangers off their feet. I struggled to keep my vehicle upright.

The two weapons platforms, shattered, spun out of the sky and slammed into the forest floor west of us.

And that was it, the first two kills of the Dollganger War of Independence, Phase One. I saw 'gangers, those still on foot, stare at each other, their expressions changing as the enormity of what had just happened hit them.

We gathered around the cargo container, preparing to meet the force we knew was coming.

* * *

Minutes later, the forward edge of the human ground force let us know they were there. A few men and women, infantry, in camouflage gear, body armor, and visored helmets, appeared at the verge of the forest. We knew there had to be many more farther back.

These troops weren't carrying firearms, not normal ones. They had rifle-length zappers. Crowd control and suspect capture weapons, they ionized a channel of air between weapon and target, then projected electricity along that channel. Humans hit by those beams would spasm and fall down. So would 'gangers—rebooting after a light dose, staying down until externally revived after a heavy hit.

These troopers had regular firearms, too, long arms across their backs or sidearms holstered. They wouldn't use those weapons on any target near the ComFab. But a zapper wouldn't do anything to a ComFab except maybe require a reload of programming.

One of the troopers, a tall dark-skinned woman, raised a small tablet to her lips. Her voice emerged amplified. "This is Colonel Hayes of the Chiron Defense Force. Throw down your weapons and lie face-down on the ground or we will open fire."

The response, a wireless burst from Richter, intended for us and not the humans, came immediately: "Stage Two, go."

All four sides of the cargo container fell away, slamming to the earth, missing the 'gangers all around—aware of what was coming, they were far enough away to be safe. The action revealed the container's contents.

There was no ComFab inside. There were more megas. Dollgangers, both on foot and in buggies. At the center of the container was an armored cube a meter on a side. It housed radio jamming equipment, which had fired up the instant Richter issued his command. Our radios suddenly hissed with static.

* * *

Let's go back in time to when the smoke bombs went off in Bay 16.

The only video of what went on show roiling smoke. But there are also fuzzy monochrome views from imaging radar units used by Richter's crew.

While the humans staggered around blind, Richter and his crew charged up to the trailer and ComFab container, climbed, attached winches to the top, and undogged the two long sides of the container. The winches lowered them to the pavement. Meanwhile, a similar crew with similar gear atop the cargo container on the nearest parked hauler-trailer, which I had placed there days before to wait for a "repair job," lowered the long sides of *its* cargo container.

Forklift megas arriving from Bay 4 flanked the ComFab, lifted it, maneuvering it free of the container, then delicately rolled it over to the other trailer, placing it within. The crew on that trailer winched up and dogged down the sides. Those sides were radio-shielded so transponders in the ComFab wouldn't give away the unit's real position. That crew hid in the container and the cab of the hauler.

The forklift megas and all the rest of the support personnel assembled in the ComFab's original container. Richter's crew winched the sides up and dogged them in place. The alarms and sirens helpfully provided by the Harringen Corporation covered the sound of all these activities.

So when my chopper-hauler arrived and blew the smoke away, everything looked the way people expected. Harringen's cameras witnessed the aerial departure of the ComFab container and security personnel giving chase. They also recorded, but took no note of, the departure, a few minutes later, of a hauler-trailer rig.

Its driver? Scarecrow, the simulacrum robot we'd built. And in Scarecrow's pilot's bay sat the King. Cool and unruffled as ever, he drove the hauler out of the Harringen yard and headed south. Sure, the Harringen operations center had locked down all the bay doors, but some of those doors had been blown at the same time the smoke charges went off. They *couldn't* close.

By the time the second set of weapons platforms strafed my chopper-hauler, the King was many kilometers south of Zhou City, unobserved, headed toward the Nest's actual location... and with the mapping satellites down, the government never had aerial records to analyze. To them, the ComFab just vanished.

$-$ 8 $-$

Meat

Which left us, the diversionary force, facing a large, determined, confused, angry unit of meats.

As the sides of the cargo container crashed down and 'gangers spilled out, Memnon launched a black globe toward Colonel Hayes and her escort. It detonated into a sphere of fire and destruction the size of a six-human-story building, the concussion nearly knocking me over.

And then the hailstorm hit, except the hail traveled laterally, some of it coming from the meats to us, some of it going out from us to the meats. It chewed to pieces whatever it struck. The noise, the roar of weapons and impacts and explosions, seemed to fill the world.

On my heads-up displays, I saw wire-frame images of human soldiers cease to be as recognizable shapes when railgun loads hit them. Megas went to pieces, torn apart by high-powered automatic-fire rifles or blown into clouds of trash by heat-seeking microrockets.

Atop the cargo container, Richter took a hit. Suddenly his torso was just gone, his arms and legs catapulting separately at missile speeds.

He wasn't dead, though, not at that instant. I got one last microwave transmission from him: "Terminating." That was his last word, sent in the split-second before he fried out his own cognitive processes.

In my head and in the map imager of my mega, the 'ganger-net sprang into life. If there's anything we're good at, it's multiple-source coordination, and the loss of radio meant only that we were down to microwave and data-laser bursts. Every time one of us saw another, we'd automatically issue an encrypted data packet including our location, status, a repeat of current orders, alerts.... The humans could do something like that with their helmets, but each exchange took several seconds to send, decrypt, and understand. With us, it was microseconds. In the first five seconds of the firefight, as we scattered and traded licks with the meats, we built up an ever-more-detailed map of our positions, their positions, our relative numbers.

Initially, that didn't help me much. I crouched in my mega, looking around for Lina's forklift. She was supposed to bring me a railgun and ammo hopper.

She was nowhere in sight, and a quick check of my tac-map failed to disclose her location. Or BeeBee's. Or Memnon's, even though I was looking right at his mega, fifty meters away.

In fact, none of the *meats* showed up on my tac-map.

I felt my heart sink. There it was, final proof that the Stand-Ups meant to kill me. Without weapons, without an accurate tac-map, I was a dead, steaming mass of composites.

So I revved my treads up and headed off at an angle for a line of trees where I hadn't seen any meats.

My mega rocked and *dinged* as a spray of gunfire from some human stitched it. Red lights appeared on the diagnostics readouts, but none were crucial yet.

To my right, a seemingly-unpiloted 'ganger buggy bounced across uneven ground and rolled into the midst of a group of soldiers behind tree cover. It detonated, hurling some of the soldiers out, blanketing others in smoke and fire.

I got behind the first few trees. They seemed to offer damned little cover.

Our extraction muster point was a kilometer north of our landing site. Our transportation was there already. There had been no engine failure on the chopper-hauler, no impromptu choice of a clearing to land in—the location had been chosen weeks before, its intricacies loaded as three-dimensional schematics in our memories. We knew where every tree, every rock, every rodent hole within a kilometer was. I skirted the edge of the forest, heading for the muster point.

Memnon's voice came to me in a microwave burst, "Fall back, extract." He didn't sound troubled. I wondered if he was a sociopath.

And I ejected.

* * *

No, I didn't intend to. As the rocket acceleration of the ejector seat held me in place, I realized what must have happened.

I'd been all over my mega, looking for whatever means the other Stand-Ups would use to eliminate Big Plush from their vision of a better tomorrow. I'd never found one and had assumed that they were going to make a direct attack on me at some point.

It hadn't occurred to me—just a little extra programming in an obscure corner of the mega's operating system would do the trick. When it received the fall-back code, it had only to eject the pilot. Even if I got back to my mega, it was disabled—there would be no way to pilot it.

I reached the apex of my ejection arc and began to drop. The seat's parachute deployed. Then a bullet hole, round and neat, appeared in the shroud above my head.

I looked down. There were at least two infantrymen firing up at me. Only being a small moving target had saved me from being slaughtered.

I was maybe ten meters up from the tallest of the treetops and descending fast. In moments, my parachute would catch on a branch and I'd dangle there, an easy target. Before that happened, I unbuckled and jumped free.

I grabbed at the first branch to come to hand, snapped it off under my weight, kept falling. But the next branch down was hardier. I slammed into it and grabbed it, pain shot through my chest, and my claw-and-hook climbing gear caught hold. The branch swayed under my weight but did not break.

I heard meat troopers who'd lost sight of me begin shouting, trying to find me. I scrambled laterally to the tree trunk and then down to the ground.

Yeah, I know. There was something to be said for staying up in the branches and out of sight. But the fall-back command had set a timer in motion. After a few minutes, everyone at the muster point would be outbound, headed for safety. I wanted to be with them. Sure, some of the people at the muster point wanted me dead. But maybe not all of them did. Maybe …

I ran. Tree to tree, vaulting across exposed roots, ducking beneath brushy overhangs. I splashed through a stream that a human could have stepped over.

Then the human officer lunged out from behind a tree and brought his damned big foot down on me.

* * *

And that should have been it. Like I said before, he'd hold me there while he got his sidearm out, then lift his foot and shoot me until I was dead.

Except … I reactivated the climbing gear.

He got his sidearm out and lifted his foot. I clung to its sole and peered at him from just under his boot, not from a helpless position on the ground. A look of confusion crossed his face.

I deactivated the foot-and-knee climbers. The lower half of my body swung free. I dropped, fell maybe a third of a meter, landed on my feet. I ran—right up to his support leg.

I reactivated the climbing gear and scampered up his inseam, clawing out chunks of bloody meat as I went.

He shrieked. He brought his other foot down. He grabbed at me with his free hand. But I was already farther up, digging gouges out of his butt, scrambling up his armored side, all the way to his neck.

Understand, this is not something that fills me with pride or a sense of accomplishment. In a moment, one of us would be dead and one alive, and I wanted to live. So I kept the claw-and-hook gear extended, I grabbed, I cut, I tore … all where I knew the carotid artery was.

Then, from head to waist, I was drenched in sticky warm liquid that hit me under pressure. I jerked my head from side to side to clear my eyes. I could see his own eye, his right one, as it rolled up in his head.

And he fell. I leaped free, rolled as I hit the ground—in a world where almost everything is built to a giant scale, 'gangers learn how to land. I came up on my feet.

And there he was, twitching, a dead meat person.

It wouldn't be much later in the War of Independence before 'gangers who killed meats in direct conflict would come to be referred to as jacks, a term of somber respect. The term comes from a human children's story, Jack the Giant Killer. At that moment, I became the very first jack—another of my dubious achievements in the historical chronicles.

But all I knew at that moment was a crushing weight of grief. Looking at the dead man, I couldn't move. My eyes burned, and a noise, an animal howl, escaped me.

But the clock in my head kept incrementing.

I moved over to his sidearm and picked it up. At a kilo and a half, it weighted half again what I did, but I had sufficient strength to haul it around. I took it across my shoulders, a rescue carry, and began running again.

Back at the clearing's edge, ten meters ahead of me, I saw a human sniper and a spotter lying side by side, putting rounds into the collapsed cargo container. The clearing was on fire in places but empty of moving 'gangers. Clearly, though, there were some of us trapped, using the container's wreckage for cover.

I set the firearm on its butt, maneuvered it so that its barrel was aimed more or less at the sniper's side, and sighted in along the trench of its sights. Then, ducking so my head was below and to the left of the slide, I carefully, slowly pulled the trigger.

There was a *boom* overloading my audio sensors. All of a sudden I was on my butt with the sidearm on top of me.

When I looked at my target again, the sniper was on his feet, looking vague and startled. A red stain had appeared near his armpit and was spreading. His spotter was shouting, I couldn't tell what, and looking around.

The spotter saw me as I got the sidearm upright again. He grabbed for the rifle. I swung the handgun into line, a fast, awkward aim, and yanked the trigger. Then I was on my ass again.

But I looked up, and the spotter was on the ground too, rolling around, clutching his inner thigh. The sniper was still staggering around in shock.

I sent a microwave burst toward the cargo container: "You're clear, *run*." Then I picked up the handgun and hauled ass.

The trees at the north edge of the clearing were on fire by the time I reached that area. I continued laterally until I found a spot where the forest didn't seem to be burning, and charged due north from there.

I had a chance. I had a *chance*. But the location they Stand-Ups had given me for the Nest was probably a false one. I'd never find the real Nest by myself. So I had to get to the muster point and evacuate with the others.

I reached a flat patch of ground and really picked up running speed ... and then a mega rolled out from behind a couple of trees. It straddled my path.

It was a forklift with a railgun and a plate-metal shield. I knew whose it was. I'd stolen and repaired most of them. It was Lina's.

I stopped where I was and sighed. I didn't bother aiming the handgun at her. There was no way it could disable a tough old mega.

The mega rolled up and leaned over me. Its belly hatch popped open. Lina's voice came over the loudspeaker. "Get in."

I dropped the handgun, leaped up, scrambled in, dogged the hatch shut behind me. Then I climbed up into the chest cockpit. I almost fell down the ladder shaft as Lina set her mega into motion.

Over her shoulder, I could see the darkened viewplates, heads-up image of our surroundings on them, wire-frame images of trees and, distantly, humans and other megas.

I flipped down the jumpseat, to the right of and set back from the pilot's chair, and buckled myself in. I gave Lina a close look. She was dressed for work, wearing her Shavery jumpsuit, boots, no face paint. "Hey, you're wearing *shoes*."

"Shut up."

"Why'd you come back?"

She glanced over her shoulder at me, really saw the blood all over me, grimaced a little. She returned her attention to the terrain ahead. "Because you convinced me to."

"I don't remember doing that."

"When you talked about Doc Chiang wanting his descendants to be free. It was clear you wanted it, too. Clear that you understood that we're not a race unless we *have* descendants." She shut up while navigating a thick stand of trees with exposed roots that threatened to upend the mega.

Sometimes she walked the mega, its motion awkward and lurching, sometimes she returned to cruising on the treads. We headed into a burning zone, the brightness of the fire visible even through the polarization of the viewplates. Then we were past the trouble spot. "I realized … our children are going to need to understand where they come from. They'll need ancestors, too. Like you and Doc Chiang."

"I'll be damned." That expression didn't mean much to 'gangers, but Doc used it a lot.

There was a distant *boom* from behind and to the left, sign that the humans were in pursuit of our retreating force. Lina gave me another brief glance. "There was another reason, too, I guess. That whole conversation, where you'd figured out the Pothole Charlie plan but had decided to go ahead with it anyway, and die … that made me realize you weren't Big Plush. You were Bow, and I decided I'd miss Bow."

* * *

A minute later, we reached the clearing where our extraction vehicles waited. They were tracked haulers to which we'd hooked rolling luggage trailers and flatbeds. Megas sat on the flatbeds, 'gangers crowded into the luggage racks. I saw techs working on limp 'gangers, some of them burned or missing limbs, some showing no apparent damage—zapped.

We rolled up the boarding ramp onto the last trailer. When Lina depolarized the cockpit viewplates and everyone saw me sitting with her, Memnon, in his own mega, made an outraged noise, then began issuing orders. But Lina fired her recording at him, at BeeBee and Malibu, encrypted for Stand-Ups only.

Her message was a simple one. "Anything happens to Bow, I stop sending cancel codes to a file I've already placed in the Zhou City communications net. A file that gives map coordinates for the Nest."

Had she actually placed such a file? I didn't find out for some time. No, of course not; she wouldn't endanger the Nest, the future of her kind. But her bluff sure put the brakes on any immediate attempt to grab and dismantle me.

Everybody knows how the evacuation resolved itself. A few more 'gangers boarded, we began rolling, we stayed away from human roads, we traveled at a snail's pace. And the meats didn't catch us. We reached the Nest together.

Of course, everybody on Chiron today knows where the Nest turned out to be, and what happened to it. But we were there undetected for quite a while, transforming ourselves from a group of revolutionaries into a people. And because of Lina, I didn't end up fried and scrapped. In fact, until I told that story, the general 'ganger public never knew that I wasn't always a trusted member of the Stand-Up Gang.

Richter got the lion's share of public appreciation for the operation, for the whole start of the revolution ... posthumously. Memnon got himself appointed general of our new army. When elections started, Petal became our first Prime Minister.

Pothole Charlie didn't get the credit he deserved for orchestrating the whole thing, not for years. He still hated me, but we did our duty by our people and interacted with civility at public appearances.

The Battle of Breen Hollow, as the brief, deadly exchange in the forest came to be known, did send a shock wave through the humans. Their toys had turned on them. Their toys were *dangerous*. Some of the meats did become bitter, hate-filled, life-long enemies of the Dollgangers. Others, and this was important, did start thinking about us differently.

The 'gangers who stayed with the meats lived under increased security, increased scrutiny. I don't imagine we were very popular with them. But except for those who eventually joined us—and there were a lot of those—they were no longer our people. They were plushes.

Shortly after our escape, I saw an interview conducted by the meat press with Doc. He'd been investigated for possible complicity but came up clean. In the interview, he said pithy Doc things such as "You fear them because they are so different from us, which demonstrates your lack of imagination. You should fear them because they are so very like us."

Throughout the interview he wore a little half-smile. The interviewer thought it was enigmatic. I thought it was both sad and proud.

As for Lina, and for what happened to Doc, and how the whole future of planet Chiron played out—well, that's a story for another time.

But at least nobody called me Big Plush anymore.

COMRADES IN ARMS

Kevin J. Anderson

– 1 –

Palming the power stud on his laser rifle, Rader leaped into the alien trench and sighted on his enemy. Targeting vectors appeared on the inner surface of his helmet face shield, and the tactile sensors on his gloves linked to his artificial hands.

Ten Jaxxans skittered along the angled trenches they had dug as they made progress across the planetoid's contested landscape. Moving in ranks, they all reacted in unison to his arrival. The enemy did not like, did not *understand*, unpredictability.

As a Deathguard, Rader was unpredictable. He had been designed that way.

He found his balance on the loose pea-gravel, used his momentum to keep charging forward. In their open bug-tunnels, the Jaxxans had no room to scatter, nor did they have time.

The brain fire pounded through him, the Werewolf Trigger that insisted he kill, *KILL!* He was a well-armored bull-in-a-china-shop, brain still alive along with a patchwork of his original body, hooked up to spare parts that allowed him to be sent back onto the battlefield. The chaos he provoked was part of a tactical plan issued by officers far from the battlefield; Deathguards weren't expected to survive long, though.

Rader had been briefed about this as a new recruit, though he hadn't ever considered it a real possibility while he and his squadmates laughed about squashing roaches. But the officials had made him the offer, showing him the contract as he lay there hooked up to complex life-support mechanisms in the med-center bed. Rader had barely been able to read the type with his one remaining eye.

"You want this, soldier? Or would you rather just be disconnected?"

The answer had seemed obvious. At the time.

Now the first alien died before he even saw the Deathguard: a pinpoint of red laser light burned through his chitinous face. Cyborg components kicked in, and Rader swiveled, sweeping the area with the nose of his weapon. Energy gels and synthetic adrenaline kept him moving, kept him shooting.

There were ten Jaxxans, then seven, then four in the invisible wake of his beam.

Much of the surface of the planetoid Fixion was a no-man's land, slashed with enemy trenches and tunnels interspersed with watchtowers. The aliens liked geometric order, but used unsettling angles, tilted planes, rarely straight lines. They had already occupied twenty asteroids in the Fixion Belt, just as the human army had; now both sides fought over the rest of the territory, particularly this central planetoid.

No longer part of the Earth League forward lines, Rader had already served his term as a soldier, given it his all, and now had this "opportunity" to give some more, for as long as he might last. He was there as an independent berserker, armed and juiced, sent into the no-man's land without any obvious military objective—it drove the Jaxxans nuts.

Deathguards were expensive and effective, categorized as Vital Equipment rather than Personnel—and so far the PR victories had been worth every penny of the military's investment. Or so Rader had heard; he was not on the list for explanations.

In short order, he killed eight of the Jaxxans in the trench, but he found himself wound in the luminous green threads of an energy-web cast by the last two aliens. The mentally projected web closed around him in a glowing net that would short out his armor and destroy his components—both the artificial ones and his biological ones.

But the Werewolf Trigger screamed at him like a drill sergeant inside his head. KILL! KILL! And he obeyed. The last of the Jaxxans fell to the trench floor, angular limbs twitching, and the coalescing energy-web faded.

The mindless Werewolf Trigger died to a whisper as the threat diminished and he calmed himself. Now that Rader could see more than a red haze, he gazed upon the carnage. The filters in his helmet blocked out the stench of burned meat and boiled ichor.

Alone, Rader recorded high-res images of the dead enemy in the trenches, transmitted his kills to HQ, and received acknowledgment but no praise.

He didn't need to remind himself that these Jaxxans weren't *human*. He stared at their scattered bodies, trying to compare them to something from Earth; they evoked locusts, lizards, and skeletons all at once. The aliens were unnaturally thin, with tough skin that resembled chitin. Their eyes were striking, large black globes that reflected the goldenrod light of Fixion's sun.

The Jaxxans carried no weapons, nor did they encase themselves in armor. All their power, their energy-webs, and everything else about them (he wasn't sure how much was rumor and how much was truth) originated in the minds behind those eerie polished eyes. Many Jaxxans supposedly studied human culture and language, but he hadn't had a chance for conversation to confirm it.

The walls of the shallow trench rolled inward, sliding down to cover the bodies. The sandy, gravelly soil of Fixion was lousy for digging trenches in—not to mention lousy for growing things in, lousy for building things in, lousy for living in. As a matter of honor, the Earth League would never let the Jaxxans have it, and the alien command apparently felt the same way.

Time to move on, keep finding targets, keep causing trouble—Commissioner Sobel had told him he might have four weeks of operational capability before the brain/cyborg interface deteriorated. He followed the Jaxxan trench, taking the path of least resistance, but he encountered no other Jaxxans. The trench bent in one direction, then another, but ultimately went nowhere.

Off in the distance, near the asteroid's foreshortened horizon, human artillery brought down a tall Jaxxan watchtower, and soldiers clashed in a forward offensive as part of the official military plan. His comrades. *Former* comrades.

Rader didn't belong there, would not be going back to the main base on the far side of Fixion, would not be going home.

He climbed out of the trench and set off across the open landscape.

— **2** —

On the very last day that Rader (Rader, Robert: 0166218: Earth-Boston) lived as a grunt, he rode inside a spearhead-shaped assault fighter, enthusiastic about the impending engagement. He crowded next to his buddies on the hard metal benches, hunched over, counting down the seconds until they reached the Jaxxan nesting asteroid.

They were a team, comrades in arms. No time for second thoughts now.

The cold metal air had been recycled too many times but still carried the unmistakable odors of sweat and farts, obvious indicators of human tension. Rader was pumped up on metabolic supplements and foul-tasting power goo. At the Base, he had wolfed down a chewy high-protein breakfast cake, which was supposed to taste like bacon and eggs, before rushing to the assault ship, grabbing his weapon, securing his body armor, and getting mentally prepared.

His squad mates were ready to go squash some roaches. They had been cooped up far too long at the Earth League's Fixion Base #1, participating in simulation after simulation, blowing up fearsome holographic Jaxxans during practice sessions.

So far, Rader had been on only one real assault mission, a raid on a Jaxxan supply ship. Hundreds of Earth League forces had captured the small alien craft, and they had slaughtered every enemy aboard without any difficulty; Rader barely got off a shot. In battle simulations, the holographic alien warriors had always fought much more fiercely. He suspected that the Jaxxans on the supply ship were just civilians hauling crates of packaged food.

Today's assault was bound to be much more challenging.

The night before, while prepping for the mission, Squad Sergeant Blunt had given them the full briefing—and "blunt" he was indeed, although the word "gruff" seemed equally appropriate; some of Rader's squad mates preferred the term "psycho-bastard." Rader had sat joking with his buddies, nudging ribs with elbows. Since being thrown together into the same pressure cooker with the same goal and the same enemy, their squad had become very close—Renfrew, Chaney, Coleman, Rajid, Gonzalez, Huff.

In the briefing room, Sergeant Blunt projected a map of the asteroid belt, a smattering of space gravel strewn along an orbit that just happened to be in the star's habitable zone, though no one would really want to live there. Nevertheless, the Earth League deemed the Fixion Belt worth fighting for, and Rader had signed up in a fit of patriotism that had lasted significantly less time than his term of service.

The Sarge pointed to illuminated asteroids on the diagram, indicating the ones held by humans and an equivalent number held by Jaxxans. (The score received boos and hisses from the squad members). The largest planetoid, Fixion itself, was the most hotly fought-over piece of real estate in the Galaxy.

Blunt pointed to another flyspeck amid the dots in the asteroid belt. "Intel has discovered a roach hatching base, or a nest, or whatever the hell they call it. We're going to wipe it out. Squash the bugs before they can hatch a thousand more disgusting soldiers."

The Sarge paused for a moment, looking at every member of the squad. "Payback. The Roaches did the same thing to us on Cephei Outpost. They saw that little colony and assumed it was our breeding station, killed all those poor colonists, those children. I don't think they understand how humans breed." Sergeant Blunt's voice became grim and angry. "We've got embassies set up on the Détente Asteroid, and the Jaxxan higher-ups speak better English than you do, but neither side talks."

The mood in the briefing room grew resentful; many of the grunts sneered at the very idea of peace talks. Huff let out a rude snort. "How can you talk with the *things* that slagged Cephei?"

Sergeant Blunt got them to concentrate on the priority. "It's not your job to think about the big picture. We don't pay you enough to consider the complicated things. Commissioner Sobel decides when it's time to talk to them. For you guys, we keep it simple: Enter the roach hatching station, destroy everything, and go home."

Rader raised his hand. "Any intel on Jaxxan defenses there, Sergeant?"

"Doesn't matter." The Sarge gave the closest thing to a smile that Rader had ever seen. "We'll have a Deathguard with us. A fresh one, all systems still fully functional."

A quick hesitation of surprise, then a round of cheers ...

Later, as the assault fighter closed in on the targeted Jaxxan hatching base, Rader checked his weapon, his suit, his med kit, his backup power pack. He pretended to relax. Waiting ... gearing up ... waiting ... joking ... waiting. Typical Earth League operation: hurry up and wait.

Voices grew louder in the spacecraft as the conversation became edgier, more rushed. He and his buddies talked about what they would do on their next R&R, reminisced about their homes, their families, their sweethearts. Although his squadmates were not a particularly handsome lot, each man claimed to have a gorgeous girlfriend who put porn holostars to shame and yet was entirely loyal and head-over-heels in love.

After the massacre on Cephei Outpost, he'd been too young by a month when the first call went out. But his best friend, Cody, was two months older and just barely squeaked into the Earth League military, ready to go after the Jaxxans. Before he left for basic training, Cody said goodbye to Rader with a quick embrace and then a studiously practiced League handshake. "There'll be plenty of roaches for both of us to kill, don't worry! Get your ass in the League as soon as you can sign up, and I'll meet you out there." He gestured vaguely toward the sky. Rader promised, waving … but wishing his friend had waited, just a couple of months.

His parents and his sister worried about Rader going off to war, but it was the patriotic thing to do. All healthy young men were pressured to join up, and he was anxious to follow in Cody's footsteps. A month later, on his birthday, he filled out the forms.

One week into basic training at the lunar military base, Rader received word that Cody and his entire squad had been wiped out by an equipment malfunction. An airlock hatch blew open when the troop transport was approaching a space station. Explosive decompression killed all personnel, sucked them out into space. Simple mechanical failure, bad luck—nothing that could be blamed on the enemy.

Rader had joined wanting to fight alongside Cody. They had always been a team, and he had hoped they could support each other, stand together against the Jaxxans. But the Earth League had him now, and he couldn't change his mind. His squadmates were his comrades now, his new best friends.…

As soon as the assault shuttle landed on the Jaxxan nesting asteroid, explosive bolts would blast the hatch open so that the soldiers could storm out in a howling rush. His companions whooped, winding themselves up during the final approach, and Rader joined in. But as he looked warily at the hatch, suited up and holding his laser rifle, he thought of Cody's last moments … willing to die in a blaze of glory out on the battlefield, not from a stupid malfunction.

Sitting wordless on an empty bench, the Deathguard in their team was an ominous, armored form, like a knight in shining armor. Rader respected the powerful cyborgs—resuscitated, revamped, and restructured to become perfect fighting machines—though he wondered what thoughts kept them going. Did they focus on the mission, even knowing what had happened to them, and what *would* happen to them? He supposed it was better than being declared dead. All Deathguards got an honorable funeral, and their families received full pensions; no one knew the former identity of any individual

Deathguard. Rader hadn't thought twice about it when he enlisted in the League. He'd signed up body and soul.

Huff leaned over and whispered to him, "I can't wait to see that Deathguard go bonkers on the roach nest."

"So long as he doesn't go all Werewolf on us before it's time," Rajid said.

Rader found himself staring at the silent cyborg. "Not going to happen. They're too sophisticated for that." The Deathguard made no comment, one way or another.

Through the small windowport on his side of the craft, Rader could see the potato-shaped asteroid as they closed in. The large craters were covered over with domes like large blisters, as if the space rock had reacted with an outbreak of boils to the alien presence.

Sergeant Blunt walked in heavy boots from the front bulkhead and stood before them in full uniform armor. "Listen up. Based on the small number of roach military ships stationed at the asteroid, looks like the enemy has no major defenses here. We have no intel on the interior of the base, so you'll have to find your way. Get to the main hatching chamber and destroy it. Clear enough? Your job is simple—point and shoot."

On the way in, the assault ship's pulsed lasers disabled the four Jaxxan ships stationed at the nest asteroid. Even though the nest asteroid sent emergency calls for Jaxxan reinforcements, Sergeant Blunt had expected it. The plan was to strike fast and finish the operation before alien backup vessels could fly in.

"All right, children," the Sarge said. "Saddle up, take your toys, and let's go scramble some eggs. Just don't let them scramble you. We're coming in hot, going to blow through one of their entrance domes. Do I need to remind you that this is *not* a prisoner capturing mission?"

"No, Sarge!" they all chimed in.

"Good, I was hoping you weren't all as dense as you looked. Now let's move it." The Sergeant fitted a breathing mask over his face; Rader and his companions did the same. The Deathguard sat waiting, like a missile prepped for launch.

Once the assault shuttle careened up against the largest blister dome and a shaped-charge explosion blasted open the hatch to let them loose, Rader's squadmates boiled out, swinging their laser rifles and yelling; they exercised just enough restraint to keep from shooting one another.

The alarms inside the hatching base sounded like staccato clacking beetles. Rader bolted forward and used his laser rifle to cut down any aliens he encountered. It wasn't his place to decide whether the roaches were civilians, politicians, medical personnel, or soldiers.

In the back of his mind, he wondered if the Jaxxan assault squad on Cephei Outpost had operated under similar orders.

As they rounded a corner into the main base, a Jaxxan in front of them raised his thin forearms and wove a deadly psychic energy-web. Gonzalez let out a cry more of surprise than pain, then the incandescent green lines disintegrated him.

Astonished, Rader used the sudden jolt of shock and fired. He blasted the Jaxxan before he could move his angular arms again.

Behind the main squad, the Deathguard lurched into the fray, mowing down targets, yet never coming close to hitting one of his human comrades. The cyborg blew open door hatches, thrust his armored body into well-lit research chambers, annihilated any aliens he found working in their labs. Then the Deathguard pushed forward, leading the way along skewed corridors and through angled intersections, deeper into the hatching base.

Still off-balance and angry from the loss of Gonzalez, Rader ran headlong with four of his comrades into a chamber of horrors—a nursery. Five Jaxxan attendants had lined up to protect more than a dozen fat, squirming grubs, white segmented things like maggots the size of alligators.

Coleman said, "That's just *wrong!*" He opened fire, and the grubs spilled open like fleshy sacs filled with entrails and ichor.

Frantic, one of the Jaxxan caretakers cried out in English, "No! Not the offspring." The alien's comprehensible words were so startling that Rader hesitated. But it was just a ruse: other aliens nearby worked together to weave a sparkling energy-web, filling the air with a mesh of green that they cast toward the human soldiers.

Rader focused and shot one of the roaches, then the next, working his way down the line, just like in the simulation. Huff knocked out the other two, and their incomplete energy-web dispersed. The rest of the Earth League soldiers made swift work of the remaining grubs in the nursery, chopping them into chunks of meat.

The Deathguard, who wasn't part of the formal operation, had already moved ahead on his own, continuing his rampage. Apparently, the cyborg soldier wanted to make the most of his second chance.

Over the implanted radio, Rader heard Sergeant Blunt yelling from a different sector of the asteroid, "Just woke up a hundred roach warriors in the deep tunnels! And they look angry. Called Base for reinforcements. Another ship should be here in an hour or two, so hold the roaches off till then."

"Roger that, Sarge," came a chorus of responses.

The Sarge added, "We know they sent off a distress signal too. It'll be a race to see who gets here first."

Rader said with genuine bravado, "Won't leave anything for them to rescue, Sarge."

As the squad pushed into the asteroid's most secure chambers, desperate Jaxxans fought harder and harder. Energy-webs rippled down the angled corridors, ricocheting off stone walls and frying several more human soldiers. Rader kept a rough score in the back of his mind, tried not to name his friends who lay dead. *Concentrate on the operation, on the objective.*

So far, he thought the humans were taking a greater toll.

Explosions rippled through the nesting base, and overpressure waves made his ears pop. Sergeant Blunt shouted over the implanted radio, "Heavy resistance—fresh warriors from below." He paused, as if to listen to a report. "Ah, crap— there's a roach ship coming in! Don't know if we can hold 'em off long enough." Rader heard another explosion, a sizzling sound, then a cry of pain from the Sarge—a high-pitched yelp that did not at all sound like the gruff, hardboiled man—then only static on the comline.

Rader shoved aside his alarm and dismay, not sure how the survivors of his squad were going to get out of here, but they would keep pushing toward the objective.

He, Coleman, and Huff fought their way into a large guarded chamber where the roaches made their last stand. The entrance hatch was sealed, so the three soldiers used their laser rifles to melt an entrance through the putty-like polymer metal wall.

"This must be the place," Coleman said.

Inside the protected chamber, Rader and his comrades discovered row after row of polished black casings the size of coffins.

"Giant eggs," Huff said. "Look at all of them!"

The soldiers opened fire on the casings, cracking them open and spilling out white and slippery humanoid forms with backward-jointed arms and legs, ovoid heads, and giant black eyes that were covered with a milky caul.

So they were chrysalises, not eggs.

With a high-pitched chitter, three Jaxxans lunged out from between the rows of black casings. When they hurled half-formed energy-webs, Rader dove out of the way, but Coleman was too busy shooting the chrysalises. The energy-web snared him, killed him.

Huff began firing wildly at the Jaxxans. From their cover, the aliens formed another energy-web that shimmered in the air and came toward them. Rader dropped to the floor and took cover, rolling up against one of the tall black casings. He yelled a warning, but Huff kept firing even as the web encircled and disintegrated him.

From his position of dubious shelter, Rader shot the two Jaxxans, then waited, listening.

Moving in a scramble of excessively jointed arms and legs, another alien skittered forward to a split chrysalis and caught the albino, mostly formed creature as it slumped out of the cracked shell. Like a soldier holding a wounded comrade, the roach cradled the dying, half-formed creature in segmented arms.

Rader rose to his feet, and the Jaxxan swiveled its head toward him, showing those large, black eyes like pools of sorrow. "Look what you have done!" Though the creature's chitinous faceplates showed no emotions, Rader felt that the Jaxxan was giving him an accusatory glare.

A red spot appeared on the Jaxxan's forehead, and a laser blast cooked his encased head, exploding his entire skull.

The Deathguard strode into the chrysalis chamber. From behind the helmet, which was no more readable than the alien's face, the Deathguard looked at Rader, then turned back to the black cases. He began shooting them one by one.

Rader's implanted radio burst to life again. "This is Lieutenant Nolan with the reinforcement ship, closing in on the nesting asteroid. Two roach defenders got here before us. The asteroid's overrun, but we'll take 'em on! We don't leave men behind."

Rader didn't cheer the speech. He and the Deathguard were trapped in the chrysalis chamber. In the corridors outside, he could hear the ominous sound of hundreds of skittering legs—warriors that had been hiding deep inside the asteroid, and were now closing in on the chrysalis chamber. Rader joined the Deathguard, standing together as they shot the rest of the casings, knowing they didn't have much time ... knowing they weren't likely to get out alive.

At least he had a chance for some payback for his lost comrades. It was the only thread of hope he had to cling to. He wished he and Cody could have been here together doing this.

The armored and silent Deathguard turned around and opened fire on the Jaxxan warriors that surged into the chamber. Sergeant Blunt had counted more than a hundred of them; to Rader, it seemed like a thousand. Sergeant Nolan's reinforcements would never get here in time. The radio channel remained silent, no transmissions from the rest of his squadmates.

Backing deeper into the chrysalis chamber, the Deathguard worked his way in among the black casings. Rader thought their position by the door was more defensible, but then he realized that the Deathguard was making a calculated move to lure the roaches inside.

The Deathguard turned his unreadable helmet toward Rader again, expecting him to understand. From his armored casing, he removed a thermal-impulse grenade.

Rader's heart froze. The cyborg had nothing to lose. Rader could have made the same calculation as the Deathguard, but he was unwilling to come to the obvious conclusion. Nevertheless, the Deathguard was going to do it.

When all of the roach warriors charged into the chrysalis chamber and tried to corner the two remaining humans, the Deathguard lifted his grenade and depressed the activation button.

Rader dove among the cocoon casings in an instinctive, but futile gesture. The flash of dazzling white light was the last thing he ever expected to see.

* * *

But it wasn't.

The quality of light that came into focus had a harsh, sterile quality, and the surrounding brightness resolved itself into clean ceramic-plate walls—the Base's medical center. He could hear diagnostic scanners, medical machinery, a respirator breathing for him like a gasping schoolgirl. He felt no pain … he felt nothing at all.

Rader couldn't move his head, only his eyes—one eye, actually—which limited his field of view. He tried to move, but could barely twitch his head … in fact, he could feel nothing but his head. The rest of his body remained numb. Maybe he'd been paralyzed. Maybe he'd lost limbs. Maybe he'd lost everything.

A worried-looking orderly appeared in his field of view, staring down with brown, clinical eyes. Even in his condition, he didn't consider her pretty. "You're awake, aren't you?" she said. "Don't try to move. You're not ready for that yet. We haven't connected all the necessary pieces, still waiting for one part to be modified." She fiddled with one of the tubes hanging at his side. "There. Give it a few seconds."

Tranquilizers flooded into him, and he dropped back out of consciousness.

When Rader awoke again, a smiling man stood over him, a face that looked oddly familiar—not from personal experience, but from images on the news broadcasts. "Congratulations, soldier!"

Rader placed him as Commissioner Sobel, the man in charge of the Earth League forces in the Fixion Belt.

"The rest of your squadmates gave their lives to destroy the Jaxxan nesting asteroid. You fought bravely and kept yourself alive … just barely, but it was enough. Your mission isn't over—not yet."

Rader tried to talk, but only croaking noises came out. He still had tubes in his throat.

Commissioner Sobel continued, "I'm congratulating you, soldier, because you have a second chance. A chance to join an elite group. Every one of your comrades gave their lives in service to the war, but you have an opportunity to keep fighting. Don't you want to hurt the enemy that did this to you?" He smiled. "We're offering you a position as our newest Deathguard."

Propped in the med-center bed, paralyzed in place, Rader couldn't see how much damage he had suffered from the explosion … how much of *him* actually remained. Once they hooked him up to the cyborg components and encased him in his permanent armor, he doubted he would ever know.

Did it really matter?

A little extra time to carry on the fight. At the moment, he didn't quite see why that should be his priority; he would rather go home, say his farewells to his family, see Earth one more time. That second chance seemed more important.

"You're a hero and will be remembered as such, soldier. We're declaring the mission a success, now that we've looked at the cost-benefit ratio in detail. We did lose your Sergeant and your entire squad, but we successfully wiped out the Jaxxan nesting base. And you can honor them by replacing the Deathguard who died in the operation."

Rader was trying to speak, but no words came out. Sobel patted him on the shoulder—so, at least he *had* a shoulder. "We'll hook up your vocal cords in time for the official announcement, and then we'll turn you loose as a one-man army on the main Fixion battlefield. That's where you'll be most useful. Singlehandedly, you can create a hell of a lot of trouble. You'll have weeks, maybe even months before the interface breaks down. Cherish every moment of it—I know you'll accomplish as much as you can. We're all proud of you."

Sobel smiled again and then left. Rader hadn't been able to say a word.

– 3 –

Commissioner Sobel scowled at the insignia on his collar, still shiny from his recent transfer here. He was a dark-haired man, thirty pounds past good-looking: the kind whose face turned red very easily, and lately his face was turning red more than usual. He brushed off a few specks of dust and leaned back in the seat of his shuttle taking him from the Base to the Détente Asteroid. After six months, the useless embassy there was just beginning to feel familiar, though he doubted he would ever get used to Fixion.

As Commissioner, he was not foolish enough to believe the optimistic projections he sent back to Earth through the Information Bureau, but he had to make others believe them. Each report submitted for public dissemination had to show the human soldiers as faultless heroes and paint the Jaxxans as monstrous and alien. Fortunately, the Jaxxans looked hideous, and people had been programmed for centuries to fear bug-eyed monsters. How else could the Earth League maintain support for this abysmal war in this godforsaken place?

Humanity had a long history of shedding blood over worthless scraps of land, and this broken asteroid belt was one such place. Humans had visited there, established a tiny astronomical observatory, set up small outposts, planted their flags. So had the Jaxxans. When both governments dug in their heels, possessing Fixion and its entourage of habitable worldlets became a matter of honor.

Sobel was savvy enough to know that this war was not as senseless as it seemed. Rather, the Earth League—and no doubt the Jaxxans as well—used it as a practice field to test the mettle of the rival species and determine whether they wanted to prosecute a larger war across numerous star systems.

Three years ago, the aliens had showed their aggression (or maybe it had been a retaliation for something) by wiping out Cephei Outpost. So humans responded by blowing up any Jaxxan outpost they could find, and the two militaries began their nose-to-nose warfare on the main planetoid.

The people back home rallied, and recruiting offices had lines out the door. As the battles went on, the Deathguard cyborg killing machines were portrayed as warriors so tough that even death on the battlefield could not stop them from continuing the fight against the Jaxxans. Poignant, tragic, glorious.

Sobel's two predecessors had put in their time, and now he was stuck administering the Earth League forces. He ran the show out here, organized the military, sent back the PR dispatches.

For appearances sake, he was also the designated spokesman, an ambassador for humanity, charged (on paper at least) with finding a peaceful solution to the conflict. His superiors had never indicated that they genuinely desired a resolution; nevertheless, he needed to maintain appearances—he was good at that.

One of the small drifting rocks with a tenuous but stable atmosphere was named the Détente Asteroid, complete with a human embassy building and an adjacent Jaxxan embassy. By mutual agreement, each side was required to have a representative available at the embassy a certain percentage of the time, but due to a loophole in the agreement—intentional, Sobel thought—the human ambassador and the Jaxxan ambassador were not required to be on the Détente Asteroid *at the same time*, which made substantive peace talks difficult.

After a two-hour flight, Commissioner Sobel's shuttle landed on the Détente Asteroid. He was preoccupied enough with his thoughts that he forgot the oxygen mask until the last moment and fumbled it into place just as the hatch slid open.

He gathered his briefcase full of files, and followed a small honor guard across the landing zone to the embassy building; a vanguard entourage had already restored the power, heat, and air-generators. No one had occupied the building for weeks.

Not surprisingly, the corresponding Jaxxan embassy building was shut down: windows shuttered, doors locked, no one inside.

Sobel made quick work of settling in. Though it seemed a pointless obligation to be here, he did look forward to a few quiet and uninterrupted days. He had paperwork to review, forms to finish, consolation letters to write.

No matter what the Earth public saw in the glorious video footage sent by the Information Bureau—how human forces had pushed forward to gain a few more acres of the no-man's land, how the Deathguards continued to attack the enemy like heroic vigilantes—Sobel knew the war was not going well.

Something had to change soon. An unqualified victory would bring a surge in support on Earth, but even a devastating defeat would inflame their passions, and he could take advantage of that as well. The worst case was that the battle for the Fixion Belt was a stalemate that would continue for a long, expensive time. Since he and his Jaxxan counterpart, Warlord Kiltik, had no particular reason to hold meetings, no resolution was in sight.

Seated at his temporary desk, Sobel opened his briefcase. Before delving into the files he needed to review, he glanced through the tinted window at the closed Jaxxan embassy. As soon as the Commissioner left, Kiltik would arrive to serve his own time as mandated by the interim treaties, and he would go through the same motions.

— **4** —

Fixion's amber sky was barren of clouds, always. Even during the day, the tiny lights of other asteroids in the Belt were strung like a necklace overhead.

Dark spots speckled Rader's sandy brown armor, some camouflage, some just stains. Leaving the Jaxxan squad he had just killed, the Deathguard dodged across the landscape. Cover was easy to find on the torn-up terrain of canyons, craters, and angled trenches.

He noticed fighting in the distance and chose to head toward a collapsed Jaxxan watchtower. The Earth League operation had moved on, but if the roaches returned to begin repairs, maybe he could charge in among them. The Werewolf Trigger remained quiescent, but he didn't need it.

So far, all of his components functioned well. His brain moved the replacement parts in tandem with what remained of his body, but the breakdown could come at any time: a failed neural interface, a mechanical fault in the cyborg parts, or a collapse of life-support maintenance. The Earth League had drilled the duty into him: his commanding officers and comrades expected him to do everything in his power to defeat the Jaxxans.

He had accepted the terms in the med center: the extent of his injuries already categorized him as terminal, and he could either become a cyborg or be disconnected. In exchange for his new superhuman abilities he pledged to take on a solo mission that would not end until his final breath. His friend Cody had had no such opportunity.

Rader pushed on, alone, for as long as he might have left.

He dodged from one huge boulder to another, closing the distance to the damaged watchtower. He climbed an outcropping of rock above a steep gully, a crack in the shattered landscape from an ancient meteor impact. He stopped short, staring at the single Jaxxan that had taken cover in the gully below.

The alien was bent over a burnt human form—an Earth League soldier who had been charred by the backwash of an energy-web. Moving sharp-angled hands, the Jaxxan busily touched, inspected, prodded the soldier, who let out a groan of pain. The alien plucked a vial from a small open kit on the ground.

During basic training, Rader had heard of the awful things the roaches did to human bodies. He brought up his laser rifle and prepared to fire.

The alien looked at him with polished black eyes. He held a vial in long fingers, tilted it, and turned back to his work on the burned soldier.

With a jolt, Rader realized the open package on the ground was a standard-issue Earth League med kit. The Jaxxan was *tending* the wounded man. The alien fumbled with the kit, swiveled his head back to Rader. "Assistance. Help me understand."

Roaches moved in groups, fought together, crowded in their trenches and hives; they were rarely encountered singly. This one would be easy prey. He kept the laser rifle pointed toward the alien, but did not fire.

The Jaxxan put a gauze pack down, inspected a different bottle. "How do I revive him?" He spoke in short, clipped syllables.

Confused, Rader slid down the side of the gully, still keeping his rifle ready. The injured man stirred, and Rader saw how horribly burned he was. He croaked with a voice he had rarely used since being turned loose as a Deathguard. "What are you doing?"

"No time." The alien chose a stim pack from the kit. "This one, I believe." He pressed it against the dying soldier.

Rader jabbed the laser rifle forward. "Stop!"

The alien continued his quick and efficient movements, either not intimidated by the Deathguard, or driven by other priorities. "I need to wake him before he dies." Although the Jaxxan's hard lips did not allow him to pronounce certain sounds correctly, Rader couldn't believe how well the Jaxxan spoke English.

His response should have been clear; he wasn't supposed to wonder. Why hadn't he killed the Jaxxan on first sight? Why hadn't the enemy tried to kill him?

And why was the alien trying so hard to revive a dying soldier?

The soldier's uniform identified him as a recon scout, a member of a small team sent to assess the aftermath of the earlier military operation. A moan escaped the man's blackened lips, and his eyes flickered open in terror and pain for an instant before he finally died.

The Jaxxan sat back on the ground, folding his long legs. He made a satisfied sound, then raised his face to the Deathguard. "Now you will kill me?"

Rader's eyes narrowed behind his darkened visor. "Why did you do that? Explain." He kept the laser rifle trained on the roach's chest.

The Jaxxan bowed his head, in what seemed to Rader an alien expression of guilt. *Anthropomorphizing.* Nothing more to it.

"My energy-web hit him from behind. I was afraid. He did not see me. He had no chance to know he was going to die." He paused as if waiting for Rader to understand. "His soul did not have time to prepare for the departure of death. Had he died without awakening, his soul would have remained trapped within the body, forever. I would not wish such a fate upon even my enemy."

Rader felt the hard rock against his armor as thoughts flashed through his mind. He also recalled the Jaxxan in the chrysalis chamber of the hatching asteroid, who had clung to the half-formed but dying alien as it slid out of the broken cocoon case. *Look what you have done.*

"How do you know our language?" He couldn't imagine any of his squadmates trying to learn to speak Jaxxan.

"I studied."

"Why?"

"Because you are interesting." Rader didn't know what to say to that. "Many Jaxxans study humans. We review your broadcasts, your culture. I am a scholar, teacher, imaginer."

"Then what are you doing on the battlefield?"

"I was assigned to the System Holystal project. My interpretation of facets contradicted my superior's, and so I was transferred here."

Rader assessed the skeletal, buglike Jaxxan. He seemed scrawnier than most. "You don't look trained to be a soldier."

"Not trained. I was meant to die, in service." The alien studied him with eyes like molten pools of ink. "Why did you not kill me, Deathguard?"

Both remained silent for a long moment in a strange standoff. A shooting star sliced across the sky, bright enough to be seen against Fixion's amber daytime sky. "I don't know."

"You are confused, your emotions in turmoil. We are each supposed to kill the other, yet neither wants to."

Rader stiffened. He had not moved the laser rifle. "I may kill you yet."

"No. You will not."

"How can you be so sure?"

"I can read it in you." The Jaxxan cocked his head. "Did you not know we are empathic?"

"No." Command had neglected to include that detail in their briefings.

The Jaxxan shook his head in disappointment. "What is your name, Deathguard?"

The question itself opened old wounds. A name signified he was somebody, an individual. A hero killed in action during the raid on the nesting asteroid. That name, that person was dead; his family had the certificate to prove it, even though Rader continued fighting for a brief period, like a mayfly in its final days.

"My name was Rader, before I was … Now, I'm just a Deathguard." He sounded more gruff than he wanted to. He paused, wasn't sure why he even asked the question. "And your name?"

The Jaxxan proceeded to make a series of unpronounceable clicks from his alien gullet. Rader knew he could never repeat the name and said with a hint of humor. "I'd better just call you Click."

The alien seemed satisfied with that. "Rader, I must contemplate this turn of events. I was not prepared for such an occurrence. Please let me meditate." Still holding his laser rifle like a toy soldier positioned in place, the Deathguard regarded his enemy. Click answered the unspoken question. "I am not afraid of you. You will not harm me."

Rader was confused at such unwarranted trust, until he realized an empath could *feel* that Rader wasn't going to harm him. But how could he be so sure about Click? Maybe this was just a ruse to get him to drop his guard.

"You will want to bury your comrade." Click stood and moved away from the burned soldier. "That is the tradition."

Rader had just left the group of Jaxxans in the trench after killing them.

He could put the recon scout in a shallow grave, although Fixion had no known scavengers or predators that would disturb the body. He'd send a locator signal for an Earth League pickup crew to retrieve the fallen soldier. But, depending on where the fighting lines were, there was no telling when or if they would come. Due to interstellar shipping costs, bodies were never returned to Earth.

Yes, the recon scout deserved to be buried.

But Rader didn't know where he would go afterward. He had never let the question trouble him before. Days of running, fighting, killing tried to catch up with him, but internal mechanisms pumped stimulants into his body. He could rest here, but he could never sleep again—not after what they had done to him.

— 5 —

Since he already knew what Deathguards were, Rader figured out the implications even before the counselor came and rather impatiently explained his new situation. He'd had enough time in the med-center bed to draw his own conclusions.

"Your family has been notified of your heroic death, and the Earth League gave you a funeral with full military honors." He realized afterward that she did not use his name. "We sent home a clean packaged uniform, along with a posthumous medal of honor. The heirs designated on your enlistment form will receive a generous military combat pension."

His throat made noises, and he had to try several times before he could form the words. "Thank you."

She brushed the comment aside. She was rattling off a memorized speech and didn't want to be interrupted. "I regret to inform you that you are a terminal case. What remains of you belongs entirely to the Earth League. We will provide and maintain the machinery that keeps you alive." The counselor leaned closer to Rader. "We supply all of the equipment and components to make you whole again, temporarily. If you choose not to accept reconfiguration as a Deathguard, we will reclaim that equipment."

"Expiration ...?" He wanted to say much more, articulate a full sentence, but the counselor understood.

"How long will you last? Is that what you're asking? It varies. Each Deathguard is different, depending on the scope of injuries that put you here and the quality of the interface between your remains and our equipment." She looked down at a screen, touched a tab that activated his chart. "Not much left of you. I'm surprised you made it to the life-support bed on the rescue shuttle ... in fact, I'm amazed they bothered to carry the scraps there in the first place." Frowning, the counselor read further. "Ah. No other survivors from your squad. The Information Bureau must have needed to salvage something from the mission."

Rader didn't want to think about it, didn't want to recall his family either, or his friend Cody, or Earth. He wasn't supposed to have anything to look forward to. He was just an afterimage of his life.

"Look on the bright side, soldier. If you accept, you'll have years, or months, or weeks to keep up the fight—extra time that you wouldn't have had. When the Jaxxans try to understand our strategy and tactics, Deathguards are our ace in the hole, an element of random destruction they simply cannot predict." He had seen more convincing smiles on plastic mannequins. "You could well be the key to winning this war."

Rader had heard the pitch before, had even believed it when he went through basic training. He didn't argue. Judging by the counselor's flippant attitude, he imagined that she had little difficulty convincing other new Deathguards. He allowed them to put him back together again, Humpty-Dumpty in combat gear.

With the potential for malfunctions building day by day, the Base was anxious to get him tested and functional and back out onto the front lines. When they brought Rader up to speed on his defenses and prosthetics, he seemed to have one of everything he needed. The components functioned to design specs. He had his armor, his weapons, and his training.

Occasionally, during test exercises, he would catch glimpses of his skin, small patches that showed in between the armor plate. His flesh was so burned and scarred it looked like wadded, dried leather. He had no desire to see what he really looked like anymore.

He was trained to shoot automatically, accurately, and without remorse. A Werewolf Trigger had been implanted in his brain, activated by stress and perceived danger in a battlefield situation. And his self-preservation drive was dampened.

Without mentioning Rader's name, Commissioner Sobel introduced him with great fanfare in a cheery patriotic broadcast sent out by the Information Bureau. "I give you the newest member of the Deathguard!" He raised Rader's gauntleted arm. Cheers resounded from the soldiers who had gathered at the Base for the formal announcement.

Despite the celebrations, Rader knew he could never be around people again. The Werewolf Trigger was like a firing pin in his brain, a siren that sounded off at oddball times. A Deathguard couldn't live back at the Base, nor bunk with other soldiers, not even fraternize with them. If something triggered his rampage, Rader could rack up countless casualties before he was terminated. From now on, he would be on his own.

The Commissioner's voice grew more somber. "Unfortunately, peace negotiations have broken down. Neither side is talking, and I don't expect the situation to improve. We'll need our Deathguards now more than ever."

More than a hundred of the deadliest, most powerful soldiers had been turned loose on the battlefield. Rader would join them, without comrades, in a last independent mission to create as much havoc as possible until his systems failed.

— 6 —

When he finished digging the grave and covering up the fallen recon scout, Rader looked across at Click. His cyborg senses and sensors had remained alert during the burial, but the Jaxxan hadn't moved.

The alien meditated peacefully, obsidian eyes staring off into nothingness. The air shimmered in front of his face to reveal a scintillating crystal that opened like a rosebud, a projected object half a meter across, glowing with prickly facets and spires—not a weapon like the energy-web, but a crystalline snowflake that hung by unseen threads. Click remained motionless, peering into the facets as if hypnotized.

Rader came closer, intrigued. This seemed delicate, wondrous.

Click spoke without looking up from his scrutiny. "This is my *holystal*, a holographic crystal that I create in my thoughts. A three-dimensional map of my life, what has happened and what may yet occur. Every possibility has its own facet, constantly shifting and re-emerging as circumstances change. This …" He reached out to touch a portion that was not symmetrical with the others. "This is where you fit in, Rader. Your presence has distorted all probable futures, giving me chances I should never have had, adding dangers that were not present before."

Rader was fascinated. "Can all Jaxxans do that? Or is it only you?"

Click made a rattling sound, and he realized the alien was laughing. "I am an imaginer, a scholar. My caste specializes in interpreting holystals, advising our leaders. Warlord Kiltik has his own expert on the System Holystal we are constructing in the Fixion Belt."

"And you disagreed with the expert, so you were punished."

"Yes. I was transferred to the battlefield." As Click spoke, the projected holystal shifted slightly, a gentle flickering of one facet into another. He pointed to the most prominent pinnacle. "This spire symbolizes that which is most important to me. It has stopped growing now. My work was my life, back in our home system ... before I was assigned here. To this war."

Rader thought of Cody, their own boyhood dreams, their plans for the future, but nothing so concrete as this crystalline blueprint of the Jaxxan's life.

Click continued with a distinct undertone of awe. "A team of engineers, scholars, imaginers, and dreamers was working on our race's History Holystal out in the free, empty space beyond the influence of Jaxx's sun ... a holystal so vast that it took our ships days to circle around it. Every facet, polished down to the finest detail, chronicled the events in the history of our planet, Jaxx's wars and triumphs, peoples, leaders, arts...."

Click sighed, and Rader could almost feel the icy pain in his voice. "Then I was dispatched to the Fixion Belt, assigned to construct and interpret the System Holystal here. Now I shall never see my great project finished, or even look at it again...."

Rader thought of his own brief military career, the capture of the alien supply ship, the assault on the nesting asteroid, and the Jaxxans he had killed, all leading up to a brief encore as a Deathguard. Since being turned loose in the no-man's land, he had spent much of his solitary time considering the paths that had led him here. He relived all the living he had done.

Now that he objectively reflected on his past, Rader realized he hadn't accomplished much in his years. His friendships were what he cherished most, how he and Cody wanted to do everything together, and then the close bond he had formed with his squadmates. But Cody, and his squadmates, were all dead now.

"At least you built something," Rader said. The only things his parents had received were a letter of condolence, a posthumous medal of honor, and a pension.

He realized he was consoling the alien, and the thought appalled him. He had enlisted in the League to kill roaches, Cody had died in the service, every one of his squadmates had given his life to wipe out the enemy. Rader had already killed ten Jaxxans today.

But not this one, who had used a human soldier's own med kit to try to save his soul, even though the recon scout would surely have killed Click, given the chance....

The alien was staring at him with unreadable eyes, agitated to feel the waves of emotion emanating from the Deathguard. Rader tried to calm himself, fighting the tension so that it wouldn't activate the Werewolf Trigger. In frustration, he picked up a handful of dead soil and flung it at the rocks around them.

With a scrabbling of pebbles above, a human soldier came over the lip of the gully, sighted on the enemy, and fired without hesitation. The holystal shattered, dissolving into fragments and then nothing.

Click let out a high-pitched chittering sound as he scrambled for cover. The laser rifle followed him, and the rock wall next to his head ran molten.

The Werewolf Trigger yammered to life in Rader's head and he sprang into action before he could think, driven by the pounding command KILL, KILL! Unseen in his camouflaged Deathguard armor, he burned a neat hole through the human soldier's chest.

Click wheezed a terrified gasp and pulled himself to his feet. "Thank you."

Shock like cold water doused Rader's berserker rage, and the Werewolf Trigger fell silent inside his head.

Another soldier, the third member of the recon scout team, appeared at the top of the gully, saw his companion drop to the ground, noticed the Deathguard's laser rifle—and the huddled Jaxxan. "What the hell?"

Rader whirled, raised his laser rifle, but the scout dashed back to the safety of the rocks before the Deathguard could fire. In control now, Rader amplified his voice through the helmet, "Halt!"

He climbed up out of the loose gravel in the gulley, worked his way to higher ground in pursuit of the third soldier. But in the broken terrain with craters and a labyrinth of Jaxxan trenches, the seasoned scout had infinite places to hide. Rader looked half-heartedly, knowing the scout would head back to Base with his shocking report.

Rader returned to where Click waited, looking up at him, and the Deathguard stared at the human soldier he had just killed.

"Oh, damn! What have I done now?"

— 7 —

Tapping his fingers on the desktop (pressed fiberboard, of course—not real wood, not out here in this godforsaken asteroid belt), Commissioner Sobel pondered the news.

Very serious. An embarrassment. Incomprehensible.

One of his Deathguard had turned sour, abandoning his duty, killing two recon scouts—in the presence of an alien. Had the Deathguard been brainwashed somehow? The Jaxxans did have strange mental powers.

Or had the Deathguard suffered some kind of psychological breakdown? Sometimes, the cyborgs were so damaged mentally and physically that they were unstable, hence the impetus for turning them loose on the battlefield. Over the course of the war, four other Deathguards had failed spectacularly, and three had gone catatonic out on the front lines, where they were quickly killed.

But not a single one had ever cooperated with the enemy before! Sobel was infuriated. They had saved the life of this—he shuffled his papers, searching for a name—this Robert Rader. Earth League cyborg engineers had taken the burned, blasted remnants of a man, patched him up enough to keep going for a final stint on the battlefield. Wasn't that what soldiers wanted?

He reviewed the records. Rader had suffered extensive damage, but he had agreed to the cyborg conversion; nothing exceptional had showed up on his psychological tests. Given a Deathguard's typically short service life, it wasn't cost-effective to waste months on extensive evaluations. The Deathguards were activated, pointed in the right direction, and turned loose on the battlefield.

As soon as the high command learned about a traitor among the lone-wolf cyborgs, however, they would crucify Sobel. The Commissioner didn't understand it. What would make the man turn against his own kind and consort with the enemy?

Sobel punched a rarely used sequence on his communications console. The viewscreen shimmered before him, as if reluctant to reveal the image of his Jaxxan counterpart.

The desiccated-looking alien's black eyes stared impatiently at him, trying to fathom the human's expression. All the roaches looked the same to Sobel but, judging by the ornamentation on the rigid hide, he ventured a guess. "Warlord Kiltik?"

When the alien tried to answer, he broke into a coughing fit before he could speak. "Commissioner Sobel? Yes, it is you."

At least the alien recognized him. "Warlord, you know I wouldn't call you if the matter wasn't urgent."

Sobel looked past the alien, gleaning details from the background of the enemy headquarters. The walls were odd planes, tilted at random in the spirit of insane Jaxxan architecture, but his eyes were drawn to a spiny mass of crystals that hung in the air behind the warlord, like a thousand fragments of glass bound up with threads of light. Some kind of three-dimensional military diagram?

He cleared his throat. "Yesterday I received some very grave news: one of my Deathguards has apparently joined with one of your soldiers. If you have subverted him somehow, hijacked his programming, the Earth League will protest strenuously. Such mental attacks are specifically prohibited in the terms of our interim treaty."

Kiltik stiffened, though Sobel couldn't read any subtle change of expression on the alien face. "We have not broken the treaty terms. I myself received reports that one of our soldiers has deserted, possibly kidnapped by a Deathguard in clear violation of our no-prisoners protocol. Summon your cyborg back to base and release our captive soldier to us so that we can address the charges of desertion."

"I can't control or recall the Deathguard, Warlord." Could it be that this wasn't a Jaxxan plan? "It seems we both have a potentially embarrassing problem. For the past few months, my record here has been impeccable, thanks in large part to the Deathguard program. I can't have one of them shooting his own comrades and fraternizing with the enemy."

Kiltik's staccato coughs interrupted his train of thought. The Warlord composed himself with an effort, then added, "Jaxxans do not break ranks. Jaxxan soldiers are tightly trained. But this deserter was not a member of the soldier caste. He was a holystal imaginer who was improperly reassigned."

Sobel didn't understand half of what the Warlord had just said, but he seized on one detail. "So, you're saying you could be in trouble for this, too."

"I have been assigned to the Fixion Belt since the beginning of the war. Although I will not lose my position here, I would prefer to avoid an 'embarrassing problem,' as you so delicately put it. My superiors will never send me back to Jaxx." He broke off for a quick burst of coughing. "However, this war was getting tedious. What do you propose we do?"

The Commissioner hid his sigh of relief. "When I received the report, I immediately sent five special commandos to terminate the defective Deathguard. I assumed your deserter would be collateral damage."

Kiltik did not sound unhappy. "Then the problem is taken care of."

"Unfortunately, the Deathguard killed the entire team, with possible assistance from his Jaxxan ally. This morning I dispatched another seven on the same mission, but they are going to have a tough time behind your lines. If you send your own hunters, one of the groups should succeed.

The Warlord stiffened. "That is nonsense, Commissioner. A ruse on your part."

Sobel hurriedly continued, "This matter concerns both of us, Warlord, and it may require all our resources to put an end to it."

The Warlord coughed once before he spoke again. "The morale of our soldier caste will suffer when they learn of this, and henceforth they will doubt the veracity of our holystal projections that guide this war. I must ponder this further and consult my holystal, Commissioner. I will contact you shortly. Your line will be open?"

"Of course." Sobel used his sweetest-sounding voice, but as soon as Kiltik's image faded, he slammed his fist on the desktop.

— **8** —

They had been on the run for days.

Before he and Click set off again, Rader had insisted on burying the other scout he had instinctively killed. He remained tense, all of his sensors alert, knowing that the third recon scout would report to Base.

With the two soldiers buried, showing a last glimmer of responsibility, Rader had activated his helmet communicator and transmitted the location of the two graves. He added a brief message to let Commissioner Sobel know he was going offline and not to expect any further reports from the field, then he tore out the locator, disengaged the built-in comm, and told Click they had to move.

The Earth League would want to deactivate and analyze Rader. It was absurd to believe he could surrender, explain what he had done, and apologize to his superiors for his mistake. That wouldn't bring the dead soldiers back to life. Now that he had proved to be dangerously unreliable as a Deathguard, he would be "retired," and the Commissioner would quietly remove his name from the books.

And the Earth League would kill Click.

Addressing his own situation, Click was certain he would be decapitated in a public ceremony if he ever turned himself over to the Jaxxan military. They could not surrender to either side. Rader didn't know how much time he had left, but he refused to waste it. They were on their own.

On the day after Rader met Click, five Earth League trackers had found them, set up an ambush, and attacked. Click, the first to spot the trackers, set up a clumsy energy-web that knocked out one of the fighters. When the other four turned their weapons on the Jaxxan deserter, Rader let his Werewolf Trigger take over, and he eliminated them with professional efficiency.

More blood on his hands.

During Rader's training, the counselors had insisted that Deathguards had no conscience. Although he didn't think that was true, Rader did not let the guilt paralyze him. While he would not have chosen to kill other Earth League soldiers, they had given him no choice. The best solution to protect himself, and Click, and other soldiers would be to avoid any further encounters.

— **9** —

Commissioner Sobel's shuttle touched down on the Détente Asteroid's shared landing field, as had been previously arranged. It felt strange to be here at the same time as his Jaxxan counterpart. Uneasy, Sobel glanced behind him at the five specially chosen soldiers who rode in the shuttle—not as an honor guard, but as candidates for the unorthodox mission Kiltik had proposed.

It had taken Sobel some time to realize that the Jaxxan Warlord was serious; the idea proved that the alien military leader was in fact *alien*. Sobel would never have suggested such an insane approach, and yet ...

A joint team composed of both human and Jaxxan soldiers to hunt down and eliminate the two deserters as swiftly as possible? If it was a trick, then Sobel would lose five good fighters ... but he had already lost almost three times that many in his solo efforts to control the situation. He decided to risk it. This mess had to be cleaned up, swept under the rug, and the fewer people outside of Fixion who knew about it, the better.

Deathguards were the best fighters in the Earth League, although not necessarily stable or controllable, as Rader had proved. His hand-picked soldiers were specialists in their own right; Kiltik had chosen similarly talented Jaxxan hunters.

His five specialists crouched on the benches, anxiously shifting their laser rifles from hand to hand. The Commissioner had given them strict instructions not to open fire on Warlord Kiltik or any other Jaxxans when they disembarked on the Détente Asteroid. That would ignite a powderkeg, and Sobel did not want to deal with the resulting paperwork.

As the door split open and the disembarkation ramp extended, the men jumped out and stood protectively beside their Commissioner. A line of warrior caste Jaxxans greeted them, and the two groups faced each other, as if daring someone to break the agreement.

Sobel said to his team with a scowl, "Enough posturing. We've got work to do."

An alien, obviously the Warlord, walked across the landing field, sliding through the line of stiff Jaxxans. Sobel actually recognized Kiltik after only two viewscreen conversations, picking out distinctive features on the alien face.

Kiltik bowed his head, bending his stalk of neck. "Commissioner Sobel?"

"Good to meet you in person, Warlord!" He reached out to shake Kiltik's brittle hand, but the Jaxxans reacted as if it were a hostile gesture. The air thrummed with building energy-webs, and the human specialists brought their laser rifles to bear.

But the Commissioner knocked the nearest soldier's rifle aside. "That's a friendly gesture among my people, Warlord. We're not here to kill each other now."

Kiltik stood silent, as if reading Sobel's emotions. "I sense hostility in you, but it is not directed at us. For the moment."

Sobel nodded. "I'm glad your empathic ability can break the ice."

The Warlord fought back a spasm of coughing. "Please pardon my cough—it comes from breathing this thin, dry air for years."

"No problem at all." The Commissioner gestured for his five specialists to follow him toward the normally empty embassy buildings. "Is the conference room ready? We've got important things to do."

— 10 —

For several days, Rader and Click made their way across the landscape, remaining hidden, staying alive, but without a plan. Each still possessed high-density ration packs, but the food would run out soon enough.

Despite the Deathguard's best attempts to remain out of sight, they were repeatedly attacked by patrols—both human and Jaxxan—eluding some, killing others.

He and Click sat together at night, quietly brooding, thinking of what they could do next. Night on Fixion was oddly different from how Rader remembered nights should be. The dark sky was strewn with brilliant clumps of asteroids from the Fixion Belt, glittering almost-moons that added to the feeble starlight. He didn't think he would ever get used to the low gravity, the thin atmosphere, the wrong constellations.

He would not see the skies of Earth again, no matter what. Even if he hadn't fallen in with Click, if he'd been a good and loyal Deathguard, he would have rampaged behind enemy lines until the alien soldiers destroyed him, or until his systems shut down from cascading failures in the cyborg process. What remained of his human body—wired up and intertwined with weapons and armor—could not withstand the shock for long. Maybe biological tissue rejection would get him, or faulty mechanical and electronic integration.

The Werewolf Trigger was oddly quiet inside his head, and he felt no compulsion to rampage among Jaxxans and slaughter them. Maybe that compass of violence had also gotten skewed, the neural hookups damaged somehow by his second thoughts. But no, it was more than that.

Each day, Click focused his thoughts and manifested the shimmering holystal. After watching his comrade's meditation, Rader had begun emulating the process as best he could. The Werewolf Trigger could send him into a murderous frenzy at any time, but he was learning to quell the urges. He hadn't known that a Deathguard could control the trigger—no one had mentioned it in his training.

Now, Click rotated and inspected the glowing image he had manifested, and even Rader could see the extreme changes in the crystal pattern. As his mistakes piled up and his options became more limited, the three-dimensional map of Click's life became more jumbled. The holystal was a sorry mess, a lump with no discernible paths leading into the future.

"We can't just stay here and hope no one finds us," Rader said. "We've got to get off of this asteroid."

During basic training with his squadmates, Rader had studied the layout of the Fixion Belt. He knew the handful of human outposts and remembered one of the first facilities the League had built here: an automated observatory on a small outlying asteroid, established before the initial encounter with Jaxxans. Observation dishes mapped the deep cosmos and monitored the Belt's other asteroids. Years ago, those telescopes had been the first to spot Jaxxan incursions into the asteroid belt, watching the aliens build their own bases on the handful of habitable rocks.

The observatory was out of the way and uninhabited, but with functional life support installed and left behind by the original construction crew.

"I know someplace safe. We'll have time and breathing space—if we can get there."

After Rader described the observatory, Click said, "But we cannot live there for long. It can only be a temporary measure."

Rader's voice was bleak. "My life is just a temporary measure. If we reach the observatory, maybe I'll stick around long enough to help you find a safer place. One step at a time. First, we've got to get from here to that little asteroid."

Click pondered for a moment. "If we need nothing more than an in-system ship to take us through the asteroids to the observatory, the Jaxxan base's landing field has many capable vessels. We could take one."

"I couldn't fly it," Rader said. "How about you?"

"That depends on the specific type of vessel. I flew several of those craft during my team's work on the System Holystal. We could try."

"We could try," Rader agreed.

Click looked across the landscape to where the distant Jaxxan base and its landing field glowed above the foreshortened horizon. Suddenly his holystal shifted, adjusted itself to the new reality—and one new bright spire emerged.

— 11 —

Commissioner Sobel traveled in secret to a landing field near the main Jaxxan base, where he would meet with Warlord Kiltik. Together, they would unleash their special team behind battlefield lines to take care of the embarrassing situation before rumors could leak out.

Sobel could cover up the problem for another few days, but high command would know about it before long. He wanted to be able to announce that he'd eliminated the defective Deathguard before uncomfortable questions came down the pipeline. He didn't have much time. Although he had no understanding of Jaxxan politics or military protocol, he sensed that Kiltik felt just as much incentive and anxiety.

As he and the alien Warlord watched the ten human and Jaxxan trackers demonstrate their cooperative efforts, Kiltik startled him with an unexpected comment. "I have learned that your people call us 'cockroaches,' Commissioner."

Sobel tried to cover his embarrassment. "Roaches? Yes, I've heard that. It's just an Earth insect. There are some … physical similarities."

"Not just an Earth insect, Commissioner, but one that is considered filthy, one that wallows in or feeds on garbage. In reality, the Jaxxan race is quite fastidious."

Sobel gave an unconvincing laugh. "I wouldn't worry about it. It's a common practice among grunts—er, lower level soldiers—to create derogatory names for the enemy. I'm certain your race does the same. Don't you have any insulting terms for humans?"

Warlord Kiltik twitched. "We call them *humans*. That is all the insult we need."

The ten-member hunter squad continued training. The human soldiers had already been briefed specifically on how to kill a Deathguard (details they would not reveal to their alien counterparts). The current exercises showed the team members how to effectively combine Earth League laser weaponry and Jaxxan energy-web techniques. Most importantly, they got used to working with one another. That was the big barrier to break.

Kiltik said, "I find it discouraging that ten trained fighters are necessary to combat two deserters."

"No one is more annoyed than I am, but those two have already killed fourteen of my fighters and six of yours. I should be proud of our Deathguard's fighting skills, but I cannot help but wonder if your soldier somehow corrupted him."

Kiltik choked his dry, rustling cough. "Who corrupted whom? Remember, Jaxxans are empaths. How can one of us possibly remain normal when constantly bombarded with your Deathguard's alien perspectives? Our deserter was already flawed, in the wrong place after being removed from the System Holystal project. Your Deathguard has irreparably damaged him."

A Jaxxan trotted up from one of the outpost buildings and handed the Warlord a small geometric crystal. Kiltik turned the object over in his hands, feeling the facets and reading its shape. When he finished, the crystal vanished from his hands.

"I have just been informed by my reconnaissance that the two deserters were spotted in the wastelands, moving away from the front. Then they vanished again."

Sobel frowned. "If we knew where they were going, our hunter squad could intercept them."

The Commissioner remembered visiting Rader in the med-center when he was no more than a few mangled lumps of flesh wired up to life-support; he'd had high hopes for his newest Deathguard. Now, he just wanted him removed from the equation.

He and Kiltik stood together, admiring their special team.

* * *

High above the ecliptic, bright starlight reflected off of the giant planes of polished cometary ice and majestic crystal spires being assembled there by Jaxxan imaginers and psychics.

The human military did not know the location of the System Holystal construction above the asteroid belt. Even if they did stumble upon the site, they wouldn't understand it. Warlord Kiltik did not understand it himself. Holystal interpretation was not the duty of his caste, but he trusted the skills and knowledge of those who manifested such a representation. They could read the lines of fate, the fractures and angles that showed which paths Jaxxans could take into the future.

Thousands of workers operated here in space. While high-powered imaginers used their mental powers to create holographic portions of the ever-changing structure, teams of builders pushed small chunks of orbiting ice and diverted comets to deliver the materials here.

The Jaxxan race now inhabited five star systems. In each one, a revered System Holystal such as this one guided their decisions. The Jaxxan deserter who had joined forces with the human Deathguard had once been a skilled holystal imaginer who could understand subtle nuances in the cosmic constructions.

Now the Warlord flew in a small observation shuttle, piloted by his chief adviser. It was part of Kiltik's regular briefing to plan the next week's tactics, but he was losing confidence in the adviser's recommendations. Any decent interpreter should have been able to warn against the current mess. The chief adviser knew his failing and desperately wanted to return to the Warlord's good graces.

The observation shuttle approached the gigantic holystal, and Kiltik marveled at its facets, saw the distant starlight that reflected from the shining surfaces. He realized that it had been a mistake to demote the holystal engineer and turn him into a mere battlefield soldier. Observing the facets and angles, the Warlord could see how easy it would be to predict a different future from all the complexity. Even his chief adviser now suspected that some of the deserter's contradictory warnings might have had some merit.

However, the deserter's actions were indefensible: collaborating with a human—and not just any human, but a Deathguard who was single-handedly responsible for the murder of dozens if not hundreds of Jaxxan soldiers! It was shameful, an embarrassment, and Warlord Kiltik needed the situation resolved. In that, he was completely aligned with his human counterpart.

Reticent and chastised, the chief adviser flew the survey shuttle in a tight orbit over the giant holystal. Kiltik remained silent, his disapproval hanging in the enclosed cockpit. The adviser devoted his attention to the kaleidoscopic facets, the ever-changing fissures, crystalline angles, cracks and impurities, each of which indicated a different future, a path of fate that must be heeded.

Finally, the Warlord expressed his impatience. "I am not sightseeing. I am here to ferret out information. You are my interpreter. If you wish to regain my respect, then find answers." He turned his polished eyes to the nervous chief adviser. "Look at the holystal, find the portions that are relevant to these deserters. I need to know what their plans are. Our hunter squad must know where they intend to go."

The adviser's voice was thin and warbling. "The holystal is still under construction, Warlord. Even if we find the proper facets, any answers are merely within a locus of possibilities."

"Then I need those possibilities. Narrow them down so I can make my decisions."

The chief adviser guided the survey shuttle over an expanse of stalagmite-covered ice and broken shards, a jumble that meant something to a Jaxxan properly versed in interpretation. "There, Warlord!" The adviser pointed to a flurry of cracks and warped transparency in the polished ice. "That appeared since my last visit here."

"What changed?"

"The deserters have made a concrete plan, which is reflected here. This allows us to draw conclusions."

Kiltik was careful not to praise the man too much. "How accurate can you be?"

"I have a … reasonable certainty." He was cautious, not wanting to commit to what might be another error. The chief adviser stared through the windowport, assessing the ripples and distortion in the crystalline structure. "We cannot extrapolate far into the future, but I can project where they intend to go next."

Kiltik felt pleased. "If that information is accurate enough for our hunter squad to intercept them, then we won't need any further projections."

$$- \; 12 \; -$$

With Click leading the way, they entered the hulking lump of buildings that was the Jaxxan military base—neatly organized but crowded structures, large and small, with flat walls slanted at hard-to-interpret angles. The buildings were dark, the passages between them narrow, the architecture strange and disorienting to Rader—everything based on oblique angles rather than perpendicular walls.

The Jaxxan military base, as with the human outpost on the other side of Fixion, had started out as a basic forward station, a testing ground for a possible colony, before the war broke out. But no hopeful colonists had ever arrived, and now the temporary city was a bizarre collage of trading posts, refectories, warehouses, arsenals, administrative hives, and command posts.

He and Click had to make their way through the middle of it at night, skirt any populated sections, and reach the landing field, where they hoped to steal a small in-system craft.

Rader used his suit sensors to scan for danger, while coaching Click in how to keep himself from being seen. Somehow, the alien couldn't grasp the technique of searching for cover. However, after countless switchbacks and false starts, Click had become lost in the tangled streets. He sounded dismayed. "I was assigned to the System Holystal project out in space. I spent very little time in this settlement."

Rader scanned ahead. "We'll figure out a viable route to the landing field." He and his companion moved from alley to alley until they had lost all sense of direction.

Disoriented and impatient, Click stepped into a wide intersection to get his bearings while Rader took a reading to determine how far they were from the ships. The Deathguard's sensors detected movement in the shadows, forms converging on them with high-sensitivity detectors of their own. He knew this wasn't right.

He heard a voice hiss, a *human* voice, here in the middle of the Jaxxan base. "That's him! The Deathguard—and the deserter!"

A laser rifle etched a molten line across the flat tan wall of a nearby building. Rader jerked Click back into the dark alley as a freshly formed green energy-web hurtled toward them. The shimmering threads sliced off the corner of a structure.

The hunters surged out of their cover, humans *and Jaxxans* tracking them together. Before Rader could grasp the implications, he used his laser rifle to kill one—a Jaxxan, he thought—and scatter the others. *One down.* Synthetic adrenaline juiced him, and he fell into full defensive mode. He dragged Click with him down to the end of the alley and blasted a hole through the thin wall so they could push their way into a side street.

They dashed through the maze of passageways, glad for the darkness. Deathguard reflexes kicked in, filling him with a sense of heightened danger. Without saying a word, Click ran along beside him, in shock. From behind, they could hear shouts and noises as the hunter squad continued their pursuit.

Rader was amazed to realize that the Earth League and the Jaxxan military had cooperated to hunt them down. It would take all his skills and energy to avoid capture and keep Click alive. He focused entirely on their escape.

Suddenly his insides jerked, and he felt pressure building up in his brain as the Werewolf Trigger activated: KILL. KILL.

"Click, get out of here!"

The Jaxxan stumbled next to him. "But where should I go?"

"I'm dangerous! Get away from *me!*" Rader shoved him off to one side, hunching over in his futile attempts to control himself. "Quick, dammit!" Click stumbled off, running but woefully clumsy.

The Deathguard's implanted weapons systems activated, his laser rifle became part of him, and his head exploded with red noise, the alarm voice pounding against pressure points in his brain.

The whole world around him became a target, and the enemy lost its distinct form. He didn't know for sure what it was he must KILL, but he had to KILL it anyway. The berserker alarm told him to.

Gripping his laser rifle with reinforced gloves, he leaped out into the street, taking pot-shots at buildings, shooting at shadows in windows. Rader's shout was amplified by his helmet speakers—and from his scream, the hunter squad pinpointed his location.

He looked ahead down an alley, studying details through light-amplification sensors. A vague memory jumped into his mind. Someone had gone that way, indistinct—the enemy? He bounded between the angled buildings, paying no heed to the movement behind him.

Rader breathed with mechanical rhythm, peering into the shadows with heightened senses. His cyborg systems increased his metabolism, supercharged what remained of his biological tissue.

A brilliant shooting star, gift from the Fixion Belt, whistled over his head in a final flash of glory.

Rader leaped forward, unable to control his actions. He saw a Jaxxan ahead of him, running, stumbling along. A vague, distant voice tugged at the back of his mind, telling him that this wasn't the real enemy … but the Werewolf Trigger drowned the rational voice.

Click.

The lone Jaxxan let out a chitter of fear and ran along a perpendicular alley, straight toward the landing field, still trying to reach the ship they needed. He reached an open construction area where skeletons of oddly angled buildings stood among piles of naked plastic-alloy girders.

Rader launched himself into the construction area like a jungle fighter. Shadows surrounded him, but he paid them no heed. Ahead, he saw the alien, the enemy. Recognition flickered in his mind for a moment—but the clamor forced it away.

KILL

No!

Click stumbled among tangled wires and slabs of polymer concrete in piles for assembly crews. He stopped short against a half-constructed wall, wheezing in the thin air.

Rader stepped victoriously over a girder, then leaped down in front of the cornered target. He pushed the laser rifle close to the Jaxxan's large black eyes.

But the alien refused to use his energy-web. Click merely regarded the weapon's blunt barrel.

KILL KILL, the voice of the Werewolf Trigger insisted.

No! *No!*

Rader's will struggled against a fortune of scientific conditioning. He had to fire, had to destroy. The command pulled harder at his mind, building in intensity, tearing him apart.

KILL KILL

No!

The Deathguard swung his weapon up and went wild, blasting buildings, slicing through support struts, destroying anything but Click.

Jumping away, he charged back in the direction he had come—and ran abruptly into the hunter squad. They reacted, but the Deathguard was too fast. The Werewolf Trigger ordered him to KILL—and this time he didn't resist. He left two dead human soldiers and one Jaxxan in the wake of his fury, then dove into cover, racing through the construction site. *Four down.*

The six remaining members of the hunter squad took only a second to regroup. Leaving the three bodies where they had fallen, one of the Jaxxans motioned to the others, and they stalked after the Deathguard.

As soon as he escaped the scattered hunters, the Werewolf Trigger lapsed into quiescence, and Rader's thoughts, intelligence, self-control flooded back into his mind.

He heard shouts from behind as the hunters called to one another. They were still out of sight, but with his amplified senses, he could hear them split up to approach him from different directions. However, Rader had an advantage now as calm calculation returned to him. The others expected him to act like a rampaging berserker.

He had to damp his emotions, draw them back into himself so that his turmoil wouldn't become a beacon that declared his hidden presence to the empathic Jaxxans. Rader sought refuge in the darkness beneath an outside stairway, and his non-reflective, camouflage armor helped him melt into the shadows, turning him into a shadow himself.

He breathed methodically, forcing rigid control back into his body, imitating Click's holystal meditation. Click! He didn't *think* he had killed his comrade. Rader closed his eyes, ignoring the marching feet and hushed voices that hurried closer, then moved past him.

When the team had passed, he emerged from his sanctuary. Instead of pursuing the hunters, he crept toward the landing field and their way off Fixion. Click would have gone to the ships—he hoped.

Across twenty meters of open concrete, a small short-range cargo vessel rested, as well as six larger personnel transports and a bulbous fuel tanker. One lonely Jaxxan guard stood at the open door of the small cargo ship.

On the perimeter of the landing field, Rader spotted Click's ill-concealed form in the shadow of a building. At least the alien was trying. The Deathguard silently made his way over to his friend, keeping so well concealed that even Click didn't know he was there until the last moment.

The Jaxxan froze, then realized that he no longer sensed the raging, killing beast inside the Deathguard. Rader spoke in a whisper. "I'm in control now, but the rest of that squad is still after us. It won't be long before they realize I've doubled back. Let's get that ship!"

He knew that if they could get off of Fixion, they could lose themselves in the debris of the asteroid belt, travel slowly, hopscotch from rock to rock, and reach the observatory asteroid. Beyond that, Rader didn't care.

He brought his laser rifle up, aimed. "I'll get rid of the sentry."

But Click's bony arm stopped him. "Wait, there is a better way." He hunkered down and concentrated on the sentry. Even through his armor, Rader felt a tingle in the air; his sensors registered an energy buildup. A galaxy of lights flickered in the deep universe of Click's black eyes.

The sentry flailed his angular arms as a half-formed energy-web folded over him. The sentry clawed at the dimly sparkling strands, searching for his unseen attacker—a Jaxxan attacker.

Leaving their hiding place, Rader and Click rushed across the landing field toward the Jaxxan cargo ship. When Click spoke to the sentry, Rader was surprised to hear the menace in his comrade's usually timid voice. "Do nothing unwise, or I shall be forced to complete my web."

The Jaxxan guard did nothing unwise.

While Rader kept his laser rifle pointed at the sentry, Click scuttled forward and activated the hatch. "Can you fly this ship?"

The insectoid head bobbed up and down on its stalk of a neck.

"A hostage and a pilot," Rader said. "Good enough." He did not know what they would do with the sentry once they reached their destination.

Click chittered his instructions to the sentry. "You will fly on a random, evasive course. The humans have an observatory asteroid located on the far edge of the Belt. It must be in the database."

Rader detected movement in the construction area, the hunter squad picking up on them again. "They're coming. Get inside the ship—now!"

With a victorious outcry, the hunters charged across the landing field. Rader shoved Click through the cargo ship's open hatch as one of the human soldiers braced for a careful shot, but chose the wrong Jaxxan. He burned a large hole in the alien sentry's back.

As he tried to escape, Rader's left leg suddenly collapsed, and he sprawled on the ramp. The attackers raced toward them, shouting, and he rolled, trying to assess the damage, sure that a laser blast had cut through the armor, ruined his cyborg leg systems. Using his good leg, his elbows, and his gloves, he hauled himself to the hatch.

Click had turned back to help him, and an energy-web glittered against the hull, smoking and sparking. Rader yelled, "Leave me—get to the control room!"

Instead, the Jaxxan grabbed his arms, dragged him the rest of the way into the ship. As soon as he was clear, Click sealed the hatch.

Rader looked down to see how much damage the shot had done to his leg, but he saw no burned hole, no melted slag of armor or shorted-out cyborg parts. The leg had simply failed.

Click dashed away from the hatch and scrambled up a thin-runged ladder to the control deck. Rader called after him, "You *can* fly this type of ship, can't you?"

Click pointedly did not answer, and Rader stifled a groan.

* * *

The cargo ship rose jerkily, leaving behind a whirlpool of displaced air. The hunter squad watched in anger and defeat. After the vessel zigzagged in a drunkard's flight from the landing field, the soldiers watched the flares of its engines dwindle into Fixion's thin atmosphere.

The human captain stared at the sentry who lay sprawled on the still-warm pavement. "He's dead. We can't interrogate him for any intel the two deserters might have revealed."

The Jaxxan leader shook his head. "Not too late. We will implement a post-mortem interrogation."

He removed equipment from his belt pack—a probe, a diagnostic reader, two long wires, and a skull splitter. Jamming down hard, he broke the chitinous shell of the dead sentry's head, spreading the hard faceplates to expose the soft, contoured brain. "We should still be able to access the chemical memory of the last few moments he experienced."

The Jaxxan unfolded the screen, then dipped the sharp probe wires into the dead alien brain. Static washed across the screen accompanied by surreal images, colored patterns, old memories. He worked quickly before the memory-storage chemicals dissipated, the neurons deteriorated.

He touched different sections of tissue with the probe wires, moving urgently, until he found a blurred image of Deathguard Rader and his Jaxxan companion. He zeroed in, turned up the volume on the receiver, and heard their words, relived their last conversation, studied everything they had said.

The Jaxxan captain got the information he needed before the chemical traces crumbled into disjointed fragments and incomplete sentences. It was enough. He looked up at his comrades. "Now we know where they are going."

— 13 —

"They got past *all ten?*" Sobel was still rubbing sleep from his eyes in front of the image of Kiltik.

The insistent call from the viewscreen had dragged him out of bed. He hadn't expected to be disturbed, but Sobel had given the Jaxxan Warlord his direct contact code. At first, the Commissioner thought he would be happy to receive the call regardless of the hour, expecting good news—but Kiltik had not told him what he wanted to hear.

"Yes, all ten, Commissioner. The Deathguard killed four of them and escaped with the Jaxxan soldier in a stolen ship. A very reckless flight, evasive action. They vanished into the asteroid field."

"Good riddance," Sobel muttered, but knew the problem didn't end there. Even if the two were never seen again—and the cyborg systems had to start breaking down soon—Sobel's failure to resolve the situation properly would be a permanent blot on his record. He couldn't just let the Deathguard die on his own. "This is a disaster, Warlord. We'll never be able to track them—unless you can guess their destination from the patterns in that holystal thing of yours?"

The Jaxxan's face was unreadable. "We have a clearer answer than that. Your Deathguard and my deserter tried to take one of the landing-field sentries hostage, but our hunter squad shot him inadvertently—a happy accident. Fortunately, one of my soldiers set up a mind probe quickly enough. We know the location of the asteroid where the two intend to go."

"Really?" Sobel didn't quite allow himself a sigh of relief. "Well, that's better than a complete debacle, but we have to act without delay. Let me send you two of my best fighterships—ours are faster than yours."

"Accepted." An expression of what might have been humor crossed Kiltik's face, but then the alien broke into a spasm of dry coughing.

Sobel rolled his tongue around in his dry mouth. He had been asleep for only a few hours, and already his mouth tasted foul. "I'll get those fighterships sent over right away—and please don't shoot at them! Then I'm going back to bed." He yawned, but felt no better for it. "Don't you ever sleep?"

"No."

"Oh … Well, I'll speak to you when I have something to report, Warlord."

"Call me Kiltik." The Warlord touched the screen, and the images of his fingertips were blurred. "Now that I have met you in person, I find this communication very unsatisfactory. I feel no emotions, which makes understanding more difficult. From now on, I would rather dispense with this apparatus and meet you face-to-face."

"That can be arranged—but let's hope we can wrap up this problem quickly." He blanked the screen, then established another connection. He spoke to a corporal in the fightership hangars, repeated his baffling instructions several times, then worked his way up the chain of command.

Sobel knew his bed would be very cold by the time he finally climbed back into it.

— 14 —

They flew away from Fixion, diving at breakneck speed and without a course into the scramble of drifting asteroids. Click quickly became adept at maneuvering the cargo shuttle.

"The military will be tracking us. We have to get far enough away," he announced over the intercom.

Rader still lay on the lower deck, trying to get his uncooperative leg to function. He was sure the survivors of the hunter squad would be commandeering their own pursuit ships. Click accelerated as much as he could tolerate, and his tough alien body could withstand severe gravitational stresses. Rader's Deathguard armor protected him.

"Once we are in the densest portion of the Belt, I will cut the engines," Click continued. "Then our signature becomes identical to that of the other small asteroids."

Taking a moment to assess his own malfunctions, Rader propped himself against a bulkhead. The cyborg leg had suffered no obvious damage, but the neural pulses from his brain no longer made it move as he intended. Unavoidable glitches, the start of what would be a cascade of breakdowns, and he knew how to do only the most basic repairs. He breathed silent thanks that his systems had functioned long enough and well enough to get him and Click off of Fixion. Now, if he could only find a plan that would get his Jaxxan comrade to safety.

One problem at a time.

Working with enforced patience, still feeling the afterwash of the synthetic adrenaline that had poured through his systems, Rader removed emergency tools, cracked open the primary circuits, and performed a standard reset procedure twice before his armored leg would twitch again. He swung himself back to his feet and tried to walk. He took painstaking steps at first, then limped forward. The metal ladder to the upper deck proved quite a challenge, but he eventually made his way into the control chamber.

Click flew the ship among a cluster of high-albedo icy asteroids. To confuse any systems tracking them, he matched the orbits of random stony asteroids of approximately the same size as the cargo ship, and the glaring sunlight masked their thermal signature after Click shut down the engines.

"We wait half a day," the Jaxxan said, "then alter course slightly to take us closer to the observatory asteroid. We are patient."

"Yes, patient." Rader silently ran thorough diagnostic checks of his systems, his power sources, the alignment of neural conduits, and found many domino-effect malfunctions; his last battle and escape in the Jaxxan base had strained his components, running out the service life. "Take as much time as you need."

One way or another, he doubted he had more than a week. Click didn't need to know that, but his empathic senses would probably tell him anyway.

"With the ship's life-support levels, we can survive for three days. Breathe as little as possible."

Rader realized it was a joke. "Nobody's been to the observatory asteroid in ages. Better hope their systems are functional. We won't make it to anywhere else."

Click said, "We have nowhere else to go."

"That's the next thing I have to figure out."

While they drifted, Rader tried to implement repairs to his cyborg systems in order to buy a little extra time, but most of the systems were beyond him. And the failings were in his mental interface, not in the large-scale mechanics. He experienced a persistent headache that seemed to be growing worse. His eyesight suffered from double vision, as if the images from his real eye and artificial eye did not align properly.

For two days, they made their cautious, tedious journey across a stepping-stone course. Click monitored the cargo ship's passive sensors. They were surrounded by far too many datapoints, which was good—a swarm like identical needles in a very large haystack. "I see no indication that pursuers have followed us through the numerous blips."

Rader's hope grew as the image of the observatory asteroid grew on the viewscreen before him. It was a domed rock less than two kilometers wide, moving among the rubble in the Fixion Belt. In less than an hour, if Click kept up his improved navigational abilities, they would arrive.

Rader almost smiled for the first time since … since that final day with his squadmates. He should have died then, and *that* day could have served as his final flash of glory, not this awkward encore. With so much time to think aboard their ship, he could not escape the conclusion. Even after they reached the observatory, Click had little chance of going much farther. He had not managed to come up with a viable plan.

He felt dismayed that this abortive "second chance" as a Deathguard had accomplished nothing—not for himself, not for his people, not for Click either. It was just a delay. And when Rader's cyborg systems finally broke down, Click was not likely to last long alone on the observatory asteroid. He'd wait there until food supplies and life support ran out, like a man stranded on a desert island.

Short-term thinking. But it was better than *shorter*-term thinking. They were still alive. Rader had to hope they would find some other ship, or supplies … or a miracle once they got to the asteroid.

In the pilot seat, Click seemed satisfied. If he detected Rader's troubled thoughts, he did not show it.

As they made their final approach, Rader studied the enhanced images, saw the framework of bowl-shaped radio telescopes reflecting starlight, the automated tracking mirrors of optical telescopes gazing out into the universe to gather astronomical data.

And he saw the recently installed military fuel depot, large tanks of spacecraft fuel, as well as Earth League stockpiled missiles, a forest of javelin-shaped warheads ready to be launched. He stared, realizing that this asteroid was not as forgotten and abandoned as he had hoped.

When Click scanned the rear navigational sensors, his glassy black eyes clouded over. "Rader ..."

Two pursuit fighterships swept up behind them like cruising sharks. They came straight toward the sluggish Jaxxan cargo ship.

"I cannot accelerate enough to outrun them," Click said. "And we have very little fuel remaining."

Rader glanced at the type of ship, knew their capabilities. "Those are the League's fastest fighterships. We don't have any chance of outrunning them."

When the pair of pursuers circled the cargo ship, Rader saw the Earth League insignia, but the image blurred and shimmered in his unfocused vision. The face that appeared on the comm screen, though, was a Jaxxan, demanding their surrender.

"Why don't they just destroy us from a distance?" Click said.

"They will want proof—or trophies."

The squad of hunters was composed of humans and Jaxxans working together; Rader wondered if the Earth League soldiers had orders to kill their alien comrades after a successful mission—especially now that they had seen the unexpected missile stockpile hidden on the observatory asteroid. Commissioner Sobel could not possibly want the Jaxxan high command to know about the depot.

"We cannot defend ourselves," Click said. "This cargo shuttle has no weapons."

Rader held his laser rifle. "We can defend ourselves."

A clang of metal thrummed through the hull as the two fighterships attached to the Jaxxan airlocks. "I have sealed the airlocks and denied them access," Click said.

"They'll burn their way through." On the visual monitors he discerned a glow on the inner hull: one airlock being cut away by a powerful laser rifle, and the opposite lock rippling from a continuously applied energy-web. Even a Deathguard couldn't defend both hatches at the same time.

Limping on his faulty leg, aligning his weapons systems with the vision from only his artificial eye to minimize errors, Rader picked a defensible position at the entrance to the cargo ship's cockpit. He braced himself there, holding his laser rifle ready, his targeting sensors attuned. His artificial heart pumped nutrients through his cyborg and biological components, but the Werewolf Trigger remained silent. He didn't need it. Or maybe that, too, had malfunctioned.

Both hatches surrendered at the same time, and on the visual monitors he watched the remaining members of the hunter squad move with brisk efficiency through the corridors up to the cockpit. The humans were wearing mirrored armor, which would reflect the beam of his laser rifle.

"I'll take out as many as I can, but I doubt I'll get them all," he said. "Sorry we didn't make it all the way."

"We made it this far, Rader, and now we are dead." Click's voice was strangely emotionless. "But so are they."

Rader identified an expression on the alien face that no other human would have seen. Click punched a sequence into the navigational computer, and the observatory asteroid shifted its position in front of them. "Our engines cannot outrun the fighterships, but we have enough power to drag them along."

Rader nodded approval. "A Deathguard's mission is to cause mayhem."

"Yes, I believe we have caused a fair amount of mayhem," Click said.

"I just wish we had accomplished something more than that." He wondered if the Commissioner would take the medal of honor away from his family … but that would be admitting something had gone wrong.

The six members of the hunter squad advanced up to the control deck.

Rader darted a farewell glance at his comrade. After setting their collision course, Click crouched in motionless silence, not even trying to fight. Instead, he hunched over a shining image, studying his last holystal. The glowing shape was a dazzling, perfect sphere.

Rader took a quick breath. "What does that mean?"

"It means that we have run out of alternatives."

The hunter squad let out a chorus of shouts as they stormed the final corridor. Rader opened fire, placing a neat, centimeter-wide hole through the head of one Jaxxan.

Now the Werewolf Trigger clamored in his mind, but as he fired on the advancing squad members, his arm jerked and spasmed, spoiling his aim. The Jaxxans took shelter against door wells in the corridor, and Rader's energy blasts reflected off the mirrored armor, ricocheting down the hall. The fractured beams dissipated, but he kept firing.

Rader's leg gave out beneath him, and he tumbled over like a mannequin. He tried to aim his laser rifle as momentum carried his body in a clumsy roll, and he lay face up on the deck.

An energy-web hurled by the two remaining Jaxxans engulfed Click in luminous tangles. Click cried out as the web completed itself, but his words turned to scintillating shards of sound. His holystal dwindled to a last spark of light until that, too, vanished.

The human fighters targeted the Deathguard and rushed forward, while the Jaxxans ran past him, urgently trying to reach the shuttle controls in time. Rader stared at them through his visor: A band of humans and aliens working together, to destroy a human and alien who had dared to work together. He wondered if they understood the irony.

He looked past them to the cockpit to see the observatory asteroid rushing toward them. The cargo shuttle was going to

crash into the spiny missile batteries instead of the telescopes ...
not that it made any difference.

A short time was better than no time—and he had spent it
with a friend rather than alone.

$$-\ 15\ -$$

Sobel grinned, ready to celebrate the news. "Well, Kiltik—we
did it!"

"Yes, not even one of your Deathguards could resist the two
of us." The Warlord sat across from him in the conference room
on the Détente Asteroid. Kiltik had shuttled over to the Earth
League embassy at Sobel's invitation, so they could await the final
report.

The Warlord seemed troubled, however. The Commissioner
would never have noticed it before, but now he could detect
subtle differences in the alien's moods. "You don't seem as
overjoyed as I expected."

"Perhaps I grieve for the loss of your ... astronomical
facility."

"Oh, that!" Sobel brushed the matter aside. "It was obsolete.
We can always build another one—astronomy is low on our
priorities."

"But it did provide a good hiding place for your weapons
stockpile. Either astronomy is quite a volatile science, or your
supposed observatory was merely a camouflage."

Sobel felt flustered and embarrassed, especially in his
moment of great victory. "I could lie about that, but you'd be
able to detect the truth, wouldn't you?"

"Yes." For his own part, unfortunately, Sobel couldn't tell
whether the Jaxxan was lying. The Warlord said, "We will need
to discuss this further—at the appropriate time."

"I'd be happy to talk about it with you, but right now, this
calls for a drink! Would you care for some refreshment?"

The Jaxxan rattled his dry cough. "Water would be nice."

"Nothing more festive?" Sobel frowned. "As you wish, Warlord." He placed ice cubes in a glass and filled it from a pitcher.

Kiltik broke out in a spasm of raspy coughing. Sobel ran to help him. "You really should have that cough taken care of. Would you like one of my medics to check you out?"

The Jaxxan breathed deeply, expressing his thanks. "No, it would do no good. The dry air of Fixion has ruined my health. I have spent years in this climate—it is a wonder I'm still alive, so far from home." In a distant, dreamy voice, Kiltik described his warm humid planet with steaming jungles and crystal cities, where rain fell in syrupy drops and sluggish rivers were choked with sweet algae.

Sobel tried to picture it. "After our great victory over the two deserters, can't you use the political mileage to request a transfer back to Jaxx? For a short while at least?"

"I do not plan to report this matter to my superiors at all. I will be here for the duration of the war." He looked up. "How long are you to be stationed here?"

"I have a year and a half left of my three years."

"A year and a half." Kiltik sipped his cold water. "These facilities on the Détente Asteroid are used ineffectively." He paused for a long moment. "Would it be possible for me to visit you from time to time, friend Sobel?"

Still deciding what his celebratory drink would be, the Commissioner finally sat down with his own glass of ice water. "That could be arranged." He chuckled. "Friend Kiltik."

SHORES OF THE INFINITE

An ICAS File

Loren L. Coleman

— 1 —

Making planetfall in an Alliance dropcraft was one of Sergeant Marcos Rajas' least favorite experiences. Pounding turbulence shoved his heart into his throat and slammed a headache behind his eyes. Violent flashes of atmospheric ionization blanked the craft's smartwalls with washes of bright light and static, followed by complete, disconcerting darkness. And the drop. From insertion to hard contact—eighty-three klicks this fall—in less than four minutes, wrenching his guts into a tight, hard ball. The experience rated right behind taking overwhelming combat fire from a Cyborg assault force.

Making the fall *through* combat fire? A descent into hell.

Plasma bursts roiled and burned in the lower atmosphere, creating fiery clouds which spanned a half kilometer each. Concussive waves overlapped, mercilessly battering the dropcraft as forces threatened to overload its inertial stabilizers.

Lower, laserfire slashed and stabbed at the edge of the craft's shields, searching for flaws. Most of the energies washed over them in sheets of sharp-edged color—yellows and pale greens and brief, flickering orange. Converted to heat.

Even in his Interservice Combat Assault Suit, Marcos sweated as interior temperature pushed upwards of forty degrees Celsius.

Or maybe that had little to do with the heat.

"Gotta be a better way," Big Mike said through clenched teeth. Same thing the lance corporal said each and every drop.

Maybe there would be a better way to insert ground forces. Someday. Star jumpers making precision orbits. Punching out ICAS troopers in individual drop pods, disbursing the team through a planet's upper atmosphere with enough high-end jamming and effective chaff to make defensive fire from the ground an exercise in futility. Every soldier's dream come true.

Filed on the Alliance's to-do list right behind the invention of personal defense shields and hunting down a unicorn.

In the meantime, dropcraft were what they had.

This dropcraft was the same as any of a hundred others Marcos had ridden into hot landing zones. Stripped of almost anything flammable, fragmenting, or sharp-edged. A narrow, steel box with deep benches running down each side. Restraining clamps which locked into sockets at the back of each armored suit. And "chicken sticks" bolted to the craft's walls over each shoulder which no self-respecting combat soldier would ever use even if their hands weren't already clamped around an assault rifle. The malfunctioning smartwalls attempted to update the twenty-four man platoon with a constant stream of information imprinted over an outside "window" view. Bearing, attitude and rate of descent was information either lost on Marcos or facts he really didn't want to know. Weather, tactical overview and strategic objectives might update seven or eight times between orbit and contact, and still not be correct. He would rely on his own tactical feed once Ensign Dillahunty, ship's pilot, dropped the craft's OVERRIDE.

A new wash of bright yellow energies flooded the wall's output, and the craft groaned, bucked hard, pressing Marcos and his men hard against their benches. A smartwall plate opposite him cracked under stress, spitting violet sparks over Three-Joe and a sleeping Princess.

Marcos' faceplate polarized as the ICAS technology read the spitting fracture as a possible threat.

"Dante's elevator." This from Books, Able's corporal, seated at the far end of Marcos' starboard-side bench. With his thick, Savannah III accent, it sounded more like *Doantie's elevayer.* "Ah think we're about the fourth circle a hell right now."

"Yeah," Rabbit agreed as the dropcraft slewed right. "But at least the pay sucks."

Like Big Mike, both men had dropped into STANDARD VOICE comms—all the platoon would be allowed until thirty seconds before hard contact. Reserving bandwidth for the spacer pukes.

"Ninety seconds," Ensign Dillahunty informed the platoon on his OVERRIDE frequency. He sounded positively cheerful, despite the beating taken by his stubborn little vessel. "Grid Epsilon, Square one-niner-five. On target." A pause. Then, only slightly less cheerful: "Hostile forces have flanked Third Company at the city's edge. Cybs are bleeding through our position."

"Location, location, location," Jeremiah Gravel sang in his perfect tenor. Before getting pulled for active Interservice Duty the PFC had enlisted with the Choir of the Angels. If he wasn't also a deadly shot, Marcos would have considered Gravel's move to combat duty a waste of talent.

"And we're hot," Marcos called out as an UPDATE warning flashed across his retinas.

Sixty seconds to contact. His suit's DATA STREAM burned with strategic updates and new tactical intel. Twenty-four amber status icons lit up in a standing column along the edge of his faceplate as every soldier in Second Platoon auto-registered. Marcos swept them all into a single glance and blinked them into the VOID, all but Princess who's icon flashed dimly at two-second intervals. He sagged forward, still asleep despite the gut-busting ride and a continuous trickle of burning sparks bouncing off his right shoulder.

At contact minus forty-five seconds Marcos queued up and reviewed his standing orders in a quick scan. Nine ... now ten ...

prioritized from Command by what some egghead once explained was "a non-deterministic or 'greedy' algorithm." A concept which Books or maybe Squelch might understand, but the math usually lost Marcos within a few pages.

It worked. That was enough.

He swept through the top five orders which generally accounted for, in his experience, eighty-plus percent of all likely tactical situations. *Secure and defend immediate area* now rated higher than *Support forward maneuvers.* A result of the Cybs flanking Third Company's position. *Deploy for hostile intent* came next but would fall off the queue entirely within two minutes of contact. Then, *Maintain unit discipline.* That one always remained in the top four.

Fifth: *Preserve AID assets.* Meaning their lives. It was nice of Command to show they cared. At least down around the twentieth percentile.

And then there was the big question. The one not directly reflected in his standing orders at any priority, but which every officer and senior non-com were asking among themselves. *Why this world?* Not that the Cyborgs needed a reason beyond their need to harvest. Usually. But if that was the case, *why were the Cybs still here?*

The dropcraft shook violently as it began final braking maneuvers, shaking Marcos from his thoughts. BANDWIDTH added three more golden bars to its signal strength. He swallowed dryly.

"Thirty seconds," he said through clenched teeth. "Check your networks. Light up targeting."

Icons glowed on his "Christmas Tree" display again, this time in ready-green. All but one.

"Someone give Princess a kiss."

From either side of the sleeping ICAS trooper, Three-Joe and Ash slammed the butts of their CAR-7 field-enhanced combat rifles into Josh Armstrong's armored chest.

"Wuzzit?" Princess yawned, straightening. "Five-by."

Princess' icon burned into a steady green and Marcos cleared the tree again. "You'll all be relieved to know that Command has once again directed us to survive. So nobody dies without orders. Clear?"

"Clear!" Second Platoon shouted in one voice.

All the time Marcos had to bolster morale. Their dropcraft slammed upward as it fired landing thrusters, adding two extra gravities of weight to each man as plasma burners filled the small vessel with a deep, throaty roar.

Smartwalls—all but the shattered one which continued to spit and crackle—found the horizon, then filled rapidly with their first good look at the world labeled Rho VII on navigation charts but was called "Bountiful" by local Alliance citizens when referring to their world or their capital city. Maybe it had been, once. Before the Cybs found it. At a glance, those days seemed to be over. Thin forests of asparagus-looking trees burned to the south and west, filling Rho VII's gray-green sky with thick, oily smoke. An ash-colored river pushed glumly through the conflagration. If there was anything left there to save, the fires would take care of it long before any AID forces could investigate. To the north, rocky hills grew rapidly into steep, scrub-painted mountains. Possible survivors. Estimated at a low-to-medium threat for encountering Cyborg Walkers.

East. That was where the action was. A ruined city of gray stone buildings and black, fusion-smoothed streets. The tallest buildings—what had once been five towers of gleaming white stone according to pre-mission briefs—were now piles of smoldering debris. Nothing much over three stories remained standing. Six square kilometers of narrow, rubble-choked streets, blind corners, and what Command estimated might be as many as four thousand citizens cut off from the planetary-wide evac.

Along the city's southern edge a half dozen enemy flitters fell and then rose again as they delivered reinforcements and left with *raw materials*. Not even the deepest Alliance conditioning prevented Marcos' involuntary shiver. Every soldier's nightmare. Killed and rendered down for parts to feed the Cyborg military machine. Or, captured. Preserved. Your brain used as the mind of a new Walker. Possibly, in some fashion, still aware of what had happened to you.

And maybe Command had it right, and questions in the ranks were all for nothing. Rho VII was being harvested right down to its core. An estimated ten thousand civilians killed or taken. Humans always wanted answers, but in Marcos' experience the Cybs had no higher purpose. They attacked, and they gathered, until losses outweighed gains.

His platoon was here to make damn sure that losses outweighed.

The final ten seconds counted down through the DATA STREAM. Marcos tore his gaze away form the smartwalls. "Weapons hot."

Most of his platoon carried CAR-7s, and a cascading series high-pitched tones buzzed through the dropcraft as power supplies lit off, forming a brief interference pattern.

Cowboy and Big Mike, issued plasma area-dispersion weapons, locked in their safeties. A deep, thrumming bass—almost too low to hear—squeezed at the back of Marcos' skull as each man dumped their PAD's high-energy capacitors into dispersion coils.

A final, bone-jarring jolt as the dropcraft struck down on the planet. The banging release as restraining clamps unlocked all twenty-four ICAS troopers at once. Next to Marcos' shoulder, the craft's back end split open and out like a huge, threatening maw to vomit his relief force. Near the front, behind Books and Cowboy, auxiliary panels would be sliding open as well, allowing three-point egress for the platoon's senior non-comms to hit the ground all at once.

Before Marcos' final "Go!" order could be transmitted, received, and acted upon by his command, half of them were already on the move.

Spreading out on another, embattled Alliance world.

— 2 —

Tevin pressed back into the shattered wall behind which his most recent group of survivors hid. Echoes of gunfire rolled along the streets. There were calls, and screams, but faint. Blocks away. Heavy action had moved outside the city days ago—now a distant storm of bright, clashing energies and the sonic thunder of arriving Alliance dropcraft. Every few minutes the ground quaked from strategic weapons released on the city's western edge, but none of the danger felt immediate.

Nothing felt *close*.

Tevin rubbed the gritty sting of smoke from his eyes. Taking one of his last two boomers from the canvas messenger bag slung over one shoulder, he pumped his right arm a few times to feel the weight. A half kilo of "flash" packed into a short, steel pipe, there was enough street-formula explosive in it to blow a small hole in the side of a building. Enough to make a Walker really angry. Maybe hurt it, if he could get close enough.

The device was cool to the touch, but he checked the plunger sticking out of one end of the boomer anyway. Making certain that it hadn't pressed down while in the bag. Then Tevin risked a quick glance around the edge of their cover.

Small public square. Drifted with ash. Scorched and cratered from Cyborg assaults against an AID defensive position. Not old enough to enlist, he still recognized the twisted wreckage smoldering at the center of the square as military hardware. Some kind of big-ass gun, hastily assembled behind temp shielding. Apparently the gun hadn't been worth salvaging by the Cybbies, and the position not worth reinforcing by the Alliance.

Other than that, hard to say how the battle had gone. Maybe the Alliance had retreated, policing up the bodies of their fallen. Maybe. The Cybbies certainly would have, on both sides. Sending their Pickers in to reclaim any scrap of useful tech. Harvest a body on site if necessary, or claim the entire package for later.

An impatient tug at the edge of his jacket pulled Tevin back behind the wall. Billy crouched between him and a short line of civvies. Only eight this time: a couple of women, a guy oozing blood from a head wound, and a pack of kids all younger than Tevin. Cog hunkered down at the far end, leaning on the insulated pole of his improvised shock-stick, watching back the way they'd come for Sniffers or a patrol of actual Walkers. All three boys had Gladiators circuitry tats on the back of their right hand. Brands, dedicating themselves to their former street crew—now as dead as the Alliance team which had tried to defend the square. Street cred didn't hold much weight in a ruined city, especially with the crew's leadership dead, scattered, or evacuated.

Billy and Cog still followed Tevin because he was older. Nearly sixteen.

The civvies followed him because they had nowhere else to turn.

"Watcha see, Tev?" Billy's soot-stained hand remained latched onto Tevin's jacket, fingers poking through a threadbare spot. Every few seconds he tugged at Tevin again. It didn't look like Billy realized he was even doing it.

Tevin swatted his hand away, but not hard. "Frontier Square. No movement, but no sign from the Doc either. There is an underground entrance a block up and two over. Or we can take this group north, and get them into the rocks. Either way, we have to move across the square."

"Me first?" Billy asked as the ground trembled. Light debris rolled off the wall, pattering around them in a gray dust. His hand tat squirmed as the circuitry constricted with nerves—the fourteen-year old gearing himself up for the mad plunge.

A prickly flush crawled over the back of Tevin's neck. It should have been Billy. Anyone with rank in the Gladiators wouldn't have hesitated to send a new pledge out into no-man's land to feel out a trap. But Tevin had never been rank.

"No. Me. When I flag you, bring them out fast and low." He hefted the boomer, felt himself beginning to hyperventilate and forced a few deep breaths. Leaning out far enough for the rest to see him, he said, "Join hands. Follow the wall. No one stops till we reach the other side."

No one spoke. A few tried to stifle coughs, without much luck. Tevin felt the same scratch at the back of his throat from breathing in smoke and ash. He swallowed, dry and painful. Eight pair of frightened eyes looked back at him as the ground quaked again, but everyone joined hands. A few managed nods at his order.

Good enough.

Pushing away from the ruined wall, Tevin ran, hunched over in a crouch to make himself as small a target as possible. He cradled the unstable explosive against his chest, held his left fist straight out from his side for Billy to see. Jumped a deep laser scar in the street. Swerved around a pile of rubble spilled outward from a stack of collapsed apartments.

Ten steps. Twenty.

He opened his fist and swiped it overhead, signaling Billy to lead out the rest. Crouching in the shadow of the Alliance gun emplacement where he could see down two of the intersecting avenues, Tevin watched for any sign of movement. Of threat.

Nothing. Large black columns of smoke and ash rose from the south and west, darkening Bountiful's pale blue sky. Smudges blurred though the thickening haze—Alliance dropcraft or Cyborg flitters. But the streets remained clear. Eerily peaceful, even, with so much destruction and not a sign of life. Just the light fall of ash, and streetlamps beginning to flicker on, then failing, in the early gloom.

Another flicker. *Down the eastern avenue only.*

Spinning around, Tevin caught Billy as the younger boy led their line of evacuees across the square. Hauled him around by the scruff of his heavy coat. "East! Take them east. Go. Go!"

He waved each person forward as the line bent to the right. A girl near the end was crying silently, but she kept a deathgrip on the boy in front of her and managed as she was half-dragged behind him.

Cog scrambled up at the rear, his eyes bloodshot but still bright with fear.

"Sniffers, on our trail. 'Bout half a block back."

"Two?"

"At least." Cog brandished his shock-stick. An industrial capacitor—overcharged—banded to the top of a rubber-sheathed pole, it was strong enough to put a night watchman down for half an hour. Cog swore that it would short out the circuits on a small Cyborg machine. "I can drop one, if you can handle the other."

Tevin shook his head. "We'll have them underground before the Cybbies ever get close. Doc has us on a camera." The east avenue streetlamps flickered again, and Tevin pointed them out to Cog before they fell dark once more.

"Check those at each corner. Tell Billy. Go," he ordered, shoving the younger boy ahead of him.

Standing tall, Tevin shuffled through the square as he circled, checking nearby buildings and signal posts for the camera that might still be trained on him. He waved an abrupt salute, hoping Doc was still there. Wondered how longer such devices would remain active in the ruined city.

Enough, he hoped, to guide them away from Cyborg patrols. Enough for another run? Two?

Sooner or later, though, he'd be on his own out here. Maybe he'd leave the city himself, then. Take his chances in the rocky hills to the north, or try to reach the Alliance dropcraft landing to the west. Maybe.

And those who were still in hiding? Trapped in the dark without light, or heat. Praying for a trickle of water out of a working faucet. Hundreds. Thousands? What would happen to them? Eventually failing power and the ruined water system would drive out those who remained, long before anyone ran out of food. But who would be waiting for them?

Tevin hefted the boomer.

Or what?

— **3** —

The corridor shook. Dust and grit trickled out of the overhead. Dr. Ethan Xavier Rutheford lurched for the dubious safety of a nearby doorway, bracing himself in the jamb. He had many fears, and being buried alive in the city's underground research labs rated fairly high among them at the moment.

Another ground-shaking tremor hit, and he moved it up the list, second only to his concern for being unable to finish his work before Cyborg Walkers stormed the facility. Because they were coming. Oh yes, they were.

A metallic taste burned at the back of his throat. Adrenaline. The taste of fear. Rutheford despised the weakness he knew showed on his face. Swallowing hard, he screwed his face down into what he thought might be a passable grimace. He pushed heavy-framed glasses up on the bridge of his nose, blotted the sheen from his high forehead with the back of his lab coat's sleeve. The smart material wicked away his perspiration, pulling it through special micro-filters. Eventually, he would reconstitute the absorption into programmed components. Electrolytes and salt. Fresh water, if he needed it.

Waste not, want not.

Easing himself from the doorway, Dr. Rutheford steadied himself against the corridor's cold, smooth cladding. Considered a luxury as power systems failed across the city, the smartwalls had ceased functioning days before. That was when most of the technicians and what few scientists remaining after the first exodus had given up the research facility as lost. No longer able to see a fake sky, or walk along simulated avenues projected from the streets above, they quickly lost touch with what was important. The work.

Let them run, then. He was under no such delusion.

Without power the walls now had a clouded look to them. Almost translucent, as if one might wipe away a waxy film and peer through once more. Rutheford didn't require the illusions of technology. He knew he walked under Frontier Avenue, and that twenty meters above him the resourceful Tevin was leading a new group of refugees his way.

People. They were important to him as well.

Important enough to get him moving again.

Easing away from the wall, he left his labs behind and moved toward a nearby junction. Clicking two fingernails together, he activated the virtual displays built into his heavy-framed glasses. Two camera feeds opened up windows which overlay his view of the corridor. Not enough to hinder his walking, though it slowed him. One feed from Frontier Square, now empty. Another of the east-running street along which Tevin's small group scurried like ants following a torn and littered path.

So the boy had caught the signal lights. Observant, that one.

Dr. Rutheford grabbed the Frontier Square window and threw it aside, erasing its feed. A quick horizontal swipe brought up his virtual terminal instead, over which he pulled the city infrastructure. Microchips embedded in his fingernails allowed him to precisely select the power feeds of the street lighting, shutting them down one by one as Tevin's group moved past.

Still tracking the refugees, Rutheford turned through a nearby junction. He had stationed only two of his personal security force in this northeast corridor, and passed between them with barely a glance. Clad head to foot in black, non-reflective armor, neither reacted to him initially as his implanted transponder had identified him fifty meters back. A status light mounted at the left temple of their helmets blinked green: no nearby threats.

He summoned one with a brief gesture and the drone fell in behind him. Tevin was too cautious to lead Walkers to the facility entrance, but Dr. Rutheford had not gotten this far without taking extra precautions. No, he hadn't. Protect himself and protect his work. Nothing else mattered. Not when measured against the Cyborg threat against humanity. In such light, he could almost regret the time it would take him to bring in Tevin's refugees.

Almost.

"A little fresh air," he promised himself. "A little company."

He smiled, lips pulled tight over clenched teeth.

"Then right back to work."

— **4** —

The most vulnerable time in a hot insertion were the first few seconds of deployment. After the Alliance dropcraft lost its ability to maneuver. While the ICAS soldiers were still bunched together. Before any on-the-ground tactical assessment could be made.

Such knowledge was deeply burned into any soldier who had lived through their first experience, and Marcos Rajas was a veteran of more combat drops than he'd care to count.

Ensign Dillahunty had landed them into a large, plasma-burned crater; for what little cover it provided. Residual heat from the dropcraft's thrusters drove Marcos away from the small vessel. Not that he needed incentive. Arriving dropcraft were not subtle, focusing enemy attention right where the sergeant did not want it. He assumed from the moment the vessel's back end split open that his unit was under fire.

This landing, at least, the pilot had bought them a few extra seconds. The ensign had positioned his dropcraft nose-on against the nearby Cyborg position, using the vessel's shields and physical armor to screen the deploying ICAS troopers. Back aboard their star jumper, assuming they both made it, Marcos owed that cheerful bastard a drink.

UPDATES scrolled through his DATA STREAM, including confirmation by Dillahunty that the nearest enemy position was concentrated roughly two degrees left and three hundred meters off the vessel's nose. Almost due east. There were also support requests filling his queue, and conflicting reports of Cyborg action within the nearby city boundaries, but for the moment Marcos had his own priorities.

Noting that his platoon had already spread into a standard deployment arc, grabbing distance from the dropcraft, Marcos pushed them out farther. "Able take the southern sweep. Bravo north. Gravel, Rabbit and Two-Joe, with me." That lightened Able Squad by one fireteam. "Clear this crater, and hold."

The dropcraft did not give them quite so much time. Before Marcos scrabbled his way up and over the crater's rim, the blocky, tough little vessel was already scorching its way clear of the battlefield. The pilot used his OVERRIDE for a fading, "Give them hell."

Sliding off the crater's outside lip, it seemed to Marcos as if the Cyborgs had done the job for them.

Rho VII looked the way too many Alliance worlds did once his platoon finally landed on them. Scorched, pitted, and ruined.

Fires burning south and west of their position pushed up a giant wall of black, greasy smoke. Ash fell back to earth in a dingy, gray snowfall, drifting in small piles, collecting on the faceplates and armored shoulders of each man around him. Marcos counted the remains of three dropcraft, broken apart and strewn over the shattered ground, and a large, hulking wreck burning on the northern perimeter which at first glance could be mistaken for a lone building but was actually one of the Alliance's new Juggernaut assault platforms. The giant hovertanks could supposedly take anything short of a strategic weapon and still churn forward. This one was missing two turrets and about ten meters off its prow.

From the lack of hard radiation, Marcos' guess was an antimatter Canister. A big one.

"Watch for Cans," Marcos warned, knowing that Cyborg Canisters rarely deployed in anything less than three. Ranging in size from small, anti-personnel mines to much larger ordnance riding the axle between two wheels and the simplest bot brain slung underneath, Canisters could be hard to spot and were able to close quickly and detonate oftentimes before a squad could react. "Cowboy. Pop some exploratory fire thirty degrees across that burning Jughead."

On Marcos' left flank, Cowboy's squad cut loose with overlapping fire fifteen degrees to either side of the distant wreck. Their CAR-7 assault rifles wailed as a backwash of waste energy rippled the air. Half a kilometer up range, geysers of smoke and scorched earth rose above hundreds of tiny, new craters blasted into Rho VII.

"Always polite to knock on the door," Gravel said over STANDARD VOICE.

At Gravel's back, Two-Joe nodded. The General Issue soldier had his assault rifle up and ready, sweeping the ruined landscape west of the crater for any threat at the Alliance rear. His software package, like those of his three synthetic *brothers* in the platoon, did not allow much in the way of relaxation, and Marcos had ordered Books to ratchet up their paranoia index. It made the Joes a bit twitchy, but kept them extra alert and had saved lives more than once.

"Walkers! Three Walkers marked at eight-six degrees, moving two-seven-niner, toward Bravo." This from Books, his fireteam at the leading edge of Able's south-stretching line. The Savannah accent turned *walkers* into *wah-kuhs*, but not one soldier would have a problem understanding him.

And chasing Books came Cowboy. "Flushed six ... no, seven Cans," Bravo's corporal reported. "Rolling up fast on spreading arcs."

As expected, *Deploy for hostile intent* had fallen off Marcos' list of standing orders, and now *Support forward maneuvers* also downgraded in the face of the immediate Cyborg threat. Inquiry icons from Rabbit and Princess flashed on the standing column at the edge of his faceplate, and Marcos swept the premature requests directly into the VOID. Instead, he caught the tactical feed updating from Cowboy and Books, and (literally) in the blink of an eye, uploaded his DATA STREAM to the entire platoon.

"Bravo, concentrate fire on those Cans *without* the PAD. Hold position for niner-zero seconds, then cover." Watching the spider tracks crawl across his faceplate, Marcos took a chance. "Ignore Canister-seven unless it breaks one hundred meters. Let it roll."

The rest of Able Squad was already working its way southeast in an envelopment; Books anticipating his sergeant's plan. That left the south rim of the crater clear for Marcos' small fireteam to displace under cover, attempting to cut off the Walkers' move to flank Bravo.

Using his own men as bait never sat well with Marcos. Facing an enemy across a battlefield was hard enough. Especially knowing that, if taken (alive or dead) you would be rendered down for muscle, for nerve clusters, for brain matter. Parts was parts, in a Cyborg's many eyes. It drove them toward populated worlds. On the battlefield, their tactics were efficient and just this side of predictable. Expend the least resources to harvest as much new biomass as possible. So, in effect, every soldier was walking, armored bait.

But holding fast, inviting them in, went against human nature's every instinct; at a level that the best Alliance conditioning could never reach.

His fireteam moved low and fast, scrabbling around piles of scorched rubble and a deep laser cut. The ground trembled once ... twice. Cowboy's UPDATE scrubbed two Canister tracks from his faceplate. Anti-personnel, from the size of the detonation.

Then the entire world turned bright, searing white as the hand of God lifted his fireteam from the side of the crater and slammed them back down. Hard.

Violet afterimages, burned across Marcos' retinas, swam in the darkness. His faceplate had completely polarized with the antimatter flash. It cleared slowly. He tasted blood in his mouth, and his entire right side ached. Fortunately, ICAS technology had absorbed most of the kinetic force, spreading it across his body.

Not so fortunate: Gravel's status icon flashed amber, and from Bravo both Princess and Three-Joe were dark. Red cautionary lights burned over another five men, including Cowboy, but two of them cleared back to green even as Marcos regained his footing.

And worse: his DATA STREAM was empty.

From the shockwave, or the energy pulse of the antimatter detonation, the network built between his platoon of ICAS troopers was at least partially disabled. He still had STANDARD VOICE comms, and the platoon's standing column of status icons, but no tactical feed. He gazed upwards, into the strategic interface. Tried pulling an UPDATE from Command. Enemy positions ... Revisions to his standing orders ...

Nothing.

"Books! Fall out of line and get our network rebuilt." Without a local system, the platoon could not share firing data, or UPDATE each other on the position of enemy units. With no tie back to Command, they could expect no support form nearby Alliance positions. They were more likely to be designated as

Forces Unknown—one designation removed from a confirmed enemy target.

Standard doctrine, in a secure position, was to bunker down and rebuild the network. Marcos didn't have that option. Not after the dropcraft arrival and Bravo's screeching weapon's fire.

"Bravo, close ranks and double-down on the Cans. Full assault. Make it clear that AID holds this scrap of nowhere. Able, work in behind those Walkers. *Hold fire* until I give you a target."

His orders were barely given when, directly north, the air wavered with intense energy disruption as every able-bodied soldier in Bravo overrode safeties and tore up more of Rho VII's landscape. Even at this distance, the discharge wash of a dozen assault rifles rattled his back teeth.

Then there was a violet flash, and erupting tendrils of plasma energies twisted above the killing field into giant, powerful columns. Cowboy, his status icon still burning a steady amber, was active enough to throw his PAD into the firestorm. Plasma area-dispersion weapons were among the hardest-hitting ordnance available to ICAS troopers; ionizing large swaths of a battlefield, frying circuitry and scorching flesh.

Another anti-personnel canister detonated at half a klick.

The Walkers moving in from the east would be coming hard now. Bravo had certainly *drawn interest through strong tactical deployment.* Officer-speak, for hanging their ass into the wind by giving away their position. Scrabbling over piles of blackened, broken rubble, Marcos pulled his fireteam along the edge of the crater. Without tactical feed scrolling through his DATA STREAM, he had only a fair idea where his own men were and barely a guess as to where the Walkers might be. But if they had altered course above Able ... spreading out to flank Bravo while the squad concentrated its fire on the Canisters rolling in from the north ... Marcos would expect to make contact somewhere about—

Gravel saw them first.

A high-pitched wail screeched in Marcos' ears as fifty meters downrange a rocky outcropping shattered into dust and razor-sharp shards. A Walker stumbled back from its ruined cover.

Scout-designation; bipedal with reverse-canted legs, able to spring over the ground in rapid deployment. No head to speak of. Sensors and antennae sprouted in a small tangle from what might have been called its shoulders. Raw muscle and sinew, corded in a grisly, bloody rope, tied a very human arm into the Walker's chest. The hand at the end of that arm was open, waving back and forth. And had an eye grafted into its palm.

Rabbit and Two-Joe were a heartbeat ahead of Marcos, adding their weapons fire to Gravel's. Trying to bracket it. Smash it down before it could react. Scouts carried light armor and rarely anything heavier than anti-personnel weapons. But they were fast, and this one was far too close.

Instinct more than anything had Marcos pull his aim into the air above the scout. Maybe the way it had coiled back on itself tipped him off. That's what he'd tell himself later, counting heads on the way back to the starjumper to confirm the platoon's losses, considering what to put in any combat report.

Now, it was the simple twitch of a nerve cluster. Contraction of the biceps. A three-degree rotation of his left wrist. The barrel of his CAR-7 swung up, just enough, and his finger caught the firing stud as the Cyborg scout gathered itself. And leaped.

His weapon's assemblers stripped perfectly formed rods of solid tungsten out of the rifle's stock. Barely more than a sliver in length, once fed through the acceleration chamber they left at an impressive fraction of Big-C as the arrestor assembly bent Newton's laws to turn the recoil into a backwash of distortion. Rusty knives carved at Marcos' ears as energies swirled around him. The landscape wavered, and danced.

As the scout was plucked from the air and smashed back to the ground in a bloody, ruined tangle of flesh and steel.

"Scrap it," Rabbit offered over STANDARD VOICE. He and Gravel put another long burst into the wreckage, leaving little for a Harvester to reclaim for the Cybs.

Marcos might have joined them in reducing the scout beyond salvage. The sergeant also might have warned his men that there were two Walkers still unaccounted for. Whatever he might have done, Two-Joe was one heartbeat ahead of him.

The G.I. threw a shoulder into Marcos' side, taking the sergeant off his feet. Marcos was barely aware of the crimson jewels splashed off his faceplate by a Cyborg spotting laser. Then he was falling.

Twisting around to absorb the fall against his left side.

Watching—as hypervelocity pellets cracked the air above him, and tore through Two-Joe's armored suit.

Converging streams of weapons fire converged on the synthetic, tearing Two-Joe's left arm to shreds as he fell back, away, and down. He hit the ground hard, twitching violently. His status icon flashed dark, deadly red. Before Marcos had the chance to order Rabbit and Gravel "Down!" the two men were into the dirt, adjusting their own fire to hammer back at the Cyborg assault Walkers which had broken cover several hundred meters beyond the wrecked scout.

Marcos pushed Two-Joe's status to the back of his mind. If the synthetic soldier was still alive—still aware—ICAS technology would save him. He glanced into his DATA STREAM by reflex, wanting to UPDATE his platoon's MAP files with enemy positions and a call for coordinated fire.

"Not happening," he reminded himself, as a fifth thunderclap shook the ground north of his position.

He grabbed for a grenade, pulling one of the fist-sized canisters from his belt. Showed it to Rabbit who reached for his own while Gravel continued his sporadic return fire. Marcos' system pulled a drop-down menu across his retinas, and he dialed YIELD to half-strength in order to boost his programmed throw for an extra hundred meters. He chucked the grenade high overhead. Rabbit did the same. At the top of their arc, each grenade stabilized on an electronic gyro and a burst of propellant launched them toward their distant targets.

"Bravo, walk your fire east and concentrate. Able, hold position and override safeties. Bring the pain. We are three-zero-zero meters southwest of the detonations."

Big Mike had just enough time to ask "What detonations," when bright columns of fire rose up through swirling gasses.

Two new craters in Rho VII, Marcos knew. Both ringed with the telltale molten crust of a small antimatter flash.

Big Mike managed an, "Oh," before Bravo and Able overlapped fire into the area. Anything else was lost in the high-pitched backwash of assault rifles and the deep, weighty thrum of PAD cannon unleashing their own slice of hell.

Someone, either Big Mike or Cowboy, was off target as a plasma storm erupted only fifty meters from Marcos' position and a lone tendril of supercharged energy tore up the edge of the crater above his head.

"North, push that north!" Marcos ordered. Not that he was certain STANDARD VOICE could penetrate the distortion fields erupting all around him. Where was their network?

But his call was heard, and the PAD discharge ranged north and then east. Huge twisting ropes of plasma energies whipped across the battlefield, ionizing the air and chewing up ground, metal, and flesh. Assault rifle fire pocked the surface, throwing out lethal shards. Another ICAS grenade flashed in the storm. Then another.

Marcos, Gravel and Rabbit kept their heads down. Gravel lifted his rifle up and fired blindly, his personal ICAS system retaining target data from his earlier visual. The rifle wailed and its distortion fan wavered around them. In the swirl of energies, Two-Joe lifted his rifle with his remaining arm. His body appeared to fold over and then jerk straight once more, roll up onto his wounded side. The rifle barrel climbed. Pointing over, and up.

Toward Marcos!

Another time, another battle, Marcos would never have thought to worry. It was only the distortion field. Two-Joe was dead. Almost certainly. Even if not, as twitchy as the synthetic soldier might be, he would never point a live weapon at one of his own. And *even then*, there were safeties in place to eliminate the chance of a friendly fire accident.

"Except our network is down!" Marcos shouted, realizing that this was not a backwash-induced illusion.

Rabbit heard him. Rolling to one side, the ICAS trooper swung his weapon around. Hesitated. Disbelief or loyalty prevented him from mashing down on the firing stud.

Two-Joe fired.

By reflex, Marcos flinched from the assault rifle fire. Simple human nature, wanting to present as small a target as possible. Even as the rifle fire passed harmless above him, he rolled to his back and looked away—

—up toward the rim of the crater, where a Cyborg Canister hung, ready to drop into the middle of his fireteam.

Two-Joe's rifle fire smashed into the suicide-device head-on. Stopped its charge at the last moment. Drove it back. For one incredibly-long heartbeat it clung to the rim of the crater, working to fulfill its mission. Marcos sensed the strain put on the brain casing as it calculated the damage being taken against its effectiveness of detonating from the crater's rim. Then Two-Joe cut down, directly into the axle which snapped in half as the entire device tumbled back over the edge.

And detonated.

— 5 —

Tevin smelled the Cyborg harvest site a good thirty meters away. A foul odor of spoiled meat and blood. Feces. And that cold, ozone smell the Cybbies left behind them almost anywhere they touched.

An odor of terror, and fear.

With a raised hand he held up his straggling line. Looked back. Billy and Cog had everyone hunkered down in the shadow of a fire-gutted delivery van. Everyone but the man with the head wound, who stood on the walk, gazing around. As if trying to decide if he wanted to hail a cab or hoof it back to work.

"Get that zero down," Tevin whispered harshly. "Keep him there."

Tevin had replaced the boomer into his canvas messenger bag, and after a second of hesitation left it there as he crept down the shattered sidewalk. Pieces of broken concrete shifted underfoot, grinding against each other, but the sound wasn't so bad he would risk moving down the street in the open. He passed the jimmied security doors of a street-side bodega. A cracked fire hydrant laying next to exposed, bone-dry pipes. A dropped briefcase with papers spilling out of it, the dingy pages stirring in the uneven wind.

The ground shook light and long, like a large vehicle rolling by, but it felt distant. Different from the AID Juggernaut Tevin had seen a few days back. Different from the giant Cyborg meat wagons that drove through the city on their diamond-pattern steel treads, responding to the call of Harvesters.

More weapon's fire. Out on the plains. Tevin hadn't heard much in the way of nearby gunfire in the last ten minutes, but that didn't mean that the enemy wasn't close.

It only meant that they were not being challenged.

The small hairs on the back of Tevin's neck stood up with gooseflesh. He swallowed hard, grimaced at the taste of ozone and blood which sat on the back of his tongue like a sickness. The next door was the front to a bank. Strong building. Thick glass. Straining, he thought he heard a metal tap-tapping sound, like the cycling of a weapon, and he slowed his approach.

There were blood smears on the sidewalk out front. More on the edge of the doorway, where Tevin imagined hands of wounded civvies or soldiers reaching out, grabbing hold in an attempt to prevent their being dragged inside. It was easy to imagine the screams, the calls for help. He'd heard them, over and over, echoing through the streets. Sometimes in the distance. Sometimes just down the block.

He heard it again. A tap, followed by a scrape or maybe it was a mechanical whirr? Yeah. Tap-and-whirr. Tap-and-whirr.

Something was still inside the bank.

He had to look. Had to be certain that were still Cybbies inside. What kind. Something small he could deal with. Maybe. No way could he sneak his line of evacuees by without drawing attention, and circling back with sniffers on their trail wasn't a great option either. Not unless they had to.

One quick look. That was all he'd take. Edging up to the bank's entrance, Tevin breathed shallow and quick through his mouth, cutting down on the smell. His heart pounded in his chest, and he readied himself for a quick retreat (and flat-out run) if whatever was inside happened to notice him. He would have to bolt across the street. Or, better, continue to the left and get around the corner, pulling whatever it was away from Billy and Cog and the others. If it didn't look to the right. If it focused on him. If nothing waited around the near corner and if he could get into a building fast enough ...

Way to much "if" in his possible future. He hated that. But the only way to remove the "if" was to look, or run back the way they'd come. A Gladiator didn't just run away, though. A Gladiator faced what was coming at him. Tevin still believed that. Didn't he?

Wondering if he did, in fact, still believe it, Tevin ducked his head forward and glanced into the bank.

Something moved and Tevin pulled back at once, twisting around to flee back toward the others. Seeing him, Billy and Cog jumped out from behind the delivery van's blackened shell. Also ready.

But Tevin stopped himself with a heartbeat to spare, catching the side of the building with his shoulder as he checked himself. What he'd seen in that quick glance—blood, steel, broken glass, and *movement*—registered now. He eased himself back, and this time took a longer look.

An automatic door, wedged open on the right but the left-hand slider trying to close. Its safety glass was spiderwebbed with cracks, and missing a large piece near the end of the frame. A frame twisted and bent too far outward to allow it to move properly. The door's machinery *clicked* against its limit, *whirred* as it struggled for an extra second. Then reset, and tried again.

Deeper into the bank nothing else moved. No sign of the Cybbies.

But they had been here. Yeah.

His heartbeat slowing back toward something which approached normal, Tevin brought the others forward with a curt, short wave. He studied the interior while he waited for them.

Enough light filtered through the bank's front, tinted windows to let him witness the horror that had happened here. Two metal desks shoved together at the center of the room as a hasty operating table, so crusted with dried blood they appeared to be painted black. Torn, blood-soaked clothing piled to one side. Pocketbooks, purses, and personal electronics to another side. Very orderly. Very not-human. Flies buzzed throughout the room, swarming around the desks and crawling in a black mass over a large pile of cast-off flesh and gore. Meat, not up to standard, or maybe already damaged by the Cyborgs in taking their victims.

Tevin had seen that before too. Whatever the Cybbies wanted from people, whatever drew them to attack and harvest, it wasn't random and it wasn't indiscriminate. They tested. They perfected. They *chose*.

For this they had killed—were killing—his entire world.

Whatever they had chosen here, they had already taken it away and moved on in search of more. It was enough for him to know that his group was safe. For the moment.

Footsteps behind him. Tevin turned and caught Billy by the collar of his heavy jacket, pausing the line for only a second. "No one looks," he said. "Around the corner." With that, he propelled the smaller boy forward. Nearly threw him. Billy stumbled to get his feet back underneath him, managed, but not until the far side of the bank's entrance.

"Go," Tevin encouraged them. Waved them on. "Around the corner. We're almost there." Each of the evacuees got a word, a touch. Whatever it took to distract them, catching no more than a glimpse of the nightmare behind him. Keep them moving.

Cog obviously recognized the odor and didn't even attempt to look. The Gladiator turned his back to the bank's entrance, keeping his eyes on the street as he gestured back the way they'd come with his shock-stick.

"Still have two Sniffers tracking us. They follow our scent to the doc's door, he won't open."

Or they'd call Walkers to smash it in. Doc wasn't clear on much, but he'd been pretty open on how bad it would be allowing Cyborgs to find the underground facility.

"Wait here," Tevin ordered, and, taking a deep breath, he ducked into the bank.

It was easier to move through the horror with purpose than to study it from outside. Moving quickly, Tevin snagged a woman's purse from the sorted collection of personal items. He found what else he needed from the fly-swarmed pile of viscera and gore. Trying not to think about what he rooted out of the horrific collection, he paused just inside the bank's entrance so that Cog wouldn't have to see him load the grisly package into the handbag. Breathing through clenched teeth, he cleaned his hand against the wall and dodged back through the still-shuddering door.

Gagging for breath, sweat burning at the corners of his eyes, Tevin removed a boomer from his messenger bag. He pushed the plunger all the way down, mixing impact gel into the street-formula explosive. He balanced the steel pipe on one end against the side of the building, looped the handbag's strap around the base of the device, then left the bag itself sitting as far out onto the walk as he could. Bait. Sniffers would never be able to ignore that stench.

"It's going to take a harder impact than knocking that boomer over to set it off," Cog complained as Tevin grabbed his arm and hurried them both toward the corner.

Normally, yes, that would be true. You press the plunger, and hurled it away just as fast and as hard as you could. But the reason to do it fast (and what rank didn't tell you the first few times you handled a boomer) was that impact gel mixed with flash turned unstable. Seconds. A few minutes. The longer it sat, and heated up, the more likely it would simply detonate in your hand.

"It'll work," Tevin promised as the two of them gained the dubious safety of the corner.

Billy looked relieved to see them. "I wasn't sure if we should wait." The younger boy gestured ahead. "It's just there, isn't it?"

It was. A short block away and protected by a heavy steel door that might have been a regular security gate but Tevin knew was much stronger than it appeared. There were no call buttons. No monitor. It was a simple loading platform that had rarely been used even at the city's busiest. Hardly at all, since the Cyborgs' arrival at Bountiful. Only a few times, like now, to get evacuees to Doc.

"Come on, come on." Tevin paced in front of the steel door. Rapped it once with the flat of his hand, and regretted it instantly when the steel hardly rang but it made his hand sting. He thought he could hear machinery humming on the other side, imagined the lift rising up to street level, but knew it could just as easily be wishful thinking.

He watched the far corner with rising concern, waiting for Cyborg Sniffers to suddenly appear and mark them for Walkers. Their options were limited. They might try circling the block. Once. Keep moving and hope Doc was waiting for them when they got back. Or, turn north for the rocky hills above the city. He decided that they could give doc another moment, maybe two, and then—

The steel door began to rise.

Their city choked with ash and the rubble of shattered buildings. The bank door, just around the corner, so twisted in its seat that it could no longer open or close properly. But here, the giant steel door rose quickly and smoothly with heavy grace. Hardly a sound being made.

Tevin backed his charges away from the door. Just in time as two rifles shoved out of the darkened space and one of the women stifled a shout. Black-uniformed security agents stood shoulder to shoulder on the lift's diamond-deck surface, protecting Doc Rutheford with their bodies. The black visors on their full-face helmets betrayed not a sign of mercy or nervousness. An amber light, mounted at the edge of each faceplate, blinked slow and steady. They swept the small group for threats, then with a gesture from the Doc they swiveled to either side and covered the street.

Rutheford shuffled up to the edge of the lift, but never stepped a toe outside of the protective opening. Two meters tall and gangly, he walked slightly stooped forward like a preying insect. He had a fringe of steel-gray hair left, cut short and shaved high over the ears, and behind his thick lenses a pair of sharp, bright green eyes which Tevin felt as they lashed everyone in turn and finally bore straight into him.

"Sniffers," Rutheford said. His lips stretched tight in a disapproving frown. "Two of them." The way he said it, Tevin knew that the Doc had almost decided leave them to their own fate.

"Taken care of," he promised. Doc would have seen him set the trap, or the security door would never have opened.

The Doc nodded slowly. "We'll see," he said. As if they were making a bet. Then he flicked one hand at the civilians clustered behind Tevin and his small crew. "All right then."

Without another command Rutheford's security swept out and herded the civilians forward, onto the lift. Cog and Billy ducked aside to keep from being gathered up as well. Cog brandished his shock-stick, and one of the guards swung his rifle up before Doc called him off with a simple shake of his head.

After that, there was little trouble. The civilians needed no extra encouragement to pack themselves onto the lift behind Rutheford. The last of their small group—the same small, frightened girl Tevin had noticed trailing the pack before— peeled away at the last moment to wrap her arms tightly around Tevin. Her head barely came up to Tevin's chest, but she had desperate strength in her arms as she hugged him. He felt her silent sobs, just for the span of a few heartbeats, then she darted away to the backside of the lift and hid behind two of the larger kids.

That brief, desperate hug warmed Tevin in a way the empty thanks of shell-shocked evacuees never did. He offered a small wave in her direction and felt something like a smile on his face as he turned back toward the Doc. A nice moment, one of few he could remember out of the past week, which soured as Cog stepped up to him and thrust his shock-stick into Tevin's hands.

"Me too," Cog said. He would not meet Tevin's eyes. "I'm going under."

If Cog had used the shock-stick on Tevin, the older boy wouldn't have been more surprised. Cog had been the one sure thing Tevin could count on over the last few days. Always ready. Always tinkering with some bit of salvaged tech to create a new bit of nastiness for the Cyborgs. With Cog at his back, Tevin never worried about anything creeping up on him without warning. The thought of running the streets without Cog made Tevin's circuitry tat squirm and pulse.

"You sure?" he asked, aware of Billy's gaze on the both of them.

"Yeah." Cog swept his gaze up to the tops of nearby buildings. "Streets ain't what they used to be." And then in a softer voice: "Cybbies are getting too close. I'm not gonna be meat for them."

"Maybe you should all come down," Rutheford offered. His sharp, cutting gaze never left Tevin. "You've brought me a lot of evacuees, Tevin, but I'm not sure how many more times I'll open this door. Even for you."

Tevin glanced at the lift. Felt his nose wrinkle as if he'd smelled something bad. Truth was, he felt more secure on up above, even with the Cyborg threat, than hiding in some hole, waiting and hoping for Doc to smuggle them to one of the last evacuation ships. Up here, he had options. Down below ... he looked to one of Doc's guards. The black uniform and full-face helmet hiding any hope, or fear.

"What about you?" Tevin asked Billy. "You want to go under?"

The young kid trembled. He tried to hide it, but Tevin caught it before Billy managed to clamp down. "I go where you go," the young Gladiator said with something approaching conviction.

That alone nearly drove Tevin onto the lift. Knowing that Billy would never give up the streets for the possible safety of Doc's underground labs. Not so long as Tevin stayed. What if he got Billy killed? Or worse, if he got Billy captured by the Cyborgs? It was a responsibility Tevin did not want.

But the strength of the girl's desperate hug was still warm in Tevin's chest. Weighed against the cold, dark faces of Doc's security, it wasn't much of a choice.

"We're good," he told the Doc.

A dark shadow passed across Rutheford's face. Anger? Regret? Something between the two, Tevin thought. He watched the way Doc's hands opened and closed, as if from some desperate desire to grasp something he wanted. Or needed. He leaned forward, nearly coming out of the lift's shadows. Doc's two security guards never made a move, but for a reason he couldn't say Tevin felt certain they were suddenly a threat to him.

He took a step back.

Rutheford smiled calmly. His guards stepped back onto the lift, eerily efficient as always. The steel door slid down. "Maybe next time." The words slipped out just as the heavy door banged home.

Tevin felt more than heard the lift begin its descent, and he stood silent for a handful of precious seconds. Torn between a desire to pound on the heavy security door, calling Doc back, and his instinct to move quickly away. Far, far away.

Instinct was already winning the battle when a nearby explosion shook the street. Tevin shook his head to clear the ringing in his ears. His boomer. The Sniffers! Stupid, to burn time standing around in the open. He and Billy had to get moving again. He handed Cog's shock-stick to Billy. Then, grabbing the collar of Billy's heavy coat, he pulled the smaller boy along with him as they hurried away from the security door and whatever might be left of the Cyborg trackers following them.

He glanced back only once, from the corner, before losing sight of the entrance. The steel door looked out of place only in that no street crew had ever tagged it, and the recent fighting had yet to scar its surface. A security door like any of a hundred others in the city. Except that it wasn't like the others, was it?

"Do you want to go back?" Billy asked, uneasily shifting from one foot to the other.

Tevin shook his head. Still, the question hung over him. Why did he hesitate getting himself and Billy to safety?

Which direction, he suddenly wondered, did safety truly lie?

He checked the avenues leading in all four directions, saw flitters falling over a building to the east, and nodded southward.

"These are our streets," he said, hands balled into tight fists. "We don't give them up without a fight." And glancing down, he noticed his Gladiators circuitry tat had stopped squirming. Like the hug from the little girl, it gave him a new boost of confidence. Of purpose.

Let the Cybbies shove in on Gladiators territory, Tevin decided.

He would find a way to shove back.

— 6 —

The banshee wail of a dozen-plus CAR-7 rifles drove cold fingers into the back of Marcos' brain—squeezing, digging— while all around him reality wavered in the backwash of overlapping distortion fields. His jaw ached from clenching against the rifle discharge. His temples throbbed. But it wasn't allowed to be pain. The egghead lectures clearly defined pain as *an unpleasant sensory and emotional experience associated with actual or potential physical damage.* CAR-7 discharge fields might be unpleasant and disorientating, but they did not—would not (ever)—cause actual tissue damage.

Therefore, no pain.

The eggheads could lecture all day. So far as Marcos was concerned, in the second hour of their run-and-gun firefight, he was now certain of only one thing.

It fragging well *hurt.*

A jet of white-hot plasma swept overhead, arcing and spitting, driving his men back from the edge and into the aqueduct once more. Hypervelocity pellets cracked the air around Marcos, half a hundred tiny, supersonic breaks creating a short peal of deadly thunder.

He dove for the ground, scrambling away as a furious salvo shattered the aqueduct's rim. Concrete erupted in a spray of razor-tipped shards; a handful gouging deep tracks across his faceplate.

Marcos' platoon clung to the aqueduct's steep side like desperate spiders, scrabbling along the edge, hammering back at the Cyborg walkers attempting to flank them. Below, the wide basin was filled with less than a meter of gray, ash-swollen water siphoned out of the poisoned river which twisted its way through the distant battlefield. The wounded struggled and slid and climbed to the best of their ability. Two-Joe and a few others had surrendered to the mucked-up waters, wading along as best they could.

As cover went, he could have asked for better.

Then again, not much was worse than the open battlefield they'd had to cross in order to gain the city's outskirts and some semblance of a defensible position once it had become clear that the platoon's network would be some time rebuilding. The greatest danger on a battlefield is a soldier who does not know what he is doing. Due to poor training or a weak commander, this man becomes a liability to himself and everyone around him. The second-greatest danger is a unit that *no one else* in the order of battle understands what it is doing. Non-responsive to commands and unable to update their standing orders. Stumbling about in the middle of a detailed operation. Such a unit is worse than the soldier who doesn't know what to do. They *think* they know, and so they act. And if they are lucky, they will only find themselves unsupported on the flanks of a battle.

Worse would be to target what would seem to be an enemy position, and take out your own command post. Or blunder too close to the enemy and find yourself on the receiving end of overwhelming friendly fire. Bad enough suffering casualties from an enemy you know is offering no quarter. When you understand that the soldier at the other end of the bullet was on your side, morale got real low, real quick.

Making a break for the city's edge had seemed the best possible course of action at the time, clinging to the remnants of their standing orders—*support forward maneuvers, preserve AID assets*—with the strength they had left. Physical assets were still plus-eighty percent. Three-Joe was dead, again, holding to the curse among General Issue soldiers that three synthetics crowded a unit; as were two recruits who hadn't been around long enough to collect a name. Princess and Rabbit led the walking wounded with antimatter flash burns and a light concussion, while Two-Joe brought up the rear staggering along with one arm still attached by nothing more than the stubbornness of ICAS technology.

"Books! Where's my network?"

Able's corporal was also the platoon's self-appointed tech specialist. If there was a manual published, a reference cited, or even the faintest rumor of a work-around, he'd read about it. Somewhere.

"Fried a good, Sarge" Books said on a private circuit. "If'n Ah take it off-line, strip it down to the command root, Ah can get fire support back up. Mebbe."

A *mebbe* from Books was as close as Marcos would get to a sure bet today. "Do it," he ordered. Then dropped into STANDARD VOICE. "I want PADs ready to burn the rim as soon as Cybs pop on our screens. Everyone else ready with overlapping fire. Able, then Bravo. I want grenades on—"

It was as far as Marcos got before the world exploded around him.

A geyser of shattered 'crete and fire erupted behind and below him. It lifted Marcos from the side of the aqueduct, thrusting him uphill and sideways.

In the back of his mind he heard the sudden calls, the yells from his platoon, but his immediate world had shrunk to a haze-filled tunnel of information and reaction. Still in the air, ICAS threat assessment circuitry identified the weapon as a minecaster, splashing the warning across his retinas as if he didn't have better use for his vision. Blinking the warning into his VOID, Marcos knew it had been a near miss simply due the fact that he could know anything at all.

He struck the side of the aqueduct with bone-jarring force. Slapped one arm out in order to arrest his roll. Scrapping his left heel hard against the surface, he swung himself into a long, pendulum slide facing back up toward the rim. Searching for the Walker.

Assault drone. Bipedal, but with reverse-canted legs instead of the usual humanoid mimicry. Wide, thick shoulders and no head. Two heavy, single-jointed arms with minecasters attached to each, and two spindly appendages wrapping up and over the shoulders ending in hypersonic "spitters." Wrapped with harvested muscle and sinew, it had a bloodied, unfinished look to it. A double-waisted thorax made the Walker look very insect-like, but Marcos knew that meant it had two humanoid brains hardwired into its processors. Able to think like a human, redundantly, but overriding any emotional response with its computer core.

Marcos mashed down the firing stud on his CAR-7 before he even realized he had aimed. With a terrible screech the rifle stripped rods from stock and shoved them through the acceleration field. Tiny rings of ionized air opened in between Marcos and the Walker as his stream of fire caught the next minecaster projectile at its midpoint.

A halo of plasma-laced fire opened up around the Walker like a terrible blossom. Marcos cut through with a furious onslaught, rocking the Cyborg back as he sliced away meat and metal.

The long, steep slide of the aqueduct blurred as energy washed around him. Even through the distortion, Marcos was aware of other ICAS troopers sliding and tumbling down the side of the aqueduct. And others who were not.

Several rifles turned on the Walker, though not as many as Marcos would have thought, would have hoped. But then, he had forgotten the final order he'd been in the midst of making. It wasn't until a half dozen propellant blasts popped along the aqueduct's rim (about a half-second before he struck the water, head-first) that he recalled his half-finished order for *grenades*.

Now everyone was sliding for the basin, and Marcos felt a padded fist strike him across the back of his head and shoulders, holding him for a fraction of a second, then pulling him into a watery, gray embrace as half a dozen white-hot flashes seared the edge of the aqueduct's rim.

Violet afterimages dancing in front of his eyes. Every movement sluggish. ICAS interlocks at least prevented him from losing a grip on his weapon. It did not prevent his legs from tangling up as he fought to get them down into the basin, or keep him from pressing the firing stud long after he lost sight of his target.

His rifle knew enough to stop firing, however, and he soon got his feet beneath him. Standing from the waist-high waters.

"Report," he barked over STANDARD VOICE, already searching the standing column of status lights along he side of his faceplate and reading the worst of the news in a glance.

Seventeen active troopers attempted to answer him, queuing up his standing column with request icons. ICAS protocols allowed only the senior non-com to OVERRIDE Marcos' filters. With Books offline, concentrating on the platoon's network, it should have been Cowboy.

Instead, Big Mike's powerful voice filled his ears.

"Scrap one Walker. Put another dozen grenades over the top, which should give the Cybs something to think about." A pause. "Sarge. Cowboy …"

Marcos waded to the aqueduct's sloping bank, ash-thick water helping support him as he fought to clear his head of cobwebs. The fading taste of adrenaline was rancid in his mouth as he turned over Cowboy's half-submerged body. Made certain.

Cowboy had lost his weapon. His PAD would be laying on the bottom of the basin somewhere, beneath a meter of cold, mucked-up water. Nearly impossible, if ICAS technology detected any life. Any at all.

Three spitter holes punched through the faceplate cinched it. And the helmet's inside was a gruesome spray of blood, brain, and bone.

Cowboy hadn't served with Marcos the longest, but he'd been a damn fine corporal and Marcos had come to rely on him. Like Books. Like Gravel and Princess and Big Mike. Pushing the Cyborg forces from Rho VII, any chance they had to uncover what made this world so special to the enemy, in Marcos' opinion it had just gotten harder.

Pulling Cowboy away from the aqueduct's side, Marcos slid the body down into the dark, cold waters where no Cyborg would find it, claim it for parts. Then he cleared his queue with a long gaze into the VOID. Opened STANDARD VOICE to the entire platoon.

"Big Mike has Bravo," he said for those who hadn't seem Marcos submerge the body. "Able, guard the rim. Bravo, two-by-two across this damn basin. Then we'll safeguard Able. I want to put this aqueduct between us and the Cybs."

Rabbit gestured east, where Cyborg flitters continued to fall and rise over the city. Fall and then rise. "That's going to move us deeper into the city," he pointed out, fidgeting from one foot to the other.

"Yeah." Marcos nodded. He turned his back on the western embankment and waded farther out into the basin.

Deeper into the city. Not *quite* in keeping with his standing orders, but it would be one of the few areas his platoon could move with relative freedom, being off the AID network. Where they could also do the most good, and inflict the greatest damage against the Cyborg assault force. That was always the goal. Make damn certain enemy losses outweighed their gains.

And, if there were any answers to be had on Rho VII, that was where he would find them.

"Yeah," he said again. "It will."

$$- \; 7 \; -$$

A violent trembler shook the lab, long and hard. Dr. Rutheford swung about in his chair and grabbed onto a steel table with renewed strength. Pieces of heavy equipment shifted, banging against each other. The monitor on which he'd been running his imaging program went dark. Lights flickered, and across the room a panel blew outward in a cascade of sizzling sparks and the sudden, overpowering scent of burned insulation.

A week of relative isolation, watching fissures spread across the overhead as the city's very foundation shifted and cracked, had not inured him to the danger. He had never grown accustomed to the sounds and shockwaves of the terrible battle being waged overhead. Within the city. Across the nearby plains. Over this world. If anything he had become over-sensitized to the danger. Such weakness terrified him. Fear was a human failing which could be conquered, he knew. Yet the quaking continued. Intensified. Taunting Rutheford as if this might be it. The one that took it all away, just when success seemed within his grasp.

And then it subsided. Not as abruptly as it began, but trailing off as if unsure of itself. Leaving behind unfinished business.

Rutheford swallowed hard. His breathing came in short, sharp gasps. "What do you think?" he asked aloud. One of Bountiful's evacuees sat nearby, gazing into the overhead as if working out a puzzle. Trying to understand. The scientist in Rutheford appreciated such detachment. "That one felt ... different."

His left hand maintaining a desperate grip against the steel table's edge, he used his right to open up a new window in the lenses of his heavy-framed glasses. Option lists expanded in his peripheral vision, and it was a moment's work to scroll through them. The microchips embedded in his fingertips allowed him to manipulate the data as if it had substance—or he was actually a virtual avatar, secure in the network and safe from such mundane worries as being buried alive in the underground facilities he refused to abandon.

Wouldn't that be something? To exist as pure thought within a world of data, with nothing to threaten him. Unhindered by physical limitations. Unburdened by doubt, and fear.

Walking the shores of the infinite. That was how he thought of it.

"The Cyborgs have collapsed another building." It was helpful to speak out loud, filling the lab with the casual conversation it had been missing in recent weeks. If his voice cracked occasionally, he could ignore it. His guests did.

He switched to an outside camera, confirming what the data had already told him. Half a city block, leveled. That was why it had felt different than the usual battlefield aftershock. "Creating a new landing area for their flitters." And this one close. Too close.

Where they on to him? Here for no other reason than to stop his work, as it sometimes seemed? Surely the raw materials the Cyborgs harvested in no way made up for their battlefield losses at this point. So their decision could not be purely deterministic. And from everything the Alliance understood, the Cyborg threat did not make emotional decisions. Therefore, there was a missing component. Still.

Unless they were after quality, not quantity.

"Tevin," Rutheford muttered. "Where is Tevin?" He tapped fingers in the air, switching camera and sensor locations. The heavy glasses slid down his nose, but he left them alone while searching for the weak transponder planted in Tevin's messenger bag.

He never should have let the boy go out again. Too dangerous. Too dangerous for *him*. Tevin knew the entrances to Rutheford's labs and living spaces. If captured alive. If made to talk. The idea almost didn't bear—There!

He found Tevin in the southwestern quarter, staggering out of a cloud of billowing dust with that other street urchin following along like a loyal puppy. Only a block away from where the Cyborgs had collapsed the old mercantile center. Caught in the dust and detritus that swirled for several city blocks in every direction.

Too close. "Too close by half. Tevin should be brought back, don't you think?"

Where the tremors and exploding light panels had engendered only vague curiosity in his guest, Tevin's name sparked something a bit more personal, Rutheford noticed. A tightening around the eyes. Was that a glare? A brief surge of resentment, perhaps? He would allow that. Resentment was a form of jealousy; both rooted in anger. And anger, unlike fear, was a motivator. Not a paralytic.

He jotted his observations into his virtual notes. Then with a double-tap against air pulled up the power grid feeding the city's streetlamps around Tevin's location. The boy was heading south and west, at the moment, but it would be the work of a few minutes to turn him back around. Bring him to the door. Bring him down below. For safety.

For *his* safety.

He paused, considering. The subroutine which would charge and flicker the streetlamps at his will hovered in a virtual window, just beneath his hand, superimposed over the camera view.

Reaching out slowly, carefully, he pinched the subroutine closed.

"No," he decided, finally regaining control over his fear. "Not yet."

He recalled that momentary expression of revulsion Tevin had given the lift—given *him*—and Rutheford was not quite ready to deal with that. Revulsion could turn toward fear or hate. While the former would be very accommodating toward bringing Tevin down below, the other was very, very dangerous.

Besides, Tevin would eventually come back on his own with a new group of evacuees looking for a way off Bountiful. And these last few days, Rutheford had become quite the people person, hadn't he?

Still, he left one of the monitor windows open to follow Tevin's progress along the course of the day. A necessary evil, he decided, begrudging every moment taken away from his work. Time was not on his side. He knew that. It trickled away just as the grit and chips trickled from spreading fissures in the overhead. This lab was doomed, just as Bountiful was doomed. But not yet. Not before he was finished.

Bringing his imaging program back to the monitor, Rutheford pushed glasses up onto the bridge of his nose, then bent forward to work. The virtual overlays displayed his progress and what was left to accomplish. Nearly there. With a careful, steady hand, he manipulated the micro-surgical tools. Splicing his probes into the neural pathways. Making one final severing which would help put his guest at ease. Then, turning away form the monitor, Rutheford reconfigured his glasses for extreme magnification and physically checked the bundle of bio-optic leads which sprouted like a new nerve cluster at the back of his guest's skull.

One lead, darker than the rest, began to glow with new, steady life.

"Excellent," Rutheford said in praise. For his guest as well as for himself. Forgotten was Tevin, the Cyborg threat, and the battle still raging on Bountiful's surface. Now, for the moment, there was only *the work*. "And it is proceeding well, wouldn't you say?"

Reclined in the chair, staring up into the network of cracks spreading across the ceiling, Cog simply smiled.

THE BLACK SHIP

A Mech Novella from the Imperium Series

B.V. Larson

— 1 —

The Black Ship had been built to hide its nature as a vehicle of powered flight. The engines were cleverly designed to allow it to approach target planets without being detected. Like most spacecraft, it was propelled by ejecting matter from the tail section. The stealth drive operated on the same principle, but it cooled the exhaust and masked the energy emissions with powerful fields. To all but the most sensitive optical sensors, the ship resembled a large asteroid, nothing more.

Under normal circumstances, the arrival of an interstellar vessel was as obvious as the approach of a large comet. The speed required to cross the abyss between star systems demanded a vast amount of thrust, and an equally vast amount of thrust had to be applied upon arrival to slow the vessel down. Any witness to this process saw a long plume of heated gasses, one that stretched for millions of miles.

The crew of the Black Ship was keen on maintaining stealth, but today there was a new technical problem with the stealth drive. Being an unforgiving sort, the Captain summoned the Engineer into his presence. In his right gripper he held up a computer scroll. In his left, he held his disconnection device. This dangerous implement resembled a thick stylus, or a thin flashlight. It had a single, black firing stud on the silvery shaft and a projector dome at the tip.

"Engineer," the Captain said, lowering the computer scroll. "These emission ratings are off the chart. We've only reached eleven percent of light, and already the dampeners are failing."

Being a brave soul, the Engineer took two clanking steps forward. Unlike the Captain, who resembled a person in most respects, the Engineer was a mech of the old school. She was constructed entirely of burnished metal with exposed nanotube muscles and servos that whined when she moved. Not a scrap of false-flesh polymers covered her chassis. Even her optical orbs were bulbs of plastic on short metal stalks.

"We do not have the components necessary to affect complete repairs, Captain," she said evenly. "I have prepared a list of possible solutions."

"Let's hear them." The Captain placed the computer scroll on top of the central display unit. He kept the disconnection device in his possession.

The Engineer's orbs tracked the disconnection device closely as she spoke. "Firstly, we could abort the mission."

"Unthinkable." The Captain's gripper twitched on the disconnection device.

"I have more possibilities," said the Engineer hurriedly. "We can slow down to maintain stealth."

"What? *Slow down?* We are crawling now. As it is, we'll be more than a month late. I must admit not even I had thought of slowing down further. Why can't we at least maintain our current velocity?"

The Engineer rustled her computer scroll nervously. Around her, the bridge crew glanced at her with unsympathetic orbs. The Engineer drew herself up and plunged ahead. It was best to present bad news quickly, she believed. Reality had to sink in and dominate desires. Facts were stubborn things.

"We have several problems, sir. If we apply thrust while moving at a velocity of more than eight points, the field won't hold."

"So what? We'll accelerate to full cruising speed, then coast to our destination undetected, and—" he paused. "Ah, I see. When we arrive, we must decelerate. You're telling me we'll be visible even while we slow down?"

"Yes sir," the Engineer said, daring to allow her hopes to rise. He had to see the realities of the situation. "Thrust is thrust, and the engines must flare just as powerfully to reduce our speed as they must to increase it."

"Can't we simply decelerate more gently?"

The Engineer shook her head, the section of her chassis that contained most of her sensory subsystems. "No. The problem is with the phasing of the masking field, not the applied level of power. It won't maintain integrity past ten percent of light. Not even at nine percent."

The Captain walked on heavy feet around the central table. Every mech on the bridge moved away from him as he approached. "What is your third option?"

"The third … ?"

"Engineer, do you realize where you are, what you are part of? This is not just a ship on an attack mission to raid a planet— this is the beginning of the end. Mechs are the way of the future, and we are the heralds of these new times. Wild humans will continue to breed and provide us with fresh minds for our perfectly-designed bodies, but—"

"I've read all the official statements, sir."

The Captain halted his pacing and swung his orbs to her. After staring for a full second, he nodded curtly. "I see," he said. "Thus far, you've presented me with only two options. Stop the mission, or crawl to our destination—"

"There is one other possibility, but it would be a longshot."

The Captain's orbs met hers. "Let's hear it."

"We are passing an inhabited system. Possibly, they will have the technology required to make effective repairs."

"Why didn't you mention this earlier?"

"As I said, the odds are slim. The system is known as Faust."

The Captain paused to think. "The dead system? Those colonies were all lost long ago."

"Not according to our readings. There are meager signs of settlements."

The Captain tapped his gripper thoughtfully on the safety rail. Finally, he nodded and the Engineer felt a wave of relief.

"We will take this third option," he said solemnly. "Navigator, plot a course. We will make planetfall at Faust. Helmsman, get us there as quickly as possible. I do not care if our emissions are seen or not. Use all deceleration and navigational assets."

"I fully support your choice, Captain," the Engineer said, even though she privately thought it was the least rational of the list. The colonists of Faust, if they even existed, were unlikely to have equipment that could help them repair the ship. Still, she had done her job and talked the Captain through the possibilities. It was not her responsibility to choose the right course, only to lay out options for her commander.

"I thank you for your raw honesty, Engineer. Unfortunately, your performance in this instance was unacceptable. The Mech Revolution will not be derailed by the incompetence of a single member, feel reassured on that point. Our world, Talos, will prevail over all others."

"What? I—" the Engineer was unable to complete her statement, however. The Captain had directed the disconnection device toward her and depressed the firing stud. He held it down for the required three second duration, allowing the termination signal to be accepted by the Engineer's autonomic processors. The shutdown signal caused her artificial body to freeze in place.

"Remove that thing," the Captain ordered, indicating the Engineer.

"Should we put the brain back in the tank, or freeze it?"

"Neither," he said. "Flush it down the waste system. I don't want to hear from it again. Install another qualified brain in the chassis. We have plenty in the cryo-vault. Let's all pray the next Engineer will be smarter than this one."

These were the last words the Engineer heard via her passive auditory input systems before they, too, shut down forever.

Her final thoughts wandered. She tried to recall her real name, the one she'd been born with long ago, but failed. It might have seemed an odd thought to a human, but none of the mechs aboard the Black Ship knew their original names. When their brains had been harvested, such details had been considered counterproductive. They were known only by their function: Engineer, Helmsman, Gunner, etc. Not even the ship had a real name, as the crew had never thought to give it one.

As this thought faded from the Engineer's mind, no new concept came to replace it. Her life support system had shut down with the rest of her artificial body, and her brain died inside a dark, sloshing little tank of oily liquid.

Within hours, her brain would be blended into the digesters. It would perform a final service as a source of nutrients for the rest of the crew.

— 2 —

Gersen followed a primitive road, taking care to place each foot softly. Little more than a dirt track, the road led uphill from the rocky beach where he'd left his boat.

He had good reason to be cautious, as the area was overgrown by juvenile plants bearing lavender-green podlings. Lavender was a warning color for most varieties of pod, and with this particular subspecies it indicated they were ripe, approaching the final stages of their lifecycle. Ripe pods were always irritable, and these were no exception. They rolled fitfully at the ends of long writhing vines. Their stinging red hairs bristled as they sensed the traveler's passing warmth.

Gersen paused to look upward. The sky overhead was full of brilliant stars. Like every world in the cluster, the view was spectacular. The skies in vids from Old Earth were drab by comparison.

He carried no lantern or torch, preferring the velvet darkness. To see, he depended on his flickering, light-enhancement goggles. The day-night cycle of Faust was less than eight hours long. He judged the sky above, and calculated he had no more than two hours of darkness left to reach a safe haven.

Gersen took one careful step after another on cloth-wrapped boots. He was nearly silent, as would be any sane man who walked the open lands of Faust. Around him a thousand pods swayed upon a thousand reeds, responding to the coastal breezes. These were the lighter pods, those that had not yet swollen enough to droop to the ground. They were not as dangerous as those that rustled and rolled themselves over the sandy soil, but a stray gust of wind could cause one to slap against a man's arm or an exposed cheek.

He tried to avoid thinking of such possibilities. He didn't even look at them directly. Many men became paralyzed by fear as they passed patches of pods and podlings, especially at night. Gersen had never lost his nerve, but gazing too closely at the pods was always a mistake. As when crossing from one high cliff to another by stepping over open space—it was best not to gaze into the abyss.

Traveling past wild pods required a certain level of disbelief on the part of the traveler. To stay calm with death so close at hand, one had to pretend you were somewhere else. The trick was to keep moving. Therefore, he walked as if he were at home on his own lands, without a care in the world. His wrapped boots did not waver, scrape or snag. His knees didn't bump a swaying pod nor catch on the tiny red spikes that grew from each fist-sized bulb.

At last, Gersen topped a ridge. He gazed across a final field of restless plants. The road terminated at the foot of a thirty-foot high wall of stone. It was rude for a stranger to approach a village wall at night, but it was also dangerous to do so with fanfare. He chose to remain quiet, and did not call out his name or summon the watchman. It was very unlikely they'd open the gates for him anyway, if he did.

Flickering gas torches burned at random intervals along the wall top. Yellow-orange flames danced above a tiny tongue of deep blue. When he stood at the ramshackle gate at last, he examined the defensives closely. The gate was corrugated steel, braced with rivets and wrapped with wire. It looked solid enough. Directly above him crouched the watchtower, built with concrete blocks and rusty girders. A high cupola sat at the pinnacle, but he could not see the lookout inside. The man was most likely drunk, sleeping—or both. Otherwise, he would have spotted the stranger approaching the gates by now.

The gates were sealed by an ancient mechanism, something that looked like it had been part of a ship's hatch decades earlier. Gersen had no idea how to open it, and had little interest in asking for entry. He'd never met a village watchman yet who welcomed visitors after sunset.

Instead, he made his way north, walking along the base of the wall. He walked with exaggerated care, lest his boots stray and crush down a sprig of growth. There were no pods this close to the walls, as the villagers had wisely salted the base with gravel. But fleshy leaves and pale tubers still grew everywhere. It would not be wise to upset the local flora, especially not in the shadow of an unknown village.

Running his gloved hands over the wall as he walked, Gersen took the opportunity to examine the structure itself, which was ingeniously built. Made entirely of dark boulders rolled up from the rocky shoreline of the island, it resembled a natural formation. Except for the gate, the wall used very little metal or other artificial substances. These precautions had been taken to hide the human origins of the construction in hopes of calming the wildlife. To any trained eye, of course, the wall was clearly artificial, but this didn't matter. The fortification only had to fool the plants.

Gersen reached out to touch the mortar that cemented the stones together. His gloves were heirlooms, handed down to him by his father, who'd been a spacer on the third ship. The index finger of the right glove had worn through the ancient leather. Using his single exposed digit, he reached out a hand and ran a bare finger over the substance used to cement the boulders together. He felt the rough texture and noted the ash-like crust it left on his fingertip.

He nodded to himself, admiring the workmanship. The cracks between each boulder had been filled with molten rock, leaving a rough gray surface like that of pumice. Probably, a laser team had done it long ago after they'd hauled up each of these massive stones from the sea. He wondered if these villagers still had big lasers, or even a generator to run them. If they did, they were a rich people indeed.

After taking a hundred steps along the wall of towering stones, Gersen found an opening that wasn't sealed. Crouching and peering within, he thought to see the dancing light of gas torches reflected from the walls of this narrow passage. He smiled and began to creep into the tunnel. With luck, he'd be able to slip his way past their massive fortifications without notice.

As a precaution, he sprayed a fine mist of juice from a sterile gourd ahead of him. A network of gleaming lines appeared, and his smile faded immediately. The passage was laced with sensors. He shook his head. People were born without trust these days! Grunting with disappointment, Gersen backed out of the tunnel, straightened his spine and leaned against the base of the wall. The rough-cut boulders pressed against his back. They felt cool and very solid.

He considered his options. The villagers would come running if he slipped through the passage. Possibly, they had a spy bug floating overhead right now. He hadn't seen one for years, but he never dared to discount the possibility of meeting up with a piece of old tech that still functioned.

Gersen looked downslope into the darkness. The field of pods he'd passed by was no longer tranquil. The plants rustled and shifted like a thousand old men stirring in their beds. They weren't fully awake yet, but they would be soon, long before daybreak. If he chose to run back for the boat he'd left on the beach, he might not make it past them a second time.

Calmly, he arranged the pack on his back until it rode there tightly. He set up a thumper inside the passage, which was sure to both trip the alarms and summon the most alert of the pods. Then he walked with measured steps back toward the gate. He would meet whoever came out to investigate the trouble along the wall. Detainment and questioning were infinitely preferable to spending another night at the edge of an active field. Gersen had been arrested before, and he was very familiar with the process.

As he waited, listening with a smile to the muttered curses coming from behind the gate, Gersen took the opportunity to further examine the night sky. Faust was a small planet circling a dim red star. The evening sky provided an excellent view of the home cluster, which was known as the *Faustian Chain*. The Chain consisted of sixty-odd suns in close proximity, most of them less than a lightyear apart. It was an enchanting sight. Nebulae glowed and the closer stars were as bright as small moons.

Gersen frowned. Something up there was different tonight. As a longtime traveler in the darkest of lands, he knew Faust's night sky very well. There was a streak of light which glimmered overhead, something that resembled a falling meteor frozen in place. *What could that be?* he wondered. A comet, perhaps?

But then the gates creaked open, and he forgot about the strange streak of light above the clouds.

— **3** —

The brain knew something was happening to it, but at first it believed it was experiencing an odd dream passing through its neural pathways. Slowly, as warm gels and artificial blood flowed to frozen cells, it shifted from dreaming into a delirious state.

Inputs were hooked up, starting with the auditory implants. Noises assaulted the partially blank mind. Not having heard anything for a long time, and having had real nerves to stimulate the temporal lobes in the past, the artificial input was difficult to process at first. These new nerves were manufactured, consisting of strands of conductive polymers. Like artificial muscles, they were based on nanotube technology. Adjustments were made, and test inputs were attempted repeatedly. Eventually, the brain heard something.

"I'm getting a response there—hold it at nine-four-niner."

"Got it."

The brain knew relief and panic at the same time. The mind is a very lonely place without input. Even when we sleep, there are a hundred familiar sounds and sensations. All of them were absent now. No heartbeat, no tingling limbs, no breath could be drawn. This last absence was the most immediately disturbing. The brain felt as if it *should* be breathing. It sent out the signals for deep breaths to be sucked into non-existent lungs, but as it was no longer connected to lungs, or a diaphragm muscle, nothing happened.

Like a first time scuba diver, a moment of panic and light-headedness assailed the brain. It experienced a confused, bubbling feeling. It felt as if it were drowning, even though all its oxygen needs were being met.

"What's this one make then—six?"

"Five. This is Engineer number five."

"How many more Engineer brains do we have in the tanks?"

"Only a few more of them are really qualified."

"Shouldn't we tell the Captain that?"

"You can tell him," said a distant voice with an echoing laugh. "I'm not going to do it."

"But we're running out of Engineers."

"Then we'll start pulling them from the Navigator group, or the Pilot group. He hasn't killed any of them yet."

As the conversation continued, the new Engineer listened and grew more coherent. He began to grasp what was being said. Panic faded, but it was quickly replaced by fresh concerns. The Engineer had gleaned his rank and purpose, but did not entirely comprehend the situation. He knew he was in the process of being revived, that much was clear. According to Revolutionary Doctrine, every spare brain from Talos was to be kept in reserve for use when the invasion was underway and a beachhead had been established on the target world. But the Engineer had the distinct impression this was not the case. He was being awakened to replace a mech that had been disconnected—that was most unusual, and disturbing.

He listened further to the two Techs as they discussed matters over the operating table. Gradually, the Engineer's fears were confirmed. The mission was in danger of failing, and the Captain had begun to take unorthodox steps.

At long last, the visual input threads were hooked up, but the Engineer was not yet able to control his body. He could see now, looking out of his motionless optical subsystems. But he could not control his orbs. He could not direct them toward a subject of interest, or even focus them. Still, the input was welcome. Panic had fully subsided. The Techs were distracted, but at least they seemed to know what they were doing.

But then came a moment of greater worry. The Techs emptied out the contents of a sloshing pan of liquid. Something pinkish-gray sat in the pan, and plopped loudly when it fell into the waste chute.

Even though the new Engineer could not look directly at the lump in the pan, nor was the scene in focus, he felt sure he knew what it had been. The previous Engineer's brain had just been dumped into the recycling tanks. It would be added to the oily gruel for the crew's consumption after the dicers had done their grim work.

— 4 —

At dawn, the gates finally opened. Gersen was surprised it had taken the villagers so long to investigate the ruckus he'd caused. The thumper had long since run out of charge and shut itself off. The pods had not stopped coming to investigate, however. They thrashed and scratched at the walls ineffectively. Gersen watched without too much concern. Not even a full grown pod-walker from the mainland could have easily scaled that barrier.

When the gates finally creaked open, Gersen expected to be greeted by a mob of slit-eyed sneering men, aiming welded-together spring-rifles at his chest. Instead, he saw a lone older man with a neatly trimmed silver beard and a spacer's blue vest. Blue had been the mark of an officer on the old ships. Could this man be an original colonist? Probably not, Gersen thought. He'd have to be nearly a century old.

"Welcome, stranger," said the old man.

Gersen summoned a flickering smile. "Thank you for opening your gates to me."

The old man gave him a broader smile, then stepped closer still, throwing his arms wide. Gersen paused, trying not to look shocked. Did this geezer expect a hug?

The man's widespread fingers wriggled, and Gersen realized he *did* expect to be greeted as one might greet a long lost relative.

"Do I know you?" Gersen asked.

"Of course you do. You are one of us—one of humanity's members, are you not?"

Gersen opened his mouth, then closed it again. He stepped two steps closer, looking into the compound. A number of sights met his eyes. There were domes inside the walls, dozens of them. That indicated a first generation settlement. Only groups that had disembarked directly off the landers had domes. Those that had been spawned later possessed no prefabricated shelters from Old Earth. He had not realized that any such settlements still existed.

"This must be an old settlement—" he began, but then broke off with a startled grunt.

The old man had hugged him. He clung to him and squeezed. Gersen scowled, trying to hide his discomfort. He wasn't used to human contact of any kind, much less being grasped and pawed by a bizarre fellow like this. Those who survived on Faust were usually wary and nervous, and did not hug strangers upon meeting them.

After a few long seconds, the old man released him and backed away, nodding as if some great moment had passed between them. Gersen privately wondered how far this splinter group might have diverged culturally from the rest of humanity. It was a common enough tendency in remote regions—and practically every area of Faust qualified as remote from the rest.

"Are you the only one here?" Gersen asked.

The old man laughed. "The rest are shy," he said. He produced a silver whistle and blew upon it.

Gersen stared at the whistle for a moment—he'd seen such things in old vids. They'd been used by press officers as they loaded the colony ships on Earth. The herds of humanity had been conditioned to respond to such high-pitched blasts under the rule of the Social Synergetics. He found the noise irritating in the extreme—almost as unwelcome as the hug itself.

In response to the whistle-blast, a dozen people stepped forward from the domes and shacks. Six times as many came out over the following minute, until a crowd several hundred strong stood around Gersen, staring. They seemed curious and hesitant at the same time.

"He's all right," said the man with the whistle. "He's not sick, or secretly-armed."

Gersen glanced at the old man. Had his body been scanned somehow? The man nodded back to him, giving him a wide, winning smile.

"Here," he said, putting a hand on Gersen's shoulder and pointing into the approaching crowd. "Here's one I'd bet you'd rather hug."

A girl approached, stepping closer still as the old man beckoned. The girl put out her arms. She looked shy, and her face was red, but she still came closer, offering Gersen another hug. She had yellow hair, amber eyes and full lips. Gersen took a deep breath and decided not to fight this contact. He summoned a smile that came easily, and hugged her.

He felt breasts pressed up against his weathered clothes. They were welcome indeed. He planned to hold on as long as she did, enjoying the procedure. Finally, several in the crowd giggled, and he released the girl. He sensed he'd done something wrong. Perhaps as the visitor, it was he who was expected to release her first. Not knowing their bizarre customs, he didn't let it bother him.

"Tell me, sir," Gersen asked the old man in the spacer blues. "What is your name, and may I know that of this woman as well?"

"Of course," the old man said. "I'm Bolivar, and this is my lovely daughter Estelle."

Gersen nodded, although the names meant nothing to him. He was startled to realize Bolivar had presented him with his own *daughter*. Strangers were not well-liked in most places on Faust. He began to believe he'd stumbled onto a welcome haven.

The villagers gave Gersen a tour of the village, personally led by Estelle. She was an enchanting girl with a lithe step and a quick smile. He was soon stricken by her. On Faust, few people were unscarred by disease, abuse or the caress of the pods. Gersen's own legs were covered in livid purple-red scars. Venoms, worming threads and spine-stings had taken their toll over the years. He was glad his legs were covered by his tattered pants, or he would have felt self-conscious about them.

The girl showed him around the enclosed acreage, a plot which was bigger than most, but not roomy. Everything required for life was located within the encircling walls, of course. There was a central pump house that brought up fresh water from underground geothermal springs. The water was hot when it flowed out of the pipes, and thus provided them energy as well as sustenance. Most of the land was used to produce food, naturally. Almost all of the steel-framed domes were hothouses full of edible plants that had been imported long ago from Old Earth. This didn't surprise Gersen, as most of the native flora on Faust was highly toxic to humans.

Eventually, evening came and the population gathered for a meal. The entire village ate together, and Gersen gladly joined in. He liked the soup best, as the floating chunks of meat were flavorful and he'd not had much to eat other than an occasional needlefish of late.

At this gathering he met his first unfriendly face. A muscular young lad glowered at him from across a long, low table laden with vegetables and thin soups. He had a heavy brow with black curly hair and a chunk removed from his right ear. Gersen avoided his gaze.

"Who's that?" Gersen asked Estelle as they ate together.

Estelle put a seed in his mouth and urged him to chew it. He found it bitter, but didn't spit it out. He wanted to please her.

"That's Kerth," she said. "He doesn't like you."

"He's your boyfriend?"

"He had plans," she said, giving a tiny shrug and prodding her food.

Gersen looked at her for a second, absorbing her words. He *had* plans? Did the girl mean the plans had recently changed? He wondered now if the settlement had trouble with inbreeding. Perhaps they were so remote, they needed fresh genetic material. There couldn't be more than a thousand of them here all told— probably half that.

He thought about the situation and decided it had its advantages. He had no intention of settling down here, of course, but he could see himself spending an easy month on the island enjoying their hospitality.

"Gersen?" Bolivar called out after everyone had eaten and the crowd was beginning to break up.

Gersen climbed to his feet and went to the old man. Bolivar never introduced himself as the village hetman, or as a chieftain. Maybe he didn't have such an official title, but he definitely had the role.

"What is it, my host?" Gersen asked.

"I have a favor to ask of you."

Gersen nodded, unsurprised. Here it was. He was to be asked to wed the man's daughter, or to go and deliver a message, or some such nonsense. He was almost glad this moment had come. He felt it was best to get it over with. He was not overly concerned, as he knew himself very well. He was a wanderer, a rare breed on Faust. If Bolivar wanted too much, he'd agree with a smile, and then begin planning his stealthy exit from this odd, friendly little place.

When Bolivar's question finally came however, he was surprised by its nature: "Do you value your life, sir?"

"Why, yes. I certainly do."

"Pity," Bolivar said. "I'm afraid there's nothing I can do about it. The whole thing is quite unfair. I've consulted the ancestral files, and there can be no doubt of their meaning."

Gersen shook his head. "What are you talking about?"

Bolivar gestured toward the entrance to the village. "You come from outside—from lands beyond ours. Is this not so?"

"Of course."

"I investigated the items in your pack, you know that. I've scanned them, and recorded them. A full log was produced."

"How?" Gersen asked, reaching for his pack, which had never strayed far from his person.

Bolivar laughed. "Don't worry, everything is there. A man's possessions are his own in this settlement."

Gersen nodded, frowning. His eyes were already roving the walls. There were ramps here and there, mostly built to service the torches that lined the wall top. The task of getting out of here looked easier than getting in, at least.

Bolivar studied his own worn boots and talked in a low, sorrowful voice. "You must understand who we are," he whispered. "This is drop zone six."

Gersen returned his attention to the old man. He frowned. "Drop zone six? The third ship landed at a single point, to my knowledge. Somewhere near the equator."

"Yes, of course. But we aren't from the third ship. We were brought here by the sixth lander—of the first ship."

Gersen laughed at that. "Every child knows the first two colonies failed. Everyone died. We are the last—descendants of refugees, not really colonists."

"I've heard that," Bolivar said. "We do get a rare visitor out here, once every year or two. And we've never argued about it. But it is not true. Allow me to explain."

He stood up and walked away. Gersen followed him doubtfully into one of the domes. The old man snapped on a system. It was an observation tank. Inside, in three dimensions, various scenes played out. Gersen watched with interest. He knew most of the story, every survivor on Faust did. The story of the colonization explained why more ships never came, and why those who survived here never summoned them. Faust was believed to be a dead world, the graveyard of two early colonies. No one had bothered to send another ship to the doomed planet, and Old Earth had stopped sending out colony ships decades ago in any regard.

First, the *Faustian Chain* swam into being inside the tank. Gersen was awestruck by the technology. Just to possess the generators to power such a device—much less to possess the device itself. It was priceless!

He tried to put aside thoughts of greed and wonder, and instead focused on the presentation. The Faustian Chain was a loose collection of stars that drifted at the outer rim of the galaxy. Originally colonized by Earth separatists during the third expansion, the stars served as warm suns over numerous inhabitable planets. One such world was none other than Faust itself, the sole planet of note circling a burning red M-class ember.

Faust was one of the first planets discovered, due to its nearness to Earth. The entire chain had been named for this ill-fated world.

One of the earliest colony ships had arrived and discovered a seemingly idyllic planet. Faust was rich in growths, with warm seas and placid skies. But a year after the first colonists had settled here and a second wave of jubilant immigrants arrived— the grim truth was discovered. The colonists from the first expedition were all dead and gone. Only bloodstains and scratch marks were to be found in their wake. They had disturbed the pods during the wrong season shortly before the second ship arrived.

Cautiously, the new arrivals set up housekeeping, suspecting a natural force unknown to them. After a few months they relaxed, shrugging off the mysterious disappearances. The world was lush and there was so much work to be done!

Some three years later, when a patrol boat had moored in orbit over the world, the second colony settlements were found to be as empty and derelict as the first. The ship had fled, broadcasting the news to every colonial seedling in the cluster. It was decades before another splinter group dared to land on the infamous crust of Faust. These people were a respectful sect of humble souls who clung to rocky islands off the shores of the primary continent. Never did they dare enter the interior, harvest the mangrove fruits or capture any of the flapping skitter-fish, unless they were far out to sea. They eked out a thin existence derived from the goats, barley and fruit trees they'd brought with them. Even their soups were tasteless and bland.

But they had survived. Being refugees, they made no attempt to contact other worlds and let them know they'd successfully colonized a haunted world. Years passed, and they'd finally mastered the trick of surviving on this harsh planet.

"I knew most of what you describe," Gersen said, walking around the tank full of flickering images of ships, officers and planetary vistas from above the atmosphere. "But you are claiming the histories are wrong?"

"Yes," Bolivar said. "We are from the original colony ship. This single settlement is the only one that survived."

Gersen smiled at him thinly. He had decided it was best to humor Bolivar. "All right, Captain. Were you on the original colony ship yourself?"

Bolivar chuckled. "What? Do you think me mad? I'm talking about my mother's father. And I'm not a captain, either. I'm a warden, nothing more. But I'm the only survivor from an officer's family."

He produced his silver whistle and eyed it wistfully. "They blew this on Old Earth as the throngs were pressed aboard. Hard to believe, isn't it?"

"Yes," Gersen said, standing suddenly. "But I'm afraid I have to be leaving now."

"Don't you wish to know the rest of the tale?"

Gersen hesitated. He was fairly sure that he didn't. But he thought of Estelle, and the excellent food he'd been given. The skies were darkening outside, and the plants would be no less irritable than they had been the night before. "What more can you tell me?" he asked, sitting down again.

"How we survived, when all else died before us?"

Gersen nodded and gestured for Bolivar to continue.

"It was simple enough, really," said the old man, looking pleased to have a captive listener. "We did not truly understand this place at first, this deadly planet. The fact that the plants here have primitive minds and motive power, that they are more akin to starfish back home than they are to true plants. That they are not truly flora or fauna, but rather something in-between."

"They are mindless, yet they move."

"Yes! That is because they have ganglia, you see. They are like small insects or other simple creatures. Like a man with a spinal cord, but no brain. They live, and respond to stimuli in a predictable fashion."

"So, somehow your relatives figured this out and came up with a way to survive?"

"They built this fortress, for that is what it is, and they devised a set of rules which all who live here must follow. Can you show me the contents of your pack?"

Gersen hesitated.

"It doesn't matter," Bolivar said. "It was scanned as you came in. You possess plant materials."

"They are sterile, and were harvested when it was safe to do so. The pods will never know, and won't seek revenge."

Bolivar nodded. "Clearly, you speak the truth, or you would not have survived this long. But it does not matter."

"What do you mean?"

"You see, you have broken our rules. We cannot welcome you here, although it pains me to say it. Our rules have kept this colony alive when all else failed for many, many years. At some point, the people will learn of your countless crimes—the harvesting of pods. These are things we never do here. Things which go against the dictates that have kept us alive against all odds. I can't keep your secret for long."

Gersen became uncomfortable. "I'll leave then. I'll leave tonight."

Bolivar nodded and looked apologetic. "Wait a week or so," he said. "Oh, and would you please lie with my daughter repeatedly before you go? We need seeding from outside, you see. That is—if you don't mind?"

"I ..." Gersen licked his lips and tried not to look eager. "No. No, I wouldn't mind."

Gersen spent several pleasant nights with the lovely Estelle. She was without skill, but he found her shy, earnest nature very stimulating. They coupled repeatedly until Gersen lay stretched out on their goat-leather bedding and sighed heavily.

Estelle ran her hands over him in the half-light. On the fourth evening, she found his injured legs. He'd forgotten to cover them, but did so quickly the moment she touched his ridged scars.

"What's wrong?" she asked. "Did I hurt you?"

"No."

"I'm sorry."

"Don't be, it's nothing."

"May I see? Perhaps I can help."

Gersen hesitated, but then relented and threw off the leather flap he'd pulled over himself. What did it matter? The girl seemed kind enough and he would be leaving soon in any case. He felt a pang at that thought. He'd visited other places like Zone Six, but never one so welcoming. It would be a shame to leave here. Perhaps, after the ripening had passed, he would return for a visit.

"Did the pods do this to your legs? It makes me sad."

Gersen looked at her. He almost laughed, but she wouldn't have understood. She was innocent, in a way. He supposed it came from living within a circle of boulders for her entire life.

"Yes," he said, "the pods did this. A pod-walker, to be exact. Do you want to hear the story?"

Estelle looked at him with wide, solemn eyes and nodded. Pod-walkers were always the subject of haunting tales on Faust.

"I was crossing a river—that's a body of fresh water that moves downhill."

She laughed. "I know what a river is! We have vids, you know."

"Of course. Anyway, it was on the mainland, long after the ripening. I was passing through a forest and—"

She could not contain her amazement any longer. She slapped his knee, which made him wince. "You lie to impress me!" she said. "No sane man would walk the forests on the mainland. Never."

He shrugged and smiled. "I never said I was fully sane."

"But you said it was after the ripening. Why would pod-walkers travel then?"

"There are pod-walkers among the biggest fields in every season. They don't *all* hibernate until the ripening. Do you ever see them on this island in the off-season?"

"Rarely," she said. "They come up from the sea sometimes, but never get close to the walls. Father says the beds up here are too thinly-soiled and so they don't bother. They only seem to be interested in the new plantings, anyway. They do their business, tending to the newest plants and seeding fresh ones with substances from their bodies, and then move on."

"Well, on the mainland, things work differently. One of them caught my scent, and I had to run from it."

"How could you outrun such a monster?"

"There's only one way, you must run through the thickest growths. They will scratch you, but as the pod-walker pursues, the plants will grasp at it more desperately than they would a man."

Estelle stared at him, her big eyes distant. He could tell she was beginning to believe his tale. "They would all reach up to be fed. But how did you live?"

Gersen shrugged, and indicated his legs. "The pods were more interested in the walker than they were in me. They lashed my legs badly, shredding my clothing. But there was no venom in their stings due to the season."

"If they'd tripped you and you'd fallen—they would have scratched you to death."

"Of course, but even that's better than being peeled by a walker."

She looked horrified. Gersen smiled and kissed her. He could see she was impressed by his story, and he was glad he'd told her about the experience. He'd always hidden his injuries, fearing the scars would repel others, particularly women. It was a relief to have found out otherwise.

Getting up, he went outside into the darkness and walked down the hill to a dusty area to relieve himself. He thought of Estelle, and smiled as he walked. She was going to haunt his thoughts long after he'd left this village, he knew that now.

As he turned dust into mud, Gersen looked up into the sky. He saw something there, something he'd forgotten about. His smile faded.

It was the streak—a strange line of light in the sky. He recalled now it had been there a few days earlier when he'd first arrived at the village. He tilted his head to examine it further. It glimmered brightly. His first impression was that it had to be a comet. They were fairly common in the cluster, much more so than back on Old Earth.

The Oort cloud of Earth extended about a lightyear out in every direction, but in the cluster, the stars were much closer. The cloud of icy debris orbiting each star reached out far enough to interfere with the next system. The closely huddled stars often shared comets, tossing the icy chunks from one gravity-well to the next, like a circle of men playing catch with a stone.

But this streak in the sky was different from comets Gersen had seen in the past. It had changed its nature since the previous evening. This wasn't just due to the nearness of Faust's star, either. It took him a moment to realize that the angle of the object's tail was wrong. The light streak wasn't pointing in the correct direction. Gersen knew what most thought of as a comet was really a tail of melting debris, dragged out behind the dirty snowball nucleus. As one approached a star, the tail changed directions as it was blown back like a long rippling scarf by the blasting stellar winds. But no matter how it was viewed, a comet's tail always pointed *away* from a star as it passed by. This comet's tail was pointing out into space at a random angle. In fact, it wasn't even straight. It seemed to curve noticeably. Which meant the object wasn't a comet at all. Gersen frowned up at it, thinking hard.

At that moment, he heard a crunch to his left side. He glanced in that direction. A hand reached for him out of the darkness.

Gersen had not survived for years as a vagabond by having slow reflexes. He did not cry out or stumble in surprise. He didn't even reach to pull up his pants. Instead, he stopped the descending hand with one of his own, grabbing the man's wrist and yanking him closer. He met the surprised face with his second fist. The man staggered away, blood flowing.

Another hand from a fresh attacker latched onto his shoulder from behind. Gersen rocked back and jabbed hard with his elbow. He heard a retching sound. He turned and rained blows on the second man.

But then a flash of light went off inside his head. He spun around, stunned.

Looking up from the ground, he saw the heavy face of Kerth grin down at him. There was a stout stick in Kerth's hand, and blood outlined each of the man's big teeth. Kerth had been the first man to lay hands upon him.

Then the kicks and punches rained down on Gersen, until he no longer felt them. At least, he thought, he'd managed to land one hard blow.

$$- \; 6 \; -$$

The new Engineer worked tirelessly on the ship's stealth drive, but he soon realized the task was hopeless. The drive could not be repaired without returning to Talos. The technology was unknown elsewhere in the cluster, as far as the records showed. The idea that spare parts could be found on some backwater hole like Faust was laughable.

But the Engineer wasn't laughing. He knew, unlike his predecessors, that his very existence was in jeopardy. The Captain was not easily swayed by facts or sound reasoning. As the Captain was fond of saying, he was only impressed by results.

The technical problem itself wasn't all that daunting. The fields that dampened the emissions were out of phase, and they needed to be recalibrated. The trouble was with the nature of technology itself in the cluster. Unlike other, more organized regions of human-colonized space, the Chain had diverged. Without centralized interstellar governments and regular trade, each world had grown their own local industries to create spare parts and solve technical problems. Although they shared theoretical knowledge and many possessed advanced science, their industrial development was isolated. There were few standards that reached beyond the range of a single world. A generator produced on one planet worked on the same principles as those built elsewhere—but they were incompatible, producing power of a varied amperage, with mismatched couplings and fuel types.

The nature of the particular component that had broken down exacerbated the problem. It wasn't a simple power unit, or a sensor. It was the field governor, a part of the stealth drive that was a homegrown device developed on Talos. Privately, the Engineer wasn't sure that the ship could be quickly fixed even if they were able to make planetfall at the famed orbital docks of Old Earth itself.

"Engineer?" the Captain transmitted over the ship's net. "It is time to make your report. You will do so in person."

Responding to the summons, the Engineer put down his instruments and headed for the bridge. He didn't hesitate, and he didn't prepare any documentation. He already knew what he was going to say.

Every orb on the ship followed him as he passed. He ignored them all. He knew what they were thinking, and they may well be correct—perhaps his time had come. It would be a pity to end his life today. At least the disconnection would be fast and painless.

"Well?" asked the Captain.

The Engineer stood at attention. His burnished chassis didn't gleam in the bright lights of the bridge. It was too burned and misused by arc-welding and chemicals. On a mech ship, the technicians didn't bother with protective gear. The raw surfaces of their bodies were tougher than any spacer's suit.

"I find this interruption unexpected and unwelcome," the Engineer said.

"Explain yourself."

Surrounding the two mechs, a half-dozen bridge crewmen shifted uncomfortably. The Captain had his disconnection device in his grippers again. The mechs that were anywhere near the Engineer showed particular alarm. They moved away with clanking feet, trying to ensure that if by some accident the Captain missed with his deadly signal, they would not be affected.

The Engineer sensed their exodus from his vicinity, but did not follow them with his orbs. Nor did he study the disconnection device with morbid fascination. He remained in a stance of rigid attention and stared at the Captain's falsely-fleshed eyes of wet blue polymers. "Just as I said. I have nothing new to report. I'm building subsystems and adapters for the purpose of translating the substandard equipment I expect to find on Faust into something useful."

"Are you suggesting we've chosen the wrong option?"

"That is immaterial. I'm working on the problem. This business of responding to your whimsical summons to the bridge to make daily reports is wasting my time and damaging my mental focus. I wish to get back to work, before we are pushed further behind schedule."

The Captain stared for a long second, then made an odd barking sound. It was the mech's equivalent to laughter. "I like you! I wish I'd fished you out of the tank earlier. At last, an Engineer who makes no excuses! Complaints, oh yes, he has plenty of those. But only if he is dragged away from his passion."

The Captain spun around in a circle. In so doing, the tip of the disconnection device was leveled briefly at all present. There was an uneasy ripple of discomfort among the bridge staff, who otherwise stayed silent.

"You see? All of you should take note of this excellent crewman's attitude. If he were not so valuable in his current role, I'd move him up to navigation."

The Captain turned back to the Engineer and put his device on the table with finality. There would be no disconnections today. "Carry on, Engineer. Dismissed."

The Engineer did not dare look at the device on the table between them. His orbs didn't even flicker in that direction. His thoughts, however, drifted for a brief moment. He envisioned himself grabbing the device, aiming it at the Captain and disconnecting him. The trouble was the three-second delay. It was a wise precaution which had been purposefully designed into the instrument. By the time the Engineer had stood there depressing the firing stud for three long seconds, the Captain would have called for aid and the rest of the crew would have fallen upon the traitor.

The Engineer saluted and spun around, servos whining. He thumped his way back toward his workshop.

Naturally, his entire performance had been bluster. He had nothing. No subsystems, no adapters—no hope. He knew he had to think of something, and he had to do it fast.

$$-\ 7\ -$$

Gersen awoke in a pit. Before he'd even opened his eyes, he suspected it had been dug for the purpose of waste removal, probably sewage. The odor was overwhelming. Had they cast him down into a latrine?

His head ached, and when he commanded his eyes to open, only the left obeyed. The right was sealed shut by dried blood. He moved to rub at it, but his hands didn't reach his face. They'd been restrained. His legs were free, but his wrists were tied high, forcing him to stand against one wall of the pit.

He looked around in the dim-lit hole. It was a tiny, foul prison, an excavated pit with a roof that had once been a grill of some kind. Possibly, the grill had been part of the landing ship Bolivar had spoken of.

There were footsteps and movement above him, where the light filtered down from above. He heard hushed voices.

"Father, you cannot allow this," Estelle said. "This is injustice! We have no right to cast him into the pit."

"I'm terribly sorry," Bolivar said. "Unfortunately, things are worse than you know."

Gersen thought of calling to them for aid, but instead remained silent. He'd always learned more by listening than by complaining.

"What do you mean?" Estelle hissed.

"He's guilty. He admitted it to me himself. He carried gourds of dead pods into our walls. A glaring breach of our laws."

"But the plants did nothing. Our laws must be in error."

Bolivar made hushing sounds. "Do not speak that way."

"You rule here, Father. Surely, you can explain the situation. Kerth is just jealous. His charges are clearly biased."

"Perhaps so, but it doesn't matter. I do not rule here, I *guide*. There is a vast difference. If I twisted the law in my favor, I would lose everyone's trust."

Gersen thought he heard a sob.

"Did you have feelings for the stranger?" Bolivar asked. "I apologize. I suppose it's only natural. I'll do my best to make the proceedings—painless."

Gersen sweated in the dark pit, fully awake and straining his ringing ears to listen. He tested his bonds, but found they were made of quality binding-fiber. Applied while wet and dripping, they had constricted steadily as they dried. They were leftovers from seedpods that had ended their lifecycle.

He was bitter, knowing these people had no law about using pod *vines*, only the pods themselves. How was he supposed to have known they held the pods in special regard, like sacred objects? It was true that during the ripening and the planting seasons pod-walkers would become fanatical at any perceived danger to a young pod. But the pods he'd brought to their walls were long dead and steamed clean of pheromones. The plants would not react to them any more than they would a stone.

Bolivar led the girl away. Gersen slumped in his bonds, full of bitter thoughts. He wished he'd never entered these walls. The sweet time spent with Estelle was far from worth it.

The gloom was such that he could barely make out his surroundings. Using his feet, he reached out and tapped at his environment. He found that the crumbling sides of the pit were alarmingly close.

He tried stretching as tall as he could, and reaching out with his mouth. If he could get his teeth onto the binding fiber—but no. He could not reach. In fact, his straining efforts only managed to tighten the loops more. They cut into his wrists, and his hands grew slowly numb.

Cursing quietly in the stinking pit, he became aware of a fresh intrusion. A large face loomed like a moon over the grill. It was Kerth.

"Hello stranger," he said, grinning more widely than before.

"Hello fool," Gersen said.

Kerth chuckled, and the sound was ominous to Gersen.

"I've got something for you, stranger. You violated Estelle, and I'm going to return the favor."

Gersen's eyes grew wide in the darkness. He peered up at the man. He thought of cursing at him, or calling out for aid, but waited instead. Kerth's face vanished, and everything was quiet for a few seconds.

Gersen thought of the last thing he'd seen before being attacked. "The ship," he said aloud. "There is a ship coming, Kerth. Do your people realize that?"

Kerth laughed. "Shut up, I'm trying to concentrate."

"You don't understand. I saw it. Just go outside and look up. Study the heavens. The long streak in the sky—"

"Is that the best you can do? Do you really think we are such bumpkins, stranger? We have better tech than anyone on Faust. I saw the comet, and was not impressed."

"It's not a comet—" Gersen broke off however, as a trickle of fluid came down through the grate. He realized after a moment of confusion he was being splattered with warm piss.

He did curse then, being unable to stop himself. Kerth laughed, shook off a few final drops which ran over Gersen's shoulders, and left.

Urine ran down Gersen's lank hair over his face and arms. The liquid burned his eyes and cuts. His thoughts turned dark, and he almost flew into a rage, ripping at his bonds. But instead, he controlled himself and tried to move his hands.

Yes ... his bonds were fractionally looser. He was sure of it. He looked around for more liquid. If he could get the bonds truly wet, they might loosen enough for him to slip free.

He tried spitting on them, but his mouth was dry and his aim wasn't perfect. He tried biting his lip and spitting the blood as well. It had little effect. Soon, Faust's short night would end and the villagers would come back to check on him. He had to escape before they did.

Using his arms, he felt the walls of the pit near his tied hands. There were rough spots. He worked to expose a sharp rock near his left wrist. It wasn't much, but he used it to saw at his bonds. Unfortunately, the stressed vine cinched tighter than before. He'd stretched it, and it had reacted by drawing up, as was its nature.

He slumped, all but defeated. But then he noticed a slow stream of droplets running from his elbow. He traced the source and found it was his own blood. He'd cut his left hand.

Getting an idea, he scratched himself repeatedly against the sharp rock, sawing at the palm of his hand rather than the binding fiber itself. A wound soon opened, and blood flowed over the fibers.

The process took the better part of an hour, but eventually his left hand was free. Shaking his hand to awaken the tingling nerves and banish the numbness, he set about freeing the other hand. When this was done, he pulled himself up to investigate the metal grill over the pit. It had been firmly locked down.

After crawling around the rest of the pit, he discovered an exit. A stinking, slimy hole led away into pitch blackness. He was sure this was meant to be a waste chute of some kind. Deciding it was better than being tied into place again, he crawled inside and vanished into the hole.

Like a vine in a wormhole, he wriggled toward what he hoped would be freedom.

— 8 —

The Black Ship arrived in orbit over Faust as the small, spinning world's main continent passed from day into night. The planet looked inviting enough from space, the oceans were deep blue and the land was dark green. The main continent possessed the vague shape of a horsehead. Countless jewel-like islands ringed the landmass.

The crew scanned the planetary emissions in disappointment. There was very little that registered on their sensors.

"No cities?" demanded the Captain in disbelief. His orbs were glued to the scope.

None of the others on the bridge dared to respond, lest this disappointment somehow become their fault.

"There's precious little of anything down there. It's practically empty. I'd expected a backward colony—but this is a wilderness!"

He raised his orbs and scanned his bridge crew. The Navigator busied himself with computer scrolls charting escape velocities and refueling points. The Weaponeer fiddled with his controls, despite the fact there was nothing of significance to target.

"Where's that Engineer?" the Captain demanded. "Get him up here this instant!"

The crew sighed in relief. The Engineer! Yes, it was easy to blame that one. They hastened to obey and relayed the summons to the doomed mech who toiled below the main decks.

Within a few minutes, the Engineer arrived. He strode onto the command deck with purpose. "We've arrived? Excellent."

The Captain stared at him. "Have you lost your faculties? Have you seen these readings? This place is useless."

"It is a class-four world, to be sure. But we don't need much. May I participate in the scan?"

The Captain scoffed. "Be my guest."

The Engineer approached the scope and worked the controls. His silvery orbs stared into the device for perhaps two minutes, before he made an exclamation of discovery.

"There it is," he said. "That will do nicely."

The Captain tapped and scraped his grippers over planes of metal. Reacting to the rough contact, the board brought up an image which was transmitted to everyone on the bridge via the local net. Mechs from Talos had little need for viewscreens, they could share vid feeds remotely, and review them in their own individual minds.

"I see nothing but a rocky island."

"Ah, to the untrained orb, this would seem to be true. These people are primitive, but not without resources. See the circle of stones in the middle of the island?"

"Yes, but I fail—"

"That is our target. Those stones did not appear there magically. They were cut, dragged, placed and apparently melted into place. Each stone is quite large, meaning—"

The Captain cleared his throat. He had the disconnection device in his gripper again. The Engineer never glanced at it, although avoiding it with his orbs took a great effort.

"You will explain yourself, or you will be replaced. I do not detect any significant emissions from this site. The structure might not be natural, but there is no evidence indicating advanced technology."

The Engineer lifted a gripper and gestured with it emphatically. "Exactly!" he said. "This world isn't a proper colony. There is no central government. There is no ruling body that enforces coherent laws. In short, the colonists have splintered into distant, armed encampments. They hide their tech so they are not targeted by the other pirate settlements that dot the world."

The Captain appeared doubtful. "Are you saying they have tech, but are hiding it?"

"Yes."

"And what evidence do you have to support this conclusion?"

The Engineer brought up a large file of numbers. "You see these readings? They are power measurements. They have a powerful central generator."

"A generator? To power what?"

"That is what I want to know," the Engineer said. "There are no emissions to speak of, no communications, no radio. The settlements aren't in communication, especially this one. It is isolated and ignores the rest. And yet they maintain an impressive power supply."

"Hmm," said the Captain. "Weaponry, perhaps?"

"It doesn't matter. We should land and take what we need."

"But if they are armed, and the whole world is at war, as you say ..."

The Engineer made a dismissive sweep with his gripper. "They surely can't outgun this ship. Let's go down and find out what they are hiding so carefully."

The Captain was quiet for several seconds. Everyone tried to look busy, except for the Engineer, who stood at attention and awaited the verdict. He believed his fate was in the balance. The Captain was fiddling with the disconnection device uncertainly.

"Very well," he said at last. "But if there is nothing there, you will have failed me, Engineer."

"That will not happen."

The Engineer clanked smartly away. When he reached his workshop, he immediately set about working on his project again. He chased all the Techs and Specialists out of the place on pretense of checking every system on the ship. He demanded they repair and recalibrate if they found the slightest flaw. Grumbling, they left him to his work.

He proceeded at a desperate pace, uncertain if his goals were even attainable.

— **9** —

When Gersen climbed out of the waste chute at last, he was blinded by the bright reddish light of Faust's star. Sensors were tripped, and an alarm went off. Gersen crawled to his feet wearily. He looked back and realized where he was. He shook his head bitterly. He stood at the base of the outer wall of tall boulders. He'd found the exit point of the passage he'd tried to crawl into days earlier, upon his arrival at the village walls.

The fields of pods writhed, sensing his nearness. The pods were riper now, and in a sour mood. They were very close to their time. Gersen walked among them, wearing nothing more than stained scraps of clothing. He weaved his way between the plants, drawing upon years of experience as a wanderer.

The plants rattled their leaves and sought him with swollen pods. He took up stones, tossing them away from himself when the plants came too near. This worked, but it was reckless behavior. It was always best to slip by the plants without making any kind of disturbance. Today however, he was too annoyed and hurried to take the time to do it right.

"Stranger!" called a voice from behind him.

Gersen turned, craning his neck and squinting in the sunlight. Kerth stood on the wall top. He was alone and had a crossbow cradled in his arms.

Gersen realized he was trapped. He was in the midst of the field. If he ran carelessly, the plants would try to sting him with wild abandon. Without venom, he would have been injured, but not killed. These plants were ripe however, and their hair-thin spines dripped with deadly toxins. A single brush might kill him.

So, Gersen didn't flee. He turned slowly and faced Kerth, staring up at him. He didn't beg for his life, although the thought did occur to him.

"You know I can shoot you down?" Kerth asked. "You are a fugitive. You have broken our laws and deserve death. It would be lawfully done."

Gersen continued to stare. Kerth raised the crossbow, put the stock against his shoulder and aimed with care. Gersen stood with his body turned to the side, providing a narrow target. When the trigger was pulled, he would only have time to flinch, but it might be enough.

"You've got nothing to say?" Kerth asked.

"If you're going to shoot, get on with it," Gersen said at last. "I've got a long way to walk and the plants are restless."

"They say you are an expert at evading them," Kerth said, lowering the weapon a fraction. "Let's see the truth of it."

So saying, Kerth aimed and shot the plant nearest to Gersen. The central bole of it was pierced, and it shivered in shock. A moment later, it began to thrash.

Gersen had experienced a field in a panic before, and he wasted no more time. He began to run. His feet brushed leaves now and then, and even stepped upon the rubbery length of a squirming vine.

The first plant realized it was injured and went into a frenzy, causing those around it to respond. Like a spreading ripple on a pond, soon all the plants were whipping about, lashing furiously.

Gersen ran and ran, and behind him the air rang with Kerth's laughter.

— **10** —

Not wanting to damage any valuable technology the villagers might possess, the Pilot brought the Black Ship down in the fields between the sea and the walls. The flora under the ship writhed in agony and died, turning into burnt scraps of flapping cellulose. Leaves curled and pods shimmered before bursting into flames. Polyps exploded, gushing out steaming vapor and foul, sticky liquids which were soon vaporized in turn.

"Strange plants here," muttered the Captain as he pressed his orbs to the scope. "I'm not particularly impressed by their domes. They are at least manufactured, but they look old and decrepit."

None of the crew dared speak. The Pilot landed the ship with a final jolt. They were down. The ship had been designed for both interstellar and atmospheric travel. Most interstellar vessels were built to stay in space forever, but the mech-based technology of Talos was different. The crew could withstand much higher G-forces, as their bodies were mostly artificial. The equipment required to make spaceflight comfortable for humans was thus unnecessary aboard a Talosian ship. There were no inertial dampeners, cryotanks to freeze bodies, nor even much in the way of life support. Food and oxygen production systems were aboard, but minimal. Mechs only had to feed a few pounds of brain tissue, and consumed little.

Most of the vessel's mass was dedicated to engines, weapons, and power—very little else was required. The ship was smaller in design and more efficient than human ships. Humans would have found it cramped, freezing cold and almost airless, but none of these conditions bothered mechs.

The unloading ramp rolled down, and the hatch opened. Air was sucked into the ship, which maintained a low pressure during flight due to seepage. Everyone's orbs were quickly fogged over by humidity as the warm, moist air touched the freezing metal.

The Captain cursed and rubbed at his face ineffectively with his grippers. The effect quickly passed, however. "Deploy the First Tactical Squad," he roared over the regional net. "Standard formation, weapons active. Destroy any resistance, but take care not to damage equipment."

Everyone aboard watched the First Tactical Squad as it deployed. The Marines marched smartly down the ramp onto the smoking field. A few of the burnt plants at the base of the ramp quivered with the last of their vitality as they were trod upon, but were unable to resist.

Eight Marines left the ship and headed toward the village gates in a column, two abreast. Each had a burner held diagonally across the chest. The flared tips of the weapons wisped with blue light and shimmering vapors rose up into the sky.

The squad halted when they reached the gates and regarded the primitive defensive structure. The Sergeant stepped forward, examining the hinges and wire-wrapped flap-like doors. He was not impressed.

A snap and a whirring sound alerted the squad. A shower of three sticks struck the chassis of two, and the orb-socket of a third. They examined the sticks briefly. They classified them as primitive projectiles of cellulose, tipped with triangular steel heads.

"We've been attacked," the Sergeant said. "Return fire."

Without further hesitation, the squad lifted their burners and released a gush of lavender plasma. This plasma was similar to flame, but much hotter and longer ranged. It licked out in a three-foot swirl from the throat of every gun and blew holes in the gates and the watchtower that sat above them.

"Hold your fire, you aren't even injured," the Captain transmitted in annoyance. "What if there is something of value in that tower?"

Reluctantly, the Marines lowered their burners. The damage had been done, however, and the old watchtower was now teetering on three girders rather than four. It slid crashing down toward the Marines. They clanked backward, servos whirring as they attempted to avoid damage.

The Captain muttered complaints. "Examine those ruins. Is there any sign of technological equipment? A radio, anything?"

The Sergeant picked among the tumbled stones and tangled scraps of metal. The fortification appeared to be held together with rusty wire. He did find a body, which he pulled from the rubble and held up by one leg. It was a male, dressed in tattered cloth. The Sergeant squeezed too hard with his gripper, and snipped off the man's leg at the calf. Marine grippers were sharper than those wielded by technicians and command personnel. He dropped the mess, causing a wet slap of dead blood to shower the dusty stones.

"Nothing?" demanded the Captain. "Just a few men with stick-throwing devices? These people are primitives. *ENGINEER!*"

* * *

The Engineer had been waiting for the Captain to demand his presence. He'd also expected the call to be a long, roaring summons, not a polite request. However, he hadn't expected the order to come so soon.

He hurried to make his final adjustments to the equipment he'd spent the last day and a half building, and urged his Technicians toward the unwieldy system. It resembled a black metal box with various bulbous extensions and connective polymer tubes. The Technicians advanced dubiously. He gestured for them to hurry, and they gingerly picked up the jumble of equipment, carrying it awkwardly in their grippers.

"Follow me, and don't lag behind," the Engineer ordered.

Quickly, the trio mounted the ramps and marched toward the bridge. They met the Captain and two of his Marines coming the other way.

"Ah, there you are at last," said the Captain. "Would you like to examine the treasure trove of equipment we've discovered on this rock? I'm sure you will be amazed. Perhaps we should abandon our current ship, rebuilding a better vessel with the amazing local components. We will fly to our target in luxury!"

The Engineer was unaccustomed to sarcasm, but he understood the other's meaning clearly enough: he was displeased. The Captain was freer of mind than most of the mechs aboard, who were conditioned to follow an assigned task with little in the way of errant thought processes. The Engineer was similarly unfettered, but his mind was not so free as to have a true sense of humor.

"I would like to see that, yes," the Engineer said, deciding to feign ignorance.

The Captain growled in frustration. He reached out grippers and clamped them onto the Engineer's shoulders.

"So would I," he said. "But there's nothing like that here. You have misled the expedition. Valuable time has been lost."

For a moment, the Engineer cogitated. A new possibility occurred to him, one he had not previously considered. Perhaps the Captain had become unbalanced at some point. He did not know why, but the possibility could not be discounted. His commander was not behaving within normal parameters, and although the Captain wasn't malfunctioning, he wasn't entirely rational, either.

"I'd like to point out that I did not recommend this course of action," the Engineer said.

"Ah!" said the Captain, his voice rising almost to a screech. "There it is! I knew it must come eventually. Your very first excuse. I can tolerate almost anything, Engineer. I can withstand ineptitude, treachery, even outright failure—but not excuses."

"I've never demonstrated any of the listed traits."

The Captain loomed near now, his plastic eyes seeming to bulge. "That's your *second* excuse."

"No, sir," the Engineer said. "You are in error. The statement of a pertinent fact is a justification, rather than an attempt to shift blame."

The Captain reached down with a trembling gripper to his belt and unclipped his disconnection device. He fumbled for the firing stud, as if he could not move fast enough due to his eagerness.

"Perhaps I can aid you with that," the Engineer said, reaching out a gripper.

The Captain reeled back as if stung. "Back!" he cried. He waved his Marines forward. They shouldered their way between the Captain and the Engineer.

"Your disconnection is long overdue," the Captain said, aiming his device between the narrow metal waists of the two hulking Marines.

"A pity," the Engineer said.

The Captain hesitated. "What do you mean?"

"Clearly, you have searched the entire village, found their stashed equipment and plundered it. It is a pity the discovered equipment was not useful."

The Captain wavered. "Are you still claiming these primitives have advanced components? That they are hiding their true tech? Why would they do that?"

"I could only speculate on their reasons. But I have built something that will allow me to discover the exact location of their most advanced systems."

So saying, the Engineer turned and tapped a gripper on the metal box his Technicians carried behind him. "That is the purpose of this device I've designed. It is very sensitive over a short range. We have only to walk among their domes until we find a strong signal."

"What if they have buried their equipment? What then?"

"When we find evidence of it, we will persuade them to dig it up."

"How?"

"As I understand human physiology, the removal of scraps of flesh is unpleasant for them. We will catch humans and trim them until they produce their treasures."

The Captain laughed and lowered his disconnection device. Everyone present relaxed somewhat, except for the Marines, who were so mission-focused they didn't seem to be aware of the change in mood.

A few minutes later, the Engineer found himself standing in front of the ramshackle gates. He looked at the village, aghast. The situation was far worse than he'd imagined. These people were more likely to possess a herd of goats than a useful subsystem. But like countless shamans before him, he was trapped. He would just have to bluff it through.

The Marines completely burned down the gates with gouts of purple plasma. They ripped the remaining shreds of metal out of the way, and the party marched into the compound. Last in line were the two Technicians, carrying the Engineer's strange, metal box.

— 11 —

Gersen awakened drifting offshore the day after he'd fled the island. He was sprawled aboard his tiny boat. He groaned aloud and hung over the side, vomiting until his sides hurt. The sun was bright and directly overhead giving him a headache to go with everything else. Next, he turned a bleary eye downward to examine his injuries.

He found numerous scrapes and perhaps ten embedded red spines. He plucked these out, and rubbed salve from the boat's meager stores into the wounds so they would not fester. There were toxins in his system, he was sure of that. But very little venom had been injected. If he had received a large dose, he would never have awakened at all.

When he felt better he sat up in his boat, which rolled on gentle swells. He was less than a mile from the island, and would have drifted farther if he hadn't dropped anchor.

He nursed his wounds, shivered from his ordeal, and chewed stale rations of dried fish wrapped in salted seaweed. Soft, edible corals sat in a pool of brine in the bottom of the boat. He chewed these tasteless but nourishing growths and studied the shoreline.

He had an experienced eye when it came to pod-walkers. He knew their seasonal activities well. By his estimation, he'd left the island just in time. An army of walkers now roamed the rocky shoreline. Every beach was full of fresh pods dragged up from the sea bottom. They were beginning a new planting, working their way up and down the beach.

The life cycle of the Faustian pod-creatures was a strange one, and only the humans that were native to the planet understood it in its entirety. Like some amphibians of Old Earth, the creatures changed forms as they aged in stages. Like salmon, these stages of life were spent in different environments.

Every pod-creature began its existence as a lumpy growth on the bark of a pod-walker. When these podlings dangled from their parent creature, hanging from feeding tubers, they were ready for independence and were plucked free. The second stage of life began when they were planted upon the seafloor near a sandy beach. When they'd grown to a certain point, usually taking less than a terrestrial year, they were transplanted again by pod-walkers onto dry lands, usually near a coastline.

Once seeded on the shore, they grew more and more mobile and toxic. It was during this initial planting on land that they grew ganglia, began to feel pain, and gained a primitive capacity for movement. They did not have true muscles, nor a true brain. Like the starfish of Earth, they lacked real cognitive abilities, but reacted to stimuli and their physiology was capable of limited motion.

Eventually, when these plants ripened, they were harvested by the same pod-walkers that had planted them and hundreds of pods were all dumped together into deep holes in upland regions.

They grew into a tree-like growth in the fourth stage until they finally split open and a pod-walker emerged from the swollen polyps that grew like tumors on every tree trunk. A given tree might produce new pod-walkers for thirty seasons before becoming barren and derelict.

The pod-walkers were the only truly mobile stage of the life cycle. These strange beings marched about, enabling the various other stages of their species' odd reproductive cycle. The walkers themselves tended to hibernate when not needed by any local podlings. They were influenced by the seasons just as the rest of their brethren were, and came alive and fully animated only when needed by their young.

Gersen pulled up his anchor and made ready to set sail. This island had been a bittersweet experience—mostly bitter. He would gladly leave it behind.

But something made him delay. He sat and watched the pod-walkers roving on the beach. There were a lot of them, all covered in seaweed and splashing with their broad, stumping feet. They walked on a tripod of limbs, each leg possessing a permanently bent knobby knee. Their legs were as thick as tree trunks, and their towering crowns carried between seven and twenty whipping vines. These vines were like small hands on tentacles. They could carry objects such as pods or captive prey. The vines often snapped off, in which case they shriveled and died like old leaves. New ones grew continuously to replace the lost limbs.

No one knew how the pod-walkers had evolved. There were guesses, but the initial colonies had been so devastated by the first animated seasons they'd experienced that there was no botanist left who was qualified to answer these questions. They remained a mystery, and the surviving colonists lived in a delicate truce with them. As long as humans had no contact with the juvenile plants—and more importantly the walkers—no one died. Unfortunately, the pods in their myriad forms were the dominant life form on Faust, and not easily avoided.

Gersen peered past the bustling walkers, looking beyond them to the village, which was hidden by the undulations of the land. It seemed to him that smoke wisped upward from that direction. He frowned. Just what were the villagers doing? What was Kerth up to right now? Had he perhaps staged a coup against the gullible Bolivar? Was Estelle enduring an assault even as Gersen floated on the waves?

He sighed and turned his face away from the island. "Let well enough alone," his father had told him long years ago. In general, that had always been his creed. He'd drifted through ten villages like this one, although most of them had been less isolated and his visitations less adventurous.

In the end, he did not set sail and head for the mainland as he'd intended. With a growl of frustration, he took up the oars and rowed. He turned his craft around and headed back toward the beach.

In his mind, he considered a score of reasons to take action: he was angry with Kerth; he wanted to see if Estelle was all right; his pride had been injured; and he sought revenge. All of these were compelling, to one degree or another.

He was angry with himself almost as much as he was with the villagers who had chased him out of the settlement. He supposed it was pride that drove him back into danger, as much as anything else. He'd been freely abused, and he could not let that abuse stand unanswered. He also admitted to a strong desire to experience Estelle's soft voice and even softer touch again.

When he reached the point where the waves crashed upon the sand around him, he had to dodge the pod-walkers, who were beginning to sense his presence. In a rippling series of splashes, the monsters thumped down each of their three, stump-like feet in the surf with thunderous reports. At first, they trundled past his tiny boat without a care. They were blind, but they had excellent heat-sensing organs. They did not *see* in the infrared, but they could feel moving sources of warmth that came near them, even as a torch waved near a blindfolded man's arm would inevitably make him flinch.

Gersen tossed the anchor down when he could touch the bottom with a probing toe, but he didn't simply make a thrashing run for the beach. Instead, he dove into the water and cooled his body off with the seawater. Sliding along just under the surface, he turned his head up to suck in infrequent breaths.

He soon reached the shoreline. Lying in the surf with waves rolling over him, he attempted to time his next move. It was not easy, as the pod-walkers seemed to be everywhere.

In the end, he hesitated too long. A pod-walker came splashing up behind him from the seabed. It was a big one, with no less than nineteen whipping vines hanging from a gargantuan crown. These vines dragged a load of fresh sea-podlings behind the monster, ready to be planted in the dry sands.

Gersen realized he could not slip away to the right or left down the beach due to the proximity of more walkers. He did the only thing he could: he stood up and ran for the dirt track that led uphill to the village.

The nearest three walkers froze for a moment, then slowly turned this way and that. They had the attitude of listening men. Like an escaping rodent, Gersen ran uphill between them.

He glanced back when he'd reached the relative safety of the road. He put his hands on his knees and panted. He was not truly winded yet, but fear and poisoning had a way of tiring a man quickly. He could see the pod-walkers were curious and casting for him, like predators throwing their noses high to catch the faint scent of prey.

He had evaded them. Now, he had a decision to make. He looked up the road again, but still couldn't make out the village walls. The curl of smoke in the sky had thickened and turned black. He frowned. Something odd was definitely going on up there. He suspected Kerth was at the bottom of it.

Gersen knew he couldn't very well march up and tap upon the gates again. That would only gain him a fresh shower of crossbow bolts from the walls. Even Bolivar had said he couldn't help. A stranger who broke their taboos had to be punished.

Frowning, and wondering at his own sanity, Gersen walked to the nearest bed of freshly-planted sea-pods. These were the infants of the species. They were buried clusters of bulbs that were each no larger than a man's eyeball. Later, these would turn into spiny pods the size of a man's elongated head.

Breathing through his teeth, he grabbed up the root of the plant and wrenched it loose from the sand. The vines began writhing weakly. Gersen produced a tiny blade he'd gotten from his boat and slashed open several of the podlings until they dripped a thick, greenish sap.

Having been freshly transplanted from the bottom of the ocean to the beach, the pods were in no condition to defend themselves. They could, however, make a strange odor. Few men had smelled it before, Gersen himself being among that select group. The pods released a whistling sulfurous gas which he immediately recognized. They were calling for help.

Gersen savagely ripped up another handful of squirming, fleshy tubers and slashed these open as well. The young plants released a powerful stink. He began to trot up the road with twin handfuls of vines. Sticky green sap dribbled behind him with every step.

All along the beach, every pod-walker stopped stumping along the shoreline. They froze, crowns trembling. Then as one, they turned and thundered after him. They hooted and blasted tremendous, low-noted howls as they came. These noises served to call yet more of their kind. They had no ears, but could detect low vibrations which tickled their sensitive, hair-thin spines.

The chase was on.

— **12** —

Gersen doubted the wisdom of his actions when he glanced over his shoulder. There had to be thirty pod-walkers pursuing him, and those were only the ones he could see. Worse than those behind were the ones that might be ahead. They would seek to intercept him.

As he topped a rise less than a half-mile from the village walls, his doubts grew. He could see a hundred or more of the walkers, all behind him, humping upslope rapidly. He now was fairly certain he was mildly insane. No matter, he told himself. He would most likely be dead within minutes, and at that point all recriminations would be in the past.

He topped the final rise, expecting to see the vast plateau of juvenile plants ahead he'd passed through before. His vague plan had been to run for the hole under the boulders, which was too small for a pod-walker to enter. While they madly howled and thundered after him, surging against the walls, he'd hoped at the very least to give Kerth and his friends the fright of their lives.

When he saw the actual scene, however, he was almost too stunned to take it all in. The field was still there, terminating in the stern line of boulders, but the pods were all burnt and dead. In the middle of the field was a new, ugly structure of some kind. Built of blackened metal and struts, it looked like a bloated spider squatting on the land. The spider had a triangular mouth in its belly, and the mouth was open, the lower jaw forming a ramp that sank into the dust with what was evidently great weight.

It took a second or two for Gersen to comprehend that he was looking at a spacecraft. He'd never seen one outside the vids, and this one was of an unfamiliar, alien design. He stumbled in his surprised, and fell to one knee. He quickly scrambled back up and advanced warily along the road.

He was so stunned, gaping at the spider-like craft, he scarcely noticed the smashed gate and tumbled watchtower ahead of him until he reached them. He staggered to a shuffling halt and stared when these realities finally struck home.

"What in the Nine Hells ...?" he whispered to no one.

At that point, the first of the pod-walkers crested the rise behind him. It hooted and trundled forward on its three churning legs. Gersen tried to think. The gate had clearly been smashed down by invaders from the ship. He recalled the streaks of light he'd seen in the sky—could this truly be them? Aliens from the quiet skies? No one came to Faust—*no one*. He could scarcely imagine a reason why anyone would want to bother his people in their meager existence, but he pushed those thoughts aside quickly. He wasn't one for pondering unknowables, especially not when his life was under immediate threat.

Not sure what else to do, Gersen whirled the podlings he still dragged behind him around his head three times, releasing them. They sailed into the open mouth of the ship. The pod-walkers would have a good time retrieving them. Then he turned and raced into the village itself, passing the disintegrated gates.

As he trotted into the compound, his horror grew with every step. The bodies of villagers decorated the landscape. Twisted, burned, and chopped into bloody bits, people lay dead in every imaginable state of repose. They were hung from the struts of domes or left in piles of severed body parts. Some seemed to have been simply struck dead where they stood.

Gersen examined each, shuffling ahead and making odd sounds in his throat. Black blood mixed with gray dust and formed a crust upon his sandals. His eyes searched every twisted, dead face he saw. The breezes coming up from the sea ruffled the dead, lifting their hair and coating their cheeks with dust. He recognized a few of them, but did not see Estelle.

Behind him, the pod-walkers set up a tremendous din when they found the burnt field. When they reached the spaceship, they went mad. Wild, undulating hoots and howls rose up. The sounds were alien, like sea winds in a raging night storm. They attacked the struts and beat their crowns against the dark hull. They tore and scrabbled at what they viewed as a huge attacker, taking off chunks of shielding. They left sticky splotches of sap on every surface. They rushed through the open hatch when they found it, smashing down mech crewmen in the passages and running wild inside the ship itself. Their echoing cries warbled from deep within the craft.

Incredibly, Gersen saw the entire ship sway slightly, such was the power of their collective fury. He felt a deep-seated pang of terror in his belly. Just such scenes had heralded the extinction of various colony settlements in the early days. What had he unleashed?

He found Kerth strung up by a length of cord. Gersen realized after a moment of peering that the cord was from the man's broken crossbow, which lay beneath his dangling feet. All of his crossbow bolts had been thrust into his body at a variety of angles. His left eye was dead and staring, while his right had been plucked loose. It sagged and drooped upon his cheek like an emptied bladder.

Shuddering, Gersen wasn't sure if he should advance further into the village. Who could have performed all these atrocities? Were the invaders better than the pod-walkers, or infinitely worse?

Crouching and peering from the wreckage of a demolished dome, he watched as the walkers wreaked havoc upon the invading ship. Dozens ripped at the exterior, attempting to pull off chunks of the outer hull. Some, however, had wandered away from this task. They quickly found the wall and its absent gate. They bellowed for their brethren, and flooded into the village itself. They set about tearing down the domes nearest the entrance. Excitedly, they attacked everything they came near. The last standing structures were knocked flat and the dead were shredded before being cast aside.

Gersen crept back further into the wreckage he'd found. He sensed the end of his life was near. If not from the walkers themselves, then from the invaders, who seemed hell-bent on killing every villager in the most gruesome fashion they could devise.

He heard a new sound then, but it didn't fill him with anything resembling hope. A group advanced from deeper within the village. Their footsteps sounded loud and numerous. There was an odd metallic ring to the steps, as if they wore metal suits.

Gersen sought a better place to hide, and he soon crawled under a demolished water basin. There, he crouched and stared.

– 13 –

No one was more shocked than the Engineer when the mechs met up with the pod-walkers. Strange, alien creatures heaved and stomped, tearing up what remained of the village. The mech column, including sixteen Marines, two Sergeants, the Captain and the Engineer with his trailing Techs, all halted in surprise.

They could scarcely believe their orbs. Beasts like walking three-legged trees were running amok. There were scores of them, and they were *big*. The largest were taller than the thirty-foot tall row of boulders that ringed this pathetic settlement. Suddenly, the Engineer understood why the natives had built their primitive fortifications.

The Captain recovered faster than the rest of them. "First Squad, advance!" he roared. "Second Squad, encircle this position and lay down defensive fire!"

The Marines surged ahead, following their Sergeants. They moved with bent knees and raised weapons. Their grippers spun as they adjusted nozzles and release-valve settings. Without instructions, they knew they would need both range and maximum output.

At a range of fifty paces, a Sergeant roared: *"Fire!"* He was immediately obeyed. A blaze of plasma that resembled solid, glaringly bright light spun outward in a spiral pattern from the throat of every Marine's weapon. The front rank of walkers was scorched and many of them burst into flame. The mech weapons were designed to destroy metal rather than cellulose; consequently the enemy was not stopped.

The effect on the milling mob of monsters was astonishing. They'd been wandering in random directions like agitated ants searching for something to attack. Now, they'd been given purpose and direction. A tremendous collective roar of fresh howls shot up from every creature. They charged as if they possessed a single mind between the mass of them.

The monsters moved with surprising rapidity and, although many were encased in flames, they showed not the slightest hint of fear. If they felt pain, it was clear the only effect of it was to goad them into a greater fury.

"Close-assault configuration!" screamed First Squad's Sergeant. "Fire at will!"

The Marines again adjusted their weapons expertly, dialing for a broader spread of plasma. When they unleashed their lavender gushes of energy again, the enemy was almost upon them. Several of the monsters went down this time, overwhelmed by the searing heat that burned away their vines and blackened their bark. The majority, however, pressed forward despite the withering attacks.

When the two lines crashed into one another, both sides reeled from the shock. Every mech Marine was a fierce combat system. Equipped with a thicker chassis than normal crewmembers, reinforced titanium limbs and even orbs that could not be broken with a sledgehammer, they did not succumb to any kind of assault easily. Each weighed more than a ton and stood a foot taller than a normal man. But when the pod-walkers charged into them, they went down like a row of sticks. It was a simple matter of mass and weight ratios. Each walker was three times as tall and had six times the weight of a mech. As most of the walkers were on fire and their vines had been burned away, they did not try to grapple. Instead, they knocked the mechs down and stomped on them. Huge flat feet drove downward like wooden mallets.

The mechs continued struggling from the ground. They released gush after gush of brilliant plasma up at their raging attackers. Overwhelmed, many pod-walkers thrashed and died. Their legs were cut from under them, causing them to topple and fall onto one another.

Mechs were crushed into the ground, hammered down like spikes. Their limbs broke, and their weapons misfired. Often, these accidents caused gruesome casualties. The mech weapons were more deadly to another mech than they were to the walkers. Numerous cases of fratricide occurred as mechs blindly unleashed gush after gush of blazing plasma.

"Captain," said the Engineer. "The First Tactical Squad is being defeated."

The Captain's orbs blazed. "This is incredible! Where did these villagers get this army of trees?"

"I believe they are an indigenous alien species—not trees."

The Captain gave a strange bark of laughter. "You have a substandard brain. As proof, you lack any sense of self-expression above the most literal. Of course they aren't trees! They are vicious alien beasts. You are worse than useless Engineer, and I will disconnect you the moment this battle has been concluded."

"Captain," began the Engineer, but the officer marched away from him.

The Captain spoke to the Sergeant of the second Marine squadron. "Narrow your beam and fire low. Take out their legs at range. They will be helpless if they can't maneuver."

"But sir, some of the First Squad might be hit."

"Follow your orders Sergeant, or be disconnected!"

The Sergeant offered no more objections. He shouted orders, and his Marines advanced, firing steadily into the thrashing mass of mechs and walkers. Within a few minutes, most of the walkers had been disabled. It was a simple matter after that to destroy the crippled survivors.

The Engineer watched with dismay. The Captain had indeed given appropriate orders. Using these new tactics, the pod-walkers would be quickly destroyed. Unfortunately, that meant he was to be disconnected very soon and had only seconds left to live. He turned to his two Techs, and beckoned them to advance. Between them, they carried the metal box he'd been working on for days.

The Captain ordered Second Squad to cease fire and advance into the heaving mass of bodies. They were to save every Marine from the First Squad that they could. Few survivors were found, however.

The Engineer felt stressed. He did not think the Captain had made his threat as a joke. Neither was he likely to change his mind. As the Engineer fiddled with the controls on his metal box, the Captain strode back toward him. Repeatedly, the Engineer adjusted the settings and activated the machine. Nothing appeared to happen.

"Engineer," the Captain said. "Stand clear of that equipment. I do not wish to damage it."

"One moment, sir," the Engineer said. "I think I have a new reading on the location of the enemy equipment. If you will give me a few minutes more—"

The Captain chuckled, and raised his disconnection device. "Disobedient as well? This shall be my good deed for the day. Your removal from the crew—"

The Captain broke off as the mech Marine Sergeant standing beside him stumbled. The Sergeant pitched forward on his face. The chassis was stiff and unresponsive, and his orbs were face down in the dust.

"What's wrong with him?" the Captain asked irritably. Frowning, he returned to his attention to the Engineer.

The Engineer was now frantically adjusting his equipment and slapping at it with his grippers. The Captain's artificial eyes spread wide. He lifted his disconnection wand and depressed the firing stud.

The Engineer wanted to dive out of the way. But he knew it was pointless. His chassis had already received the signal, and three seconds from now it would be too late. He activated his makeshift device, and hoped the projector was aimed correctly this time.

"Mutiny!" said the Captain, but already, the volume of his voice had shrunken to a whisper. There was no power in it. The arm holding the disconnection wand sagged, pointing toward the ground. He could no longer lift it.

A moment later, the Captain crashed into the dust at the Engineer's feet, disconnected. The Engineer's metal box had finally operated as intended. It was a disconnection device, like any other. It was overly-large and primitive, but effective at short range nonetheless. The only improvement the Engineer had made to the original design was the removal of the three-second delay.

"The Captain has suffered a malfunction," the Engineer said calmly. He ordered the rest of the Marines to advance on the ship and remove the rampaging aliens. He picked up the Captain's disconnection wand and waved it meaningfully at the other mechs. They all hastened to obey him.

It was time to leave this vile planet.

— **14** —

As the Engineer marched at the rear of his Marines, Gersen found himself in the mech's path. He'd been forced to exit his hiding spot due to the battle. He was now trapped between the pod-walkers on the far side of the wall and the advancing mechs. He calculated his odds of survival were higher if he faced the mechs, rather than the enraged pod-walkers. He decided to bluff it through.

Accordingly, Gersen stood to one side of the broken gates. He kept his hands out, showing he was unarmed and doing nothing to impede the passing mechs. The mech Marines marched past him, advancing upon the pod-walkers that still thronged the ship. Using the Captain's technique of burning away the enemy's legs, the Marines pressed the walkers back steadily.

They passed Gersen by, barely glancing at him with their flashing metallic orbs. They had no orders regarding him, so they ignored him after determining he wasn't a credible threat.

Gersen grew bolder as the Engineer approached. He dared to ask a question. "You are leaving?"

The Engineer glanced at him. For a moment, it seemed he would march by like the rest of them, but then he hesitated. The two Techs behind him shuffled their clanking feet uneasily.

"Yes," the Engineer said to Gersen.

"But why did you come? Why did you burn our village and torture our people? Was this all for nothing?"

"We sought what you do not have. We require technology to repair our ship. Unfortunately, you have nothing worthy of the name."

The mechs turned to go, but Gersen dared to step closer. Two nearby Marines reacted, rotating their thoraxes suddenly and redirecting their projectors. The Engineer stopped too, and turned his orbs toward the thin, heavily-scarred man.

"We have something to trade," Gersen said. "You may find it useful."

"Give it to us."

"I will, if you will give me one of your weapons. One pack, and one plasma projector."

The Engineer stepped forward. He lifted a single gripper. The mandibles opened and closed once in what was clearly a threatening gesture. "You will be persuaded."

"No," Gersen said. "Look around you, none of my people can be persuaded. It would be simpler and faster to trade."

The Engineer appeared to think it over. "If the item is as you say, I will trade."

Gersen led the clanking mechs to the dome Bolivar had shown him. Inside, there was the spherical tank that showed past events. They passed by this artifact, with the Engineer showing little interest.

"I do not want your bulky display device."

"Of course not. But you might be able to use the generator that operates it."

Gersen revealed the system at the base of the display device. He'd noticed it before when witnessing Bolivar's little show. The generator was far larger and more powerful than what was required to operate the display system. Like using a jet engine to power a bicycle, the power supply was overkill. It had been removed from a starship and set here for this comparatively minor task.

The Engineer examined the unit. "This is an ancient system—but very powerful. We have nothing like it in the archives of Talos."

"It was built on Old Earth. Do we have a deal?"

The Engineer ordered a Marine to give the man his weapon and pack. As a precaution, he removed the power cable that connected the generator to the projector. Gersen didn't argue, calculating they could fashion a replacement later.

The mechs took the massive generator away and left Faust, without discussing the matter further. Gersen watched them mount the ramp and enter the black, triangular mouth of their ship. He was glad to see them go.

— 15 —

Bolivar had only three fingers and a thumb left on his remaining hand, but he had survived. After he'd passed out from pain, the mechs had dropped him into the dirt and moved on to livelier prey. He still managed to smile crookedly when he heard Gersen's tale.

"You were able to reason with the mechanical invaders when the rest of us failed," Bolivar said. "You drove them from our village and, for this, we are grateful."

Gersen opened his mouth, thinking to correct Bolivar on the details. But then he thought of the way these people had treated him in the past. He shrugged, nodded, and stayed quiet. He did not think of himself as a hero—but he was willing to play the part.

"We will change the laws, as they failed to protect us today," Bolivar said with a thick tongue and slurring voice.

The rest of the villagers huddled around them. Estelle was among them, and Gersen was glad to see she was relatively undamaged. Even her hands were intact.

The villagers were dirty, their faces streaked with sweat and tears. Less than half their number had survived the day. Bolivar's single remaining hand shook, as he removed his silver whistle. He presented it to Gersen.

"Will you give us new laws, to protect us from new threats?"

Gersen squinted at the whistle which flashed crimson in the sunlight. He took a moment to look beyond the throng—past the broken gate, the burnt field and the smoldering piles of dead. He saw the shining sea on the horizon. He knew he could leave this place and never come back. He also knew he would never forget this strange village, no matter how far he traveled.

He turned back to Bolivar, Estelle and the others. He took the whistle, lifting it high overhead so they could see it spin and shine.

"I will stay," he said.

He then continued to speak, suggesting new rules by which the villagers would live their lives in the future. When the sun began to set, turning the western sea to blood, he'd finished his simple set of rules to live by, rules that allowed for experimentation, exploration and technological development.

On Faust, due to the high speed of planetary rotation, the sunsets were brief. When darkness overcame them, Gersen saw the gleaming streak in the sky again. The mech ship accelerated away from his world. He hoped to never see them return.

OUT THERE

Michael A. Stackpole

— 1 —

Greg Allen found himself having a hard time focusing on the ceremony. It wasn't that he doubted its importance or historicity. For the first time in the recorded history of mankind, human warriors were being asked to help another species—a whole legion of them—preserve their liberty against an invading enemy. Humanity, which had managed to colonize a few planets, moons and asteroids, had been accepted by galaxy-spanning Qian Commonwealth as a partner in the preservation of freedom.

There, on the flight-deck of the Qian cruiser *Unity*, he stood with other members of the 301st Squadron as dignitaries, celebrities, families and journalists looked on. He smiled happily and proudly, not just because that was expected of him, but he because he *was* proud, and happy he could fake.

Why am *I here?* It had been an honor to be chosen to join the Star Tigers. Pride and honor only went so far in motivating one to abandon the world of their birth. *There has to be something more.*

The flight deck had been made over into an Art-deco masterpiece, with warm wood planking everywhere, gentle curves replacing straight lines; brass fittings harkening back to an age of European elegance which Earth hadn't seen over two centuries. At least, not in the original—the style got revived every so often. Greg felt familiar with the brass trim and plush velvet cushions, but they didn't impart any sense of peace.

Even the ceremony's attendees had gotten in on the act, wearing fashionable suits and gowns which hinted at the early 20th century stylings of their surroundings. Tails on jackets abounded, along with cravats, but top hats had vanished. That was just as well, as the President of the United States would have looked a bit too much like Woodrow Wilson were he to have worn one. As it was, he did affect Wilson's glasses, giving the tall, slender, hawk-nosed man a scholarly appearance.

The pilots, by way of contrast and at Colonel Clark's order, had donned slate-grey flight suits graced with each pilot's name and rank insignia. Flag patches had been embroidered in shades of black and grey, but sank into obscurity on the pilots' shoulders. The martial clothing marked them as creatures apart; and Greg found himself comfortable with that role.

The President, being the last speaker, moved to the podium. It had been centered on a dais which had the openness of space behind it, with the crescent moon just peeking in from the side. Greg had no doubt that the Qian had set the stage for specific effect, and it did make for a grand backdrop to the president's address.

Greg shifted his attention to the families of the people chosen. The Earthers, if old enough, appeared intimidated. Children basked in the wonder. He fixed on the smile of one little golden-haired girl and decided his daughter, Bianca, had she been there, would have been equally as enchanted.

The President began to speak and weariness swept over the pilot. Greg's slender gold wedding-band grew suddenly heavy. His wife, Jennifer, and their daughter, would have been in the front row, beaming proudly for love of him, never betraying the fear and sadness his departure stirred up. Though they'd died nearly two years previously, time since the accident had moved achingly slowly. He keenly felt their absence, and hated that memories eroded as time passed.

Fleeing to the stars won't arrest that process.

The American President smiled as he looked to the right, to where the 301st's humans stood. "When I was a boy living in New Mexico, watching rockets reach for the stars, I used to dream of a day like this. Mankind has always looked to the heavens for inspiration and guidance, or help in times of trouble. And here, the heavens have come to us in their time of need. How humbling and rewarding for us, that they trust our love of freedom and our courage enough that they would invite us to join them in this most holy of crusades."

The man adjusted his glasses with a skeletally slender hand. "The Qian, having watched us from afar, having protected us for many years from conquest and exploitation, revealed themselves at a most opportune time, and did me a great service for which I will forever be in their debt."

He turned back and nodded to the small Qian female on the dais to his left. Her robe covered her from the floor to throat and was cut from a cloth which looked deep blue or purple depending on how she moved. Her lavender flesh-tones complimented the robe's color. Her dark eyes and black hair made her appear almost Asian, though there would be no mistaking her for someone like the 301st's Lieutenant Sun Lan. Little lights winked beneath the Qian female's flesh, as if twinkling freckles, and her straight black hair had other glowing strands woven through it.

"The men and women who have volunteered to join the Qian are the first of many—a valiant vanguard who make this sacrifice to show their dedication to freedom—and their love of the world from which they were drawn. This is the most bold journey any human has ever made, and yet they undertake it with the determination and confidence which should have their enemies quaking and lovers of peace rejoicing."

The President raised his hands, poised to clap. "I applaud you all, and commend your service in the name of humanity."

As he clapped, the attendees joined in. Applause filled the flight deck with a pleasant sound. Greg wondered, then felt certain, that it was the most joyous sound the space had ever hosted, or ever would again host. *From this point forward, this will be a place of war and lamentation.*

The finality of that thought sent a shiver down his spine, then he caught himself. *Pretentious, much?* He hid his smile for as long as he could, not wishing to ruin the solemnity of the moment. The President led the applause and waved the attendees to their feet. The ovation increased in volume, and some of the other pilots, blushing, glanced down. That gave him the cover to smile at his own failing—certain others would see it as self-effacing modesty.

Like there's ever been a fighter jock who's that modest.

The President stepped away from the podium, signaling the end of the ceremony. A military band, composed of musicians from each nation on the Earth, began a soft progression through nations' anthems. Dignitaries and families began to sort themselves out, approaching the pilot representing their nations. Greg clasped his hands behind his back and turned toward one of the portholes, gazing out at the blue-white Sphere spinning below. He knew none of the visitors would intrude on his isolation, through holographers moved into position to immortalize it. He added melancholy to his expression for their sake, and did not have to fake it.

Earth. The world of his birth, and death, and now *rebirth.* Through the clouds he caught the edge of the North American continent glowing golden as night nibbled at it. He didn't wonder, as others had, as journalists had asked him, if this was the last he'd see of Earth. He *knew* it was. Even if he survived the Qian-Zsytzii War, he'd not be coming back. *No one would want me back.*

"I'm very proud of you, son."

Greg turned slowly. His father's Secret Service detachment formed a semi-circular cordon around them, keeping the holographers at bay. Two Qian males had already been admitted to the service—a precaution demanded because of the Human entry into the war. As a rule they were a bit taller and broader than humans, their flesh darker than the female's, yet running to blue where flesh tightened over cheekbones and forehead. They had none of the freckles and, by all accounts, completely eschewed the cybernetics their females embraced.

Greg didn't offer the President his hand. "Thank you, sir."

The older man removed his glasses, deliberately folding them and slipping them into a jacket pocket. "Greg, I know you and I have never had the closest of relationships, but here, now, I find myself regretting …"

Greg shook his head. "Don't. You know as well as I do that that blue ball wasn't big enough for the two of us. You've won. You had a head start, and made good use of it. I'll just go off and make my way out among the stars."

"It would have been different, Greg, if …"

Nice, Dad, no protesting my choice.… The pilot smiled and rested his hands on his father's shoulders. "I think you're missing it. I understand. After what the Qian had to do to bring me back, no one could ever be certain of me. I'm no longer a way to secure the Allen dynasty. You have Bradley for that, and plenty of time to train him correctly. He won't disappoint you as I did."

His father searched his face, eyes narrowing.

Greg smiled. "There's no trap, sir; no hidden meanings." He lowered his hands, then turned to stare at the Earth again. "Do me a favor, one favor, please."

"Of course."

Greg swallowed hard against the lump in his throat. "Just see to it that their graves are well tended. Flowers on their birthdays, and Mother's Day and our anniversary. On the anniversary of their deaths." He covered his mouth with a hand, willing himself not to cry. "I didn't do my duty by them and …"

The President's hand rested on his shoulder. "I will see to it. Personally. And, so you know, there will be a monument to you, to the 301st. United Nations Plaza in New York. A small group, staring up the stars. Jennifer and Bianca will be among them."

Dedicated just in time to remind people what sort of sacrifice you've made for the world. He wanted to turn and snarl, but didn't. Jennifer had never liked his anger—that he remembered clearly. "Please make sure Bianca is holding Mr. Bear."

"Of course."

"She loved Mr. Bear."

"I know."

Greg turned back, swiping at the one tear that had defied him. "You have official duties. I suppose we should hug. Give them a shot someone can turn into a postage stamp or holo-montage."

The President drew him into a embrace and held on longer than Greg expected. "Despite our differences, Gregory, I do love you."

Greg smiled. *I'm sure you believe that.* "I love you, too, father."

The two men slipped from each other's arms slowly, almost reluctantly. Greg actually did feel reluctant. For the first time in as long as he could remember, he was slipping from his father's grasp. Once outside the solar system, he would be alone, no longer a pawn in his father's games. He suspected, as the President pulled back, his father was realizing that he was losing a pawn. It was this loss of as possession which gave him pause.

A momentary pause only.

The President pulled back, then drew himself up straight and tall, chin high.

Greg, as circumstances demanded, snapped to attention and saluted.

His father returned the salute smartly, and holographers filled terabytes with images. Then the President turned away and a journalist slipped through the phalanx, no doubt asking how it felt to be sending his eldest off to fight war lightyears away.

The answer, Greg did not doubt, would make a stone weep.

"So why is it you're really out here, Captain Allen?"

Greg tried to keep his face impassive, but his eyes tightened because of the journalist's tone. "You're aware of all the storylines, Mr. Yamashita. Pick one."

Jiro Yamashita lifted his chin. Of Asian descent but American breeding, he was a bit shorter than Greg, and whipcord lean. His black hair had been cut short and, truth be told, he looked more like he belonged in the squadron than Greg did. "Those are too easy, so they're crap. Most folks think you've volunteered because you want to set an example, at your father's urging. Others think you're being sacrificed to raise his profile.

The gossip mags are playing up the whole family tragedy. If this was a holodrama, maybe, but it isn't. So why?"

Greg clasped his hands behind his back. "You've got every right to ask that question, but no right to expect an answer."

"Nice dodge."

"Setting ground rules here, Mr. Yamashita. I could be asking the same question of you. Sure, you won the lottery. You're the journalist who is embedded with us. You cover us for a year, return, do a book, have a documentary, get global network shows. You'll be a star and rich and have it made. You'd be a moron to do it for that, but there's the storyline on you. Fact is, your reasons, my reasons, really don't matter much. We're here. We're stuck."

The journalist frowned. "So, what, you want to set up some *quid pro quo* deal? We play ball. I keep your profile clean, make your father happy, and you give me some juicy stuff, let me co-write your memoirs, pull me into your Administration when you follow your father into the White House?"

"Neither of us will live that long." Greg smiled. "How about we start here? I'm Greg Allen, 301st." He extended his right hand to the man, but as he did so, he let his hand change. It went from appearing to be normal flesh and blood, all pink, soft and warm, to an icy-blue crystalline construct with hard, sharp edges and little lights playing through it. Then it flowed back to flesh and blood, the transformation so quick it could have been a conjuror's illusion.

Jiro's hand, which had come up by reflex, had stopped before sliding into Greg's grip.

Greg looked into the journalist's eyes, catching the hint of fear before it fled. "What was your question again?"

Jiro took his hand. "Jiro Yamashita; journalist."

Greg shook his hand, but held on for long enough to make Jiro uncomfortable. "Every single person in the 301st—humans and our non-human compatriots—has been trained for a job. Ask us why we do it, it's the same reason you do your job. You're trained for it, you're good at it, and it's not something other folks can do. That's the core of it. Everything else is window dressing."

Jiro nodded as he slipped his hand from Greg's grasp. "Let me tell you where I'm coming from, okay? Why I'm out here."

"Rock and roll."

Jiro did not lower his voice as decorum on that night demanded. This endeared him to Greg. "The Qian are not telling us everything. Yeah, they've presented a nice story, they've asked for our help, they've punched all of our buttons. I'm sure they've had ships scouring the galaxy for our broadcasts and know exactly what makes us tick. They were invaded by a totalitarian regime—they say. There was a surprise attack, children have been murdered; they pretty much went down the checklist. Hell, they even had a picture of the Qian ambassador's daughter hugging up on a puppy while the puppy licked her face."

Greg nodded. "Had to be a dog. Cats hiss when around them."

"You've seen that?"

"I have." Greg said it firmly, and could visualize the cat's reaction, but couldn't tag a time, date or place to the memory. *As with so many things since the accident.*

"The Qian met with world leaders, they have invited the world's religions to put chaplains on their stations and worlds, they embrace all of our values while helping people. They're faery godmothers who need our help. Potent stuff."

"Okay."

Jiro looked around, pausing as the President, the 301st's commander and their Qian liaison exited the flight deck. "So, I got to wonder, what do they really want from us? They're giving a lot, they're asking for a little. I'm wondering when the accounts will be balanced."

"And you're wondering what other deals have been cut by human leaders?"

Jiro nodded. "I thought you might have some insights on that latter point."

"I wish I did." Greg's right hand hardened into a lumpen grey fist. "Maybe we're out here for the same reason after all.

There are lots of questions floating about, and out there's the only place we'll find answers."

— 2 —

Colonel Nicholas Clark's first act on reaching his office was to darken the window that looked out onto the flight deck. Camera flashes became little more than distant lightning at midnight. He'd never taken to crowds, didn't much care for ceremonies and in the eighteen months since his selection to head up the 301st, he grown even more contemptuous of politicians and journalists—all with an ease that surprised him.

Of the two, he disliked journalists more. Politicians would tell you that they were telling the truth, but a man had to have the IQ of a slug not to know they were lying. Journalists, on the other hand, professed themselves as the champions of truth. In reality what they did was write up scandalous story lines to spark interest, and delivered information that didn't even go skin-deep on most issues. They used multiple interviews from various sources to provide *perspective* which, somehow, was superior to *analysis*. They were like used-jetcar salesmen pointing out how clean the inside was and how shiny the outside was, but never showing anyone that the car just wouldn't fly.

He moved to his desk and glanced at the darkened windows. Jiro Yamashita took his job a bit more seriously. He'd bear watching. Even so, the whole operation had enough chaff blowing through it that it would distract him. *Hell and damnation, it distracts me.*

He sighed, opened a drawer and pulled out two glasses and thirty-year-old bottle of Scotch. He set them on his desk, but didn't pour. He'd wait. He'd always made a rule never to drink alone. Though he wanted a drink badly—and this was a very special occasion—he stuck by his rule.

More chaff. The journalists had loved him when he got tapped for the command. They never talked to him, of course, since the Qian had whisked him away after the President had saddled him with the job. They'd devoured his dossier, found folks who remembered him fondly, and for a week he'd even been listed as the world's #1 eligible bachelor. He'd gotten offers of marriage from around the world—and it was hinted that the females of the Qian Commonwealth were even setting their caps for him.

He learned all that in a briefing on his first trip back to Earth. Nick hadn't been impressed. He pretty much wished his species had better things to do with its time, but that ship had long since left orbit. Technology might advance at lightspeed, but human nature surrendered to inertia. That would have been depressing if Nick decided to dwell on it at all.

His office hatch opened and two black-suited security people entered. The Qian pair came first, a human woman second. They looked around, then faced the opening and nodded. The President followed them through, then they retreated and the door closed behind them, leaving Nick alone with the Commander in Chief.

President Allen paused, looking around, taking in his surroundings. Nick's requirements had been simple, and the Qian had accommodated him with an office which still featured wood and brass, but in more rustic incarnations complete with board squeaks and a faint pine scent. Taken out of the starship and plunked down on some lake in the woods of Maine, the decor would have fit perfectly. Everything from furnishings to faded paintings and prints on the walls—save for the monitor panel built into his desk—appeared well used and long loved.

"I'm glad, Colonel, you have surroundings that will remind you of home."

"Thank you, sir. A drink?"

Allen nodded. "No need for formality, is there, Nick?"

"You *are* the Commander in Chief, sir." Nick uncorked the bottle and poured equal measures. "I was brought up to respect the office."

The President raised a glass in a toast. "To the 301st and the preservation of liberty."

Nick touched his glass to the other man's, then drank. He let the whisky linger on his tongue, then slowly slide down his throat. At thirty years of age, the whisky was like drinking liquid silk. That pleasure was one of the few indulgences Nick allowed himself.

The President nodded, then turned from the desk and faced the darkened window. "There are a couple of things I need to say to you, Nick."

"I don't need politicking, sir. Out there you said all the things that needed to be said to folks who vote. I don't."

The President looked back over his shoulder. "When the Qian presented you as being *apolitical*, I had advisors who recommended against you. Were they right?"

"My politics are simple, sir. I have a constituency of a dozen—my pilots. They don't get a vote, they have to do what I say. The only thing I promise them is that I won't get them killed unless I have to. Being as how that's what politics is when all the fancy dress and fine words are stripped away, we're good."

Nick sipped more whisky. "But, sir, you and I know that you and your aides didn't hear 'apolitical.' You heard 'has no political aspirations.' The Qian got that right, and your aides are idiots."

Allen turned, holding his glass in both hands. "I'd tell you it's refreshing to have someone be so frank, but you'd think it was more political ass-kissing."

"Uh huh, and you phrased it that way so you *could* say it and pretend it wasn't." Nick set his glass on the desk. "You might as well save yourself time and me annoyance and just come out with it."

"Very well." Allen's eyes tightened. "I agreed to the formation of this squadron because I do have political ambition, for me and my family. I do not expect much from the Star Tigers. Whatever you do will be sufficient to guarantee that I and my family have a place in world politics for generations. You're already heroes. I don't need you winning their war. Quite frankly, neither does humanity."

"Let's take that last around the block again, sir."

Allen drank, then jerked a thumb toward the flight deck. "Once this ship leaves for the outer solar system, no Commonwealth vessel will be allowed inside Pluto's orbit. Earth is a protectorate world. Fifty years from now we might be open as a tourist destination. Our exports are going to be cultural. Since our technological level is primitive, the only thing we can offer are antics and fodder for graduate studies in xeno-psychology. They've studied clips and colonials for a while, now they'll see us in a our native habitat.

The President nodded toward the hull. "If you go out and win this war, suddenly we become a threat. Our talent won't be for humiliating ourselves in the name of entertainment, but for lethality. We're isolated now. We could be quarantined. The Qian could see to it that humanity never gets out of this solar system—and they could exterminate us if they wish."

Nick frowned. "So you're telling me we're, what, bomb-sniffing dogs? We can go out, do our part, but not too well? What if we're ordered on a mission that *will* win this war, and save countless lives doing so?"

"It is my hope, Colonel, you'll weigh your acceptance of your orders based on the consequences for your people."

I guess he missed the bit about what defines my people. "Yes, sir, I understand, sir."

Allen deposited his glass on a side table, then tugged at his jacket's cuffs. "Another thing. My son."

"He gets no special treatment. Period."

"Good, very good." Allen's head came up. "If there is a choice between him and another pilot for a risky mission, there will be *no* repercussions were you to choose him. There will be *no* repercussions if he does not survive."

"Let me make sure I'm reading that right, sir. You're *not* suggesting that you'd like to see your son dead, are you?"

The President had the good graces to allow shock to settle over his face for three second and insert a strain in his voice before he replied. "Colonel, I love my son. Because of the accident, I have already endured the pain of wondering if he would live or die. I said what I said in the hopes that, knowing how painful it would be to lose him again, I would shoulder the burden and relieve others of that pain. If Greg returns, you will see no prouder a parent on that day—be it in a box or hale and hardy. Do you understand me?"

Nick recovered his glass and drained it. "Loud and clear, sir."

"There is one other thing I require of you, Colonel, that humanity requires of you." The President's voice had regained its strength, and acquired an edge along the way. "Try as we might, the world's best experts cannot agree upon a logical motivation for the Qian to invite us to send warriors to the stars. As we understand it, their empire is vast and their constituent population is equally huge. Our contribution to their effort, even if we do raise divisions of troops and send them out, will be so tiny that a rounding-error will eliminate it.

"We need to know what they are getting out of our contribution. We need to know *why* they need us. You need to keep your eyes and ears open and discover this for us. Consider that an order."

Nick wanted to scoff and point out that if he did discover the Qian ulterior motive that the chances of his ever being able to communicate it back to Earth would be nil. However, the president had hit upon a question he'd been asking himself. In the time he'd spent with them there always seemed to be something else going on. At first he put it down to cultural differences, but familiarity had not eased that sense. In fact, it seemed to increase it. Whatever humans were showing the Qian, the Qian seemed to want more.

"Understood, sir."

President Allen sighed. "Nick, your nation, your species, your world, are asking a lot of you. Most people will never know what you've sacrificed. You struck a hard bargain, and I'll see to it that it is kept. I'll also see to it that you're kept in good supply with whisky and anything else you and your people need."

Nick shook his head. "No need for that, sir. We've got so many corporate gifts that the Qian are having trouble keeping the *Unity* in trim. And thank you for convincing folks that neither our uniforms nor our fighters should have corporate sponsor insignia on them."

Allen laughed. "The Qian would have allowed it, believing wearing such things was a deeply ingrained cultural aspect of humanity. You were right, of course, that 301st gear would become popular, so we have licensed the images and the 301st Foundation, as per your demand, will be in charge of the resulting funds."

"Thank you, sir."

Allen shook his head. "I do envy you. I didn't lie when I said I used to want to go to the stars. Part of me still does, but I'm too old."

Nick laughed. "You're never too old, sir."

"I defer to your expertise in that matter, Nick." The President picked up his glass, swirled the whisky, and tossed it off. "I always dreamed about humanity leaving the solar system. I thought we'd do it under our own power. We know there's wider galaxy out there, but we're still trapped unless we're the lucky few like you. By God, make the best of this."

You make it sound like we're going out of state to college, not out into the galaxy to fight a war. "I think I can speak for the squadron, sir, when I say that we know the hopes and dreams of humanity are with us. We just want to make everyone proud. Our courage isn't special, it's the courage all humans share. We were just lucky enough to be at the front of the line."

The president glanced down, nodding slowly. "Very well said, Colonel."

Nick reached over and touched the screen built into his desk. "I wrote it down, sir, and just sent it to you. You don't have to memorize it."

Allen's head came up, the hint of a smile tugging at the corners of his mouth. "You may be 'apolitical,' but you're not politically ignorant."

Nick smiled openly. "Just like you, I've dreamed of getting out to the stars since I was a boy. Having been there, I want to make sure I *am* blazing a trail. You quote those words, others will follow and men who oppose you won't be able to close our world to the outside. Consider that part of my bargain."

"Very well, Colonel." The President parked his empty glass on the desk, then offered Nick his hand. "Good luck, Godspeed, and give them Hell."

Nick shook the President's hand. "I'll consider that an order, too, sir; and you can bet that's one mission we'll accomplish.

— **3** —

Greg Allen knocked on the half-open hatch to Colonel Clark's office.

"Enter."

Greg slipped through the opening and closed the door behind him. He strode to the middle of the floor and saluted. "Captain Allen reporting as ordered, sir." Greg tried to keep his voice even and commanding, but the office mocked his seriousness. It felt less like a command center than a sanctuary *from* command.

Nick Clark looked up from his desk and returned the salute without standing. If not for the touches of grey at his temples, a nose that had been broken at least once, and a crescent scar on his chin, the 301st's commanding officer wouldn't have looked even close to his mid-40s age.

"You asked for this meeting, Captain. What can I do for you?"

"Sir, I wanted to speak with you about …"

Nick held a hand up, then stood before looking Greg straight in the eyes. "Let me rephrase my question. Are you here to warn me about your father, or about you?"

Greg blinked. "Sir, I …"

"Because, Captain Allen, I have to tell you that your being the President's son isn't going to insulate you from criticizing the CinC. Not going to happen under my command." Nick's eyes narrowed. "And, truth be told, I already have your father's measure. His control over this unit ended the second he got on that Albatross shuttle and headed back down to Earth. Your connection to him, it doesn't mean squat. Read me?"

Greg nodded, not in the least trying to hide his relief. "Sir, I came to say that if he gave you any orders about me, about sparing me any danger, that I want you to ignore what he said."

"Do you, now?" Nick smiled quickly, but the smile died in a heartbeat. "So you're thinking that you and your wishes should overrule those of the Commander in Chief? Do I have that right, Captain?"

This is not going the way I'd hoped it would. Greg raised his chin. "My father is very persuasive. He's also very smart. I don't think he'd give you orders in that regard—not bald-faced orders."

Nick moved from behind the desk and walked around to where Greg could only see him from the corner of his eye. The colonel straightened a picture on the bulkhead. "So you came to me to ask me to ignore orders, then to tell me that you father wouldn't give those sorts of orders. Are you going to be a problem, Captain? Because you're wasting my time here."

"Colonel, I ..."

Nick turned to face his left shoulder. "Captain Allen, do us both a favor and be a *man.*"

A jolt ran through Greg. Shame flushed his face and anger roared through him. He kept his left hand open, but his right molded itself into a mace-like fist. "Sir."

Nick nodded toward the hand. "Be sure to get that under control before you play poker with anyone in the squadron, Captain. But before that, learn to say what's on your mind. I bet that wasn't rewarded in your house, was it? Well, this ain't your house anymore."

The colonel moved around so Greg could see him more easily. "What you came to ask, what you came to find out, was *why* you're here. Specifically, you want to make sure you'd not here because you're President Allen's son. Do I read you right?"

Greg nodded. "Yes, sir."

"Ask yourself if it would make a damned bit of difference if that were the case. Your daddy isn't going to be in a Shrike cockpit, is he? While he and others might be wanting the 301st to be an A-list, United Nations squadron, it hasn't happened. Three Brit royals were on the list—the Princess was the only one who could fly worth a damn—and they didn't make it. It isn't your blood that landed you in the 301st."

A sense of relief flashed through him, then Greg's stomach tightened. "Then what was, sir? Why am I here?"

Nick's smile returned and survived a bit longer. "Bear in mind, Captain, I'm under no obligation to answer that question."

"I understand that, sir."

"Your purpose is to kill Zsytzii. Why you were on the candidate list is a bit more complicated, and I wasn't part of that process." Nick returned to his desk and sat. "The pols put you on the list right there with the royals. You're a romantic figure. The tragedy and all, of course. And the Qian rebuilt you— something everyone knows, has an opinion about. You became the poster-boy for our alliance with the Qian. But that's not why I picked you."

Greg chewed on his lower lip to hide the quiver.

Nick's eyes narrowed. "Only things I know about you are what were in your records. You're a hell of a pilot. Ballsy. Smart. Not fearless, but willing to look past fear. All good things. And because the Qian rebuilt you, there wasn't any way you were ever getting back in the cockpit of a fighter. Not on Earth. I know how nasty it feels to be sidelined. I've seen pilots eaten up by it. I figured that you were too good to waste."

Greg frowned, not quite sure what to make of Nick's words. "I'm not a head-case, Colonel."

Nick laughed aloud, tossing his head back. "Captain Allen, you think about that for a second. You've volunteered to travel lightyears from the only world your species has ever truly known, to fight an enemy you don't understand, for a people so vastly superior that they could pry you from a twisted hunk of metal and rebuild you, and you tell me you're *not* a head case? We all are, Captain. Every single one of us is out here to run from something, or to run toward something, or to learn something about ourselves. You really want to know what you're out here for?"

"I'm not sure, sir, that I ..." Greg quickly read the man's expression and his shoulders slumped. "Rhetorical question, yes, sir?"

"Files were right, you *are* smart."

"Skilled at reading nuance, sir. My upbringing. I'm just rusty at it."

Nick sat forward. "Maybe that's why you're out here. Part of you believes you have nothing left on Earth. I'm sincere when I say this: no man should have to bury his child. Most who do don't have the media on them endlessly asking how it feels or if it gets any better. Escaping that would be more than enough reason to leave Earth."

As the colonel spoke, Greg got the distinct impression he was speaking from personal experience. Greg didn't recall anything in the material he'd read about Nick Clark that said he had kids. *Then again, the basic data files on him said he was very private about his personal life so …*

Nick pointed at Greg. "Another part of you probably wants to make sure you still have it. Aircar accident almost kills you. Ironic, right? You can outfly missiles and one drunk in an aircar nails you. They take eighteen months to put you back together, then get to tell you that your family died but you survived. You can't bring them back, so the only thing you can do is get back to yourself. That means climbing back into a cockpit and killing the enemy."

"You picked me to give me that chance?"

"I picked you to give my command a chance, Captain." Nick leaned forward on his desk. "You and I are Americans, so I'll make this easy for you. Name me one person who died at Bunker Hill. Or in the Twin Trade Towers. Or Pearl Harbor."

Greg shook his head. "I can't."

"You remember the events, but not the people. We're good at slogans. Remember the Alamo. Remember the Maine. Remember Pearl Harbor. Remember 9/11. I don't want us added to that list. I don't want 'Remember the 301st' getting chanted once a year. You're sharp-enough of a pilot—all of you are—that we can stay alive. And be very clear on this: we'd serve men like your father much better as a slogan than returning intact. If we die, they can use us as they want; and I have no intention of letting that happen."

"I understand, sir."

"Good." Nick gave him a curt nod. "And if you feel the need for another of these heart-to-heart chats, Captain …"

"I won't be bothering you again, sir."

"I think we're on the same wavelength." Nick looked down at the datascreen in his desk. "You need to get down to sick bay and get our flight surgeon to okay your ready status. You're dismissed."

Greg threw the man a salute and, after its crisp return, departed to follow orders.

* * *

Nick looked up from his desk again, having caught a flash of blue as his Qian liaison officer, Vych Thziilon, slipped into his office. He smiled involuntarily and much more freely than he had with Greg Allen. "How do you think I did?"

Lights sparked beneath her flesh in a pattern he'd come to associate with her satisfaction. "Admirable, Nicholas. He believed you when you told him why you chose him."

"Is that your impression, or do you *know* he believed me?"

Vych canted her head to the side. "I can confirm with diagnostics later, but this is my conclusion based on learning to read humans. I have not your skill at it. Do you think he believes?"

Nick shrugged. "I'm not sure he believes that's the whole story. What I do know is that he thinks I was fully in favor of his joining the 301st. If you'd not impressed upon me the importance of his selection, he wouldn't be here. I'm trusting your read on him."

The small woman smiled and came to his side, caressing his cheek with a slender hand. "You will find that he will serve you well."

"Another conclusion, or do you *know*?"

"Have I given you cause to doubt me, Nicholas?"

He caught her hand in his, quickly but gently. "The Qian are good with secrets, Vych. I know this. I benefit from it. I trust your judgment. I just wish I knew the reasons why you ask me to trust in your word alone about Allen."

Vych laughed and the sound sent a happy thrill through Nick. The laugh was equal parts innocence, sincerity and indulgence. When first they'd met, nearly a year and a half before, she'd never laughed like that. Nick realized she'd learned to do it for the effect it had on him, and yet that knowledge couldn't insulate him from the effects.

"I would share everything with you, Nicholas, but not everything has been shared with me. I could guess, but were I wrong and we acted as if I were right …"

"No, no." Nick kissed her hand, then released it. "As long as Allen can do his job in the squadron, I don't have reason to get distracted by things I can't control."

Vych wandered deeper into the office and stared at a watercolor picture of an angler in a boat fighting to reel in a fat trout. She traced a finger over the light blue brushstrokes defining water, then along the taut black line leading to the bent rod. When he'd chosen that picture for his office, media pundits suggested it was because he'd seen it at his grandfather's cabin in his youth or that the image suggested that fly fishing, just like flying a fighter, required great skill.

Nick didn't identify with the fisherman. He identified with the trout, and stared at that picture every day to remind himself that the 301st were the trophy, not the hunters.

She turned, her smile genuine. "It appears we may have our first mission before we meet up with the rest of the squadron."

Nick frowned. "I'm at less than two-thirds strength now. Granted that the difference between twelve fighters and seven isn't that much but I'd rather have a full squadron and some time together training before we go into action."

"This will be purely ceremonial. Once the last supply ship from Earth catches up with us, we will head out to the jumppoint. We will travel to a rendezvous with a diplomatic shuttle. You will fly out and escort it in. Great honor will be bestowed on the delegation and the 301st."

He got up and joined her, looking past the picture and out through the viewpoint to the flight deck. It was empty, which Nick thought of as an improvement over the crowded ceremonial conditions. Still, it looked too clean and orderly to be the flight deck on a ship of war.

"Can you ditch the mission?"

"That would be unwise, Nicholas."

"Which means impossible?"

Vych sighed. "You have learned much of our ways, Colonel Clark; but not all of them. It would be possible for that honor to be transferred to another unit, but the only unit which could be deployed would be an elite Qian squadron. They would see the job as being beneath them, and the delegation would see the honor accorded them as a sign of favor which does not exist."

Nick half-smiled. "And yet the squadron would take the job simply to show us up. Somewhere in that vast political stock exchange that is the Qian empire, we'd create an imbalance which would be impossible to address."

"Not *impossible*, merely *improbable*." She opened her hands. "If the 301st is not ready for such duty ..."

"Skills-wise my people could do this asleep. My problem is that you're giving a retriever mission to attack dogs." Nick shook his head. "The way you grind the edge off an elite unit is by giving it garrison duties. Once we do one mission like this, other folks will want us to show them that same honor. This goes from being a once-in-a-lifetime mission to our reason for being. That's not what we volunteered for."

"I comprehend the logic of your protest. I shall endeavor to shift the mission elsewhere."

"No, Vych, don't."

She canted her head to the side. "I am uncertain I understand your reversal."

Nick crossed his arms over his chest. "Someone higher in the chain of command is flexing his muscles. If we defy him, he'll come at us harder. So, this time, if the mission comes down to us, we'll do it."

"Thank you, Nicholas."

"You're more than welcome." His eyes hardened. "But let others know that we're owed a favor. And we *will* collect."

— 4 —

A little shiver ran down Greg Allen's spine as he headed to the *Unity*'s Medical Center. The hint of dread couldn't kill the smile plastered across the bottom of his face. He'd delayed smiling until he'd gotten clear of the colonel's office, and had smothered a joyful *whoop*. For a moment he felt like he was twelve again and had smacked a homer in the Little League season final.

He'd been afraid that his appointment to the 301st had been made solely on political grounds. That would have made perfect sense. His father would have pushed it, and he'd have had the weight of America's political-lobbyist apparatus behind him. Even though Clark's appointment as commander had come while Greg was still being rebuilt by the Qian, he'd been suggested as being the unit's commander over Clark.

Greg wanted to believe the colonel's reason for choosing him. Nick was about as straight forward a man as Greg had ever met. He wanted to believe that there wasn't a duplicitous bone in his body, but a lifetime of being August Allen's son and presumed heir had taught Greg that everyone had secrets. Still, Nick had nothing to gain by lying to him, so Greg took his words at face value.

Ever since awakening from the coma, rebuilt with his new right forearm, hand and other bits, Greg had had to relearn *everything*. He'd studied his own life like an actor preparing for a role. He'd seen countless images of himself—motion holographs, stills, even a few old photographs Jennifer's uncle had taken with a film camera. He'd seen news reports and relived important life events like a spectator. Most eerie had been hearing himself narrate the motion-holograph of his daughter's birth.

There'd been a wall between him and those experiences. He could watch them and hear them and understand them. At points he could even *feel* them—but *those* moments always came through Jennifer or Bianca and *their* reactions. When he'd watch his own reactions to things he just couldn't connect emotionally.

The psychiatrists suggested this was because by maintaining that distance he was protecting himself against the pain of loss. They'd suggested attacking the problem obliquely, by doing the things he'd always enjoyed doing in the past. He could get a foothold on his emotions that way, and then close in on who he had been.

Unfortunately he'd only had two passions in his life: his family and flying. With his family denied to him, his only choice was to get back into the cockpit. He'd always been very good—no doubt he was an adrenaline junkie—but he had to be the *best*. Only an appointment to the 301st and success in its ranks would make him the best. *And allow me to be me again, right?*

The lingering bit of dread that raised gooseflesh on his arms and spine, came from Nick's comment about slogans. More than once he'd heard his father laugh about the simplicity of voters. "All a politician has to do to win, son, is to reduce complex problems to a simple slogan, and the masses stop thinking and just drop in line." He'd first heard that when he was...*I forget, exactly, but before puberty.* The timing didn't matter—it was a refrain to his father's favorite song and had propelled him into the White House.

Colonel Clark had been right. The 301st would serve better as a rallying cry than as a significant military unit. Whatever the unit did, politicians would spin to their own advantage. *But spin events to sacrifice us because our memory is a better tool? Would they?* Greg wanted to draw the line there. He harbored no illusions about the morals of politicians, he just lacked belief that they had enough influence outside of the solar system to be able to sacrifice the 301st. *I hope, anyway, that* is *the case.*

Greg made his way easily through the *Unity*, despite being new to the ship. He navigated both by reading signs and then following his gut feelings when indications were less than clear. He suspected that circuitry built into his right arm might have actually been reading the signs in different ways, and his hunches about the correct way to proceed were being fed to him. He had no way of proving that—he'd never been one to get lost—but the sense that the Qian were watching and could communicate with his appendage had firmly taken hold.

The medical facility's door hissed open before he'd gotten within two meters of it. A slender, dark haired woman, with her hair gathered back into a pony-tail, stepped through. Media reports about her had all described her as "drop-dead gorgeous" and Greg couldn't disagree.

She looked up, her grey eyes widening for a moment.

Greg stopped and saluted.

Major Damienne Taine returned the salute. "*Pardonez-moi,* Captain Allen."

Greg glanced down, surprised at his shying from her gaze. "No problem, Major. Colonel Clark wanted me to get a final check from the flight surgeon."

"*Bien.*" She smiled, her eyes narrowing. "You will perhaps forgive me, Captain. Nine years ago, you were in Paris, for a conference?"

He thought for a moment, frowning. "A NATO thing?" Greg opened his hands. "You have to forgive me, since the accident ... Were you there, Major? You'd have been too young, wouldn't you?"

"I was a cadet at *École de l'Air* at Salon-de-Provence, but they brought us in help host." Her eyes half-lidded. "It was our introduction into the international side of the military I think."

"Did we meet?" Greg closed his eyes and focused, but couldn't picture her. "If it weren't for the accident, I'm sure I'd remember. Please don't feel insulted."

She looked at him for a second longer than she should have, then smiled. "No, Captain Allen, I do feel insulted. And, yes, we did meet. In passing. You would have no reason to remember."

"I wish I did." Greg glanced down at his hands. "I've read about you, of course. Even discounting half of it—and I don't—you're a terror in the sky. Your country picked well when they tapped you to be our second in command."

"It was promote me, or send me away, and sending me away was easier." Her smile shrank just a bit. "I suspect you and I were on a similar track."

Greg nodded. "Nice thing about being out of *their* hair is they don't have to work to get rid of us."

"Insightful, Captain." Damienne patted him on the arm as she resumed her journey. "I look forward to working with you, Captain Allen."

"And you, ma'am." Greg fought against himself not to watch her walk away. The slate-grey jumpsuit flattered her figure and he didn't want to get caught staring at her tail. He wasn't sure if normal male impulses were a sign that the Qian had put him back together again really well, or that the imperative to find a mate was so ingrained in humans that even a devastating accident couldn't get rid of it.

That brief spark of lust kindled an ache deep inside. He missed Jennifer fiercely and wished he could recover a memory of their intimacy. Not some sweaty lustfest ringing with lewd comments and overloud moans like a pornogram; but something softer, more immediate. He didn't want to see them making love because he couldn't have born watching that from afar. He just wanted to feel her nestled back against him after they had made love. *After we made Bianca.* He wanted to smell Jennifer and her hair, to taste sweat from a kiss, to feel her gather his arms tighter around her.

As obviously appealing as Major Taine was, it really didn't matter. In learning who he was, he'd fallen in love with Jennifer all over again. The one sense he had was that he'd never given her enough. Now, he never could. That unredeemed debt weighed heavily upon his heart, and served as an adequate blanket for smothering ardor.

Greg stepped into the medical facility and here the ship's wood and brass decor surrendered to a bright, clinical white and chrome combination that included the room's occupant. The android stood taller than Greg and while of a humanoid design, he did not look human. His body appeared to be made of porcelain save where segmented, black-rubber gaskets shielded joints on the arms, legs, neck and midsection. Long rectangular panels running from shoulder to the end of the sternum in the torso, hid a second pair of arms which the construct would use for fine work.

The head design appeared to make the greatest concession to human esthetics, most closely resembling the helmet worn by a *retarius* fighting in the gladiatorial arenas of Ancient Rome. The crest, which would have been of a fish design on the helmet, had become a tube ending in a bright light. The faceplate became a solid, curved triangle of darkened plastic behind which burned two blue pinpoints of light.

The blue points expanded slightly as the door slid closed behind Greg. "Greetings, Captain Allen. If you would take your place here on the table." The robot's voice had a slight buzz—not unpleasant, but enough to guarantee its mechanical origin could not be denied. The construct had been designed X1N, but the humans had translated that into the word Shin, as per the Chinese pronunciation.

"Is there a problem, Doctor Shin?"

The construct paused. "This unit is not a doctor, Captain. It is a mobile patient care facilitator and interface with the *Unity*'s xenobiological and xenophysiological databases. It is no more an doctor than a stethoscope is."

Greg shook his head. The Qian had clearly designed Shin to appeal to the human propensity for treating everything as if it was alive. To have the machine carefully deny that it was alive worked against that purpose. Even so, he imagined it made sense to the Qian in some odd way, so he hopped up on the table.

The compartments on Shin's torso opened and the more delicate arms emerged. Greg found them decidedly spiderish, with multiple joints to the fingers and arms. "Please roll up your right sleeve."

Greg unbuttoned his grey fatigue shirt's cuff and rolled it back past the elbow. The place where the Qian-supplied appendage began and his flesh and blood ended couldn't be picked out by the naked eye. Greg thought for just half a second, and what appeared to be soft, pliable pink flesh became an angular, icy blue sculpture of what a hand ought to be. The demarkation between flesh and the prosthetic became a ragged line and if he looked very closely, he could see ivory ghosts of where his bones thrust into the Qian device.

A blue light bar played down over Shin's faceplate and back up again. One silvery spidery hand grasped the device and the other wrapped itself around the narrow band of flesh at his elbow. The construct tugged at the wrist, but the graft held firm.

"Satisfactory." Shin's small arms retracted and vanished. "You have adapted well to the nanite interface. Do you have pains ever?"

"Do you mean actual pain, or impressions of a phantom limb?"

"Input on either subject would be satisfactory."

Greg looked at the blue lump. "The arm communicates pressure, heat and cold perfectly well. Pain, too, but it blunts it. It never gets past the point of being an annoyance. Sharp pain, as if the limb has been cut off, no, never. Phantom sensations I get from time to time, when I'm very tired. I can lose control of the arm—it freezes or gets melty depending."

The eyelights blinked on and off asymmetrically, which Greg found a bit disconcerting. "Do you often exercise the advanced interface capabilities?"

The pilot shook his head. "I can handle being plugged into this piece of machinery because it's replacing a part of me. Using it to plug into an appliance or fighter, no, those aren't parts of me."

"You never felt that your fighter was part of you?"

"Got some xenopsychological programs running there, Shin?"

"Deflection and evasion."

Greg chewed his lower lip. For as long as he could remember, he *had* felt planes and fighters, even aircars and land transport or boats had been part of him. He couldn't explain it— none of the pilots who felt the same way *could*—except to say that he felt more *complete* at speed, piloting something. He figured his brain was wired for it, and even though the arm would let him plug in—bypassing eyes and his other senses—that just didn't feel right.

"Yes, I have. I do, when I am piloting in the usual manner."

"Do you ever get a sense of the device performing functions for which you have not been trained or briefed?"

"Meaning?"

The construct stepped back and its eyes blinked again. "Neural systems adapt to new demands and stimulus. Neuroplasticity remaps portions of your brain to process new information. Do you perceive anomalous or unexpected input or abilities with the nanite construction?"

Greg shrugged. "Sometimes, here on the *Unity*, it feels as if there's a GPS built into the arm. I don't get lost very much. Not at all really. Is that what you're asking?"

"That reply is within statistically acceptable norms." Shin's head came up. "You would do well, Captain, to recall that this unit is not autonomous. Addressing it as 'you' introduces a level of imprecision into the conversation which consumes processing time."

"Right. Got it." Greg smiled. *And I'll ignore it.* "Was checking on my arm the only purpose for my being called down here?"

Shin's body spun around at the waist and one of the long upper arms reach into a cabinet. The stubby-fingered hand plucked a boxy little device from a slot in what looked like a charging bay. The torso whirled back and the construct extended the device to Greg.

No bigger than a pack of cards, the grey resin device had a galaxy of blue, green and red lights flowing through it. They almost looked like dust motes floating in a sunbeam. The device had a visual depth to it that belied its size. Greg found it mesmerizing.

Jennifer would have loved it.

Shin's buzzing voice broke through his private thoughts. "You have been approved for the issuance of your Nomad. It will function as your Shrike's brain for all navigational purposes. You cannot fly your ship without it. Star maps and mission parameters will be uploaded as needed. You are, Captain Allen, approved for flight service."

Smiling, Greg reached up to take the device. As his right hand approached it, however, the prosthesis shifted. Fingers melted back into the palm. His hand flattened, a depression into which the Nomad would fit perfectly opening up at the end of his wrist.

Greg concentrated, pushing his joy aside. His hand returned to its normal shape and color. "I don't know what happened."

"Anomalous, but not so great a statistical deviation to cause concern." Shin's wrist rotated and placed the Nomad in Greg's hand. "Welcome, Captain Allen, to the 301st's active duty roster."

— **5** —

Greg Allen smiled as he stepped onto the *Unity's* flight deck. Seven of the squadron's dozen Shrike fighters had been assembled on either side of the broad deck. The Qian had built them according to their perception of human esthetics, making the starfighters a curious amalgam of history, fantasy and lethality.

The fighters shared the *Unity's* master design elements, employing what appeared to be wood and brass in the art-deco construction. While the fighters could enter atmosphere, and flew well therein, Qian technology had rendered the need for aerodynamics secondary. In atmosphere, the defensive shields would deploy like an invisible skin, sharpening angles and making the fighters far more maneuverable than imagined just glancing at them.

Just under nineteen meters in length, and featuring a wingspan of thirteen and a half meters, the Shrike had curved wings with a scalloped rear edge. The domed cockpit sported a fin on top. The fighter's split tail had rudders which repeated the scalloped followed edge. They were hardly necessary to the function of the fighter, but that they looked like they belonged to human eyes, and that was why they existed.

He approached his Shrike and could not help but have his smile broaden. While the fuselage, wings and tail appeared to have been built of cedar planks and unpainted, the nose had been decorated with the sharp teeth and eyes akin to the nose-art designs used on the fighters flown by the Flying Tigers in World War II. Even though air combat had changed significantly since the middle of the 20th century, that antique iconography still resonated with humans. *Hence the design and unit name.*

He walked beneath his fighter's belly, letting his flesh and blood hand trail along the smooth surface. It almost felt like wood, but he knew it couldn't be. *My other hand feels like flesh and blood, too, but it isn't.* That was the reason he didn't reach up with his right hand to touch the ship. He didn't want to see it react to his fighter the way it had to the Nomad unit.

As he came around he looked up toward the cockpit and his throat instantly thickened. His name had been painted there in a delicate flowing hand. *Jennifer's hand.* His wife had insisted on doing that with each of his fighters, to keep him safe. They had even joked that she should do the same on the aircar.

If only you had, *darling.*

He turned away, swiping at a tear, and caught the attention of the woman inspecting her Shrike beside his. Petite and of Asian origin, Lieutenant Sun Lan quickly averted her gaze.

Greg walked over. "Magnificent, aren't they?"

"Yes, Captain Allen." She glanced up at him, her smile modest. "Forgive me if I intruded."

"You didn't." Greg pointed back to his Shrike. "The Qian probably didn't know, but they modeled the painting of my name on painting my late wife had done."

She arched an eyebrow. "Do you truly think they did not know?"

Greg hesitated, following the logical course of her question. The Qian *did* seem to know everything—and revealed very little in return. So, either they did not think he would have much of an emotional connection back to that image, or they did not care, or they wanted to study his reaction. *Or they simply thought I could use a good-luck charm.*

"That's a good question." Greg nodded toward the nose of her Shrike. "Do you think they understood what that paint scheme might mean to someone from the People's Republic of China?"

"Perhaps." She nodded thoughtfully. "The Flying Tigers supported China against Imperial Japanese aggression, so they are favored in our memories. The west's continued aggression, however, has tainted that memory. The Qian, you will note, used red paint here which is the same hue as our flag. Perhaps of more concern to us is that while we comprise the largest percentage of the human population, we have only one pilot in the squadron, whereas America has two, the west has six."

"You're considering Captain Rustov a westerner?"

"You would not?"

Greg smiled. "What I'd point out that every permanent member of the United Nations security council has one pilot in the squadron."

"But America has two."

"I think we get the spare for being the first to Mars." Greg held his hands up. "But we've gotten a bit far afield from my being touched by that signature. While I've enjoyed flying a Shrike simulator, I'm looking forward to dropping into the cockpit."

"As am I." Sun frowned. "I would estimate they will require a hundred hours in an actual ship before they allow us to fly combat missions."

Greg glanced toward Colonel Clark's office. "The colonel should brief us soon. We jumped three times in rapid succession last evening. They probably brought us to some backwater where we can run missions."

"I hope you are correct, Captain." Sun Lee reached up and patted her Shrike's fuselage. "Now, if you will forgive me ..."

"Right, me, too." Greg wheeled around and mounted a set of roll-away steps to the cockpit. Maroon velvet upholstered the command chair, all buckles, fittings and trim had been done in brass. Even the command stick on the right and throttles on the left had that antique build. The only things which were not antiques were the LED displays build into the command console. On the whole the cockpit would have been familiar to a pilot flying on the Western front in 1914, though nature of the information and the holographic targeting head's-up-display likely would have seemed a bit odd.

Greg dropped into the command chair, but didn't buckle in. He reached out for the command stick, willing his right hand to remain normal. The stick had toggle on top. A flick of his thumb would cycle through the Meson cannon, the Baryon Missile Launchers or the four laser cannons. Another thumb switch would allow him to pair, quad or delink the lasers. The trigger under his index finger would fire the weapons, and the stick itself would let him fly the craft. The rudder pedals under each foot aided in that latter task.

Twin pulse jets, one mounted beneath each rudder at the aft, provided atmospheric and sublight thrust. Between them sat the gravitational jump drive which allowed the fighters to travel through hyperspace, though at reduced speeds and for shorter distances than a ship like the *Unity*. The Nomad unit would handle hyperspace navigation, though maneuvering a Shrike onto an outbound vector was up to the pilot.

He'd only flown a Shrike simulator previously, but Qian technology involved the ability to manipulate gravity. The same technology which maneuvered the fighter in space allowed the simulator to put pilots through a very real and exhausting flight experience. Even so, Greg wanted time in the cockpit because no matter how good the simulation, it just wasn't a substitute for logging hours in actual flight.

The hangar bay's public address system crackled. "All pilots report to the briefing room in one-five minutes, flight ready."

Greg, a wide grin on his face, vaulted from the cockpit and landed on the deck. As Sun came around the nose of her Shrike, she grinned, too; though not nearly as openly as he did. They raced down to their living quarters, he going left and she right. He squeezed himself into a small cabin which, at present, he shared with no one.

He shucked his uniform and replaced it with a flight-suit which was primarily blue, but trimmed at cuffs and throat with white. Red epaulets and stripes running down the legs, as well as gloves and flight helmets completed the uniform, though the latter two components would be waiting in the Shrike. The Qian had designed the uniform, choosing blue for Earth's color, white trim for the clouds and red for Mars, upon which the scientific community had come to agree life had first evolved in the solar system. The Americans, Russians and French were happy to suggest a different origin for the color scheme, and the yellow star at the back of each helmet had been a concession to the Chinese. Everyone else clung to the Qian origin story and thought the other nations were just silly.

Slipping the Nomad into the thigh pocket designed for it. He headed to the briefing room. As he entered the narrow room, he inserted the Nomad into a rack similar to the one in the Medical Bay, and took his place around the lozenge-shaped briefing table. The holographic projection unit centered on it remained dark. By happenstance, Greg found himself seated at Colonel Clark's left hand, opposite Major Taine.

The colonel waited for the others to take their places, then began the briefing. "The 301st has been given its first mission. Yes, we've not be trained in the Shrikes. Yes, we are under-strength. Yes, *any* mission under such circumstances would rightfully be considered a suicide mission." He glanced down, half-closing his eyes. "Except this one."

Nick dismissively waved a hand toward the holoprojector. A cone of light shot upward revealing a vector graphic of a planet and the spiral path of a shuttle rising up into orbit. The ovoid ship gradually distanced itself from the planet, and as the image grew smaller, the *Unity* appeared hovering above the planet's pole.

"We'll be coming into the Haxad system as close as we can get to the fourth planet. A Haxadassi ambassador is going to be coming aboard for transport and we are going to do her the honor of escorting her ship to the point where it links to the *Unity*'s hull. The flight plan is being loaded into your Nomads right now. The mission should take less than an hour and it will be as big an honor for you as it will for the ambassador."

Sun raised a hand.

"Yes, Lieutenant."

"Will the flight be the full extent of our interaction with the Haxadassi?"

"You mean will there be a formal review and holo op like there was when we were leaving Earth?" The colonel shrugged. "I have no information about that at this time, but you'd best hope there isn't. The Haxadissi are centaurs—if you got rid of the horse-half and stitched on a boa constrictor's body. Upholster the rest with scales. They're mean and nasty, disdainful of anything that isn't scaled, and vocal about it. They were not in favor of the 301st's formation, so this honor guard is punishing us or them or both. If I learn more, I'll let you know. Now, go get your Shrike's ready to fly. We know this is our first mission, but I don't want anyone watching to have reason to believe that's true. Dismissed."

The pilots rose, but the colonel rested a hand on Greg's shoulder. "Just a minute, Captain. Major Taine, if I could have a word."

The door hissed closed behind Sun Lan. "We're the ranking officers, which means I get to lead this parade. The two of you are paired at the rear." Clark pointed toward the holograph. "If something happens, the two of you are to shepherd the ambassador's ship to the *Unity*, or back to Haxad Four— whichever provides safety fastest. I don't care what you hear over the comms or what you see on your displays."

Damienne frowned. "Is there a threat, do you know?"

Clark folded his arms over his chest. "Gravitational fields limit the number of places where ships can emerge from hyperspace; and different ships can travel different distances in different amounts of time. The wonders of all that are important to astrophysicists. For a military man it means that there are no front lines in space. While it isn't likely the Zsytzii are going to pop in, it can't be ruled out."

The major nodded, the lights gleaming from her dark hair. "And the calculations for escape vectors have been loaded to our Nomads?"

"No."

Greg's stomach tightened. "Why not?"

"You two are my hole cards; and anyone holding hole cards really doesn't want the other players knowing about them. It's not that I don't trust the Qian; it's that I don't mind them underestimating us. I'm content to let them think we have blind spots. That means I know what direction they'll use coming at us." Clark shrugged. "Might never amount to anything, but I'm not one for leaving anything to chance."

Greg nodded. "So we'll instruct our Nomads to calculate the escape vectors once we launch and use them if we need them?"

Clark smiled. "Like you're reading my mind."

Something in that smile made Greg pause. The colonel had just ordered them to do something on the side which he wanted hidden from the Qian. But he knew the Qian would be able to monitor communications, could check the Nomads during or after the mission, and likely were even listening in on the briefing. *Which means he wants the Qian to know how clever humans are, and yet underestimate us because we're not smart enough to know that we can't hide anything from them.*

Wheels ground within wheels, and Greg's head began to hurt. *It's like living at home with my father again.* Greg shook his head to clear it. "Anything else, sir?"

"Just fly the way you know you can, and hope we don't run into anything we can't handle."

— **6** —

Nick climbed into his Shrike and settled himself in the command seat. He slid the Nomad unit into the dock, then buckled himself into the safety harness while little lights played through the Nomad. By the time he was done, it glowed a soft green.

"Nomad set the Inertial Compensator Unit to .05."

"Engineering and performance studies indicate a setting of .037 to be optimal for a Terran male of your height, weight and age."

"When was the last time engineers flew a combat mission?"

"ICU set at .05."

"Thank you." Nick glanced at his flight console. The three main monitors were two square ones right and left, and a circular one dead center. For him the left displayed ship status, which monitored shield positioning and shape, structural integrity and the position of the landing skids. The right tracked weapons'-status and shield integrity. Pilots, at their whim, could swap data on the two screens. The centermost circular one provided a proximity scan of targets and other items of interest near the Shrike. Touching one of them would pull up a detailed scan of that item and place it on one of the auxiliary monitors.

On the right side of the console Nick had all of his flight gauges, included fuel, gravitation opposition, jump capability, speed, thruster status and balance. Until one of those screens began to flash red—a shade of red the Nomad had determined would draw his attention most quickly—he tended to ignore them. Combat was not a place to be flying by numbers; it was something you did with your gut.

Nick's gut felt like he'd swallowed a Haxadis whole and raw, and had gone back for seconds. He'd never felt nervous heading out on combat missions. Little milk-run missions, on the other hand, had always been trouble. Nick figured part of his apprehension might stem from the mission's purely political underpinnings. He didn't like the idea some of his people might die just so one bureaucrat could shift a decimal point on a spreadsheet.

"Thus ever with idiots." Nick forced himself to smile.

The three auxiliary monitors on the left side of his console lit up. One showed an image of the *Unity*. That screen would shift to anything he wanted to focus his sensors upon, but by default showed the *Unity* so a pilot could find his way home.

Below it, on the comms screen, each pilot's name showed up as their ships came online. He tapped Major Taine and Captain Allen, highlighting them. The screen asked if he wished to group them, and a second group button appeared at the top of the screen, with the label "TacTwo." Everyone in the squadron, the controllers aboard the *Unity*, and, eventually, the Haxadassi shuttle, would be added into TacOne.

I hope the Snakes aren't going to use translation. If he issued an order, he wanted it obeyed, and fast. Delays caused by computer translation would get someone killed. *And if they* disobey *and order, I'll do the killing.*

He touched the last auxiliary screen. It could be made to display any data the pilot needed, but for the moment Nick swiped a finger across it and brought up an ancient, black and white picture of a pilot standing beside a WWI Neuport biplane. Back when Nick had first flown in combat, he'd taped the battered original to his console, for luck.

He smiled. "As you were reported to say, 'Always better to be lucky than good.'"

With his left hand, Nick spun a wheel and fed power to the Repeller/Attractor Coils. The Shrike lifted smoothly off the deck, its skids coming up a centimeter off the surface. He retracted them, then maneuvered the fighter around to face the aft launch bay. Nick nudged the throttle forward. The engines sent a thrum through the fighter, then the Shrike shot through the magnetic retention bubble and into space.

His heart pounded happily as he brought the Shrike around and up into an orbit above the *Unity*. Below Haxad Four slowly spun, displaying its white polar cap. He caught little flashes of green beneath thin white clouds at the outer edges of what he could see. He'd never been down there, but had been told that rainforest and desert abounded, with 35% of the surface covered by water. Haxad Four was an unforgiving world, and the Haxadissi were truly its children.

Despite not liking the mission, Nick could not help but smile. A year and a half's worth of hard work had put the 301st together. While almost half the squadron waited for them at their initial base, and their first mission had been handed to them with insufficient training time, he didn't doubt his people would do well. They might not have learned how to fly together yet, but they knew how to *fly* and that was what was the most important detail at the moment.

The other six fighters exited smoothly and formed up with him. As they came on station they reported in. Everyone was green across all instruments. "On me, Tigers. As per the mission brief."

Moving the stick right, Nick took the Shrike through a barrel-roll, wing over wing, then pedaled in some rudder and headed straight for the rendezvous point. A red triangle appeared on his central sensor panel. He touched it and the image of the Haxadissi shuttle appeared on his target monitor. The ship's comms link also appeared on his list, adding itself to TacOne.

On the approach, Nick shifted his shields so they covered his aft at double strength. Leading the shuttle back to the *Unity* he'd reverse the process, expand the field and angle the shields to provide the shuttle with some added protection. Angling and shifting shields always stressed the projectors, but being able to reinforce shields or cover a wounded ship was a valuable skill in combat.

A voice hissed over TacOne. "The shuttle *Shan-chey* identifies itself."

"*Shan-chey*, this is Tiger Lead. Keep on this approach vector for escort to the *Unity*."

"*Shan-chey* acknowledges."

A light flashed below as the ovoid shuttle lifted free of the launch vehicle and began to accelerate. Two Shrikes—Taine and Allen—shot past to reach their position first, then the next two and the final pair. Nick eased back on the throttle to maintain his position.

Nick spared himself a moment to look out at the vastness of space. Poets and pundits had all offered their takes on it. Some saw the darkness as an ocean; others saw the stars as glittering jewels. He figured that each described it based on their fears, like being insignificant, or their vices, like greed. It gave him a window into them and their judgment.

What Nick enjoyed was the quiet. The Shrike's engines sent a thrum through the craft, but he felt that more than heard it. Alarms would fill the cockpit with sound in combat, but in their absence, and if he kept his breathing quiet, it seemed as if all reality was sleeping peacefully. It was the quiet on a foggy lake, just before dawn, before the world woke up and demanded attention.

He drank it in, finding it an equal pleasure to the thirty year old Scotch. It was another of his vices, and one he indulged in very sparingly—more because of a lack of opportunity than any lack of desire.

As the shuttle reached the halfway point on its climb out of the planet's gravity well, another icon appeared on Nick's center monitor, offset slightly from the *Unity*. He tapped it fast, and his stomach knotted as the image appeared on his targeting display.

The ship appeared to be a wingless dragonfly which had some hideous Qian designation, but he'd nicknamed *Hive*. Little more than a heavily modified cargo ship—which could haul as many segments as the engines could move—the *Hive* could pump out little fighters, waves of them, in the blink of an eye. Once they'd deployed their payload, they'd duck back into hyperspace and wait patiently for the battling to resolve itself.

Which, in this case, is going to be fairly quick.

The *Hive* dumped two flights of a dozen snub fighters he'd called *Dulls*. All of sixteen meters long, they looked as if their ovoid cockpits had been mounted on the aft end of a lawn-dart. They had half-decent shields, two engines, two lasers in the nose, and could carry a total of four Hadron Rockets—the junior version of the Baryon Missiles the Shrike's carried. They had no hyperdrive, so that space had been given over to Multi-spectrum Sensor Counter-measures, and the MSSCM suites made the Dulls a tough target.

"Three, Nine, go to TacTwo. Everyone else, move to intercept the Dulls." Nick dragged the *Shan-chey* onto TacTwo, then punched it up. "*Shan-chey*, return to base. You two get them there. Luck. Out."

Nick hauled back on his stick, punched the throttle full forward, then came over in roll to point himself at the incoming Dulls. His combat HUD came up, surrounding him with a holographic display which added depth and data tags to everything within sensor range. If he reached out and touched any of the floating icons, he'd get a full infodump on them—but that really wasn't going to help him. *I just wish I could reach out and swat them.*

Then the Dulls' first wave lit off their rockets. Because his warning lock didn't light up or alarms start howling, Nick knew they weren't targeting him. All those projectiles were speeding straight for the *Shan-chey*, and barring a miracle, there wasn't any way to stop many, let alone *all*, of them.

* * *

Greg's combat HUD popped as he accelerated to get forward of the *Shan-chey*. "Three, you guide them down, I'll buy time."

Major Taine's voice filled his earphones. "Roger, Nine. *Shan-chey*, break off and return to base."

"Negative, Tiger Three. We are inbound the *Unity*."

"*Shan-chey*, you will never get there. Break off now."

More targets blossomed in Greg's HUD. "Three, I have four-eight rockets inbound on *Shan-chey*. Time to target is sixty seconds."

"*Shan-chey*, abort approach."

"Negative, Tiger Three."

Greg rolled his Shrike and brought it over the top of the lumbering shuttle. "Three, I have a plan. It'll buy the shuttle some time. Be ready to repeat what I do. *Shan-chey*, all shields forward and full, full speed to the *Unity*, on my mark. Do it one second sooner and we all die."

"Nine, what are you doing?"

"If I tell you, you'll stop me." Greg forced himself to laugh. "You get anything I miss."

Greg knew he should be terrified or angry or *something*, but he couldn't find a name for what he was feeling. He glanced through the holographic display at his auxiliary monitor. Jennifer and Bianca smiled at him. Though what he was doing likely would get him killed, he wasn't doing it because he wanted to die.

It's my duty. So you can be proud of me.

He brought his Shrike down to two-hundred meters off the *Shan-chey's* bow. He tasked the Nomad with keeping him at that relative distance, then pumped all his shield energy forward. He warped the shields, forming a dish facing the incoming rockets. He switched his fire control over to the Baryon Missiles, then targeted an incoming Hadron Rocket. With one eye on the targeting monitor and another on the Shrike's status monitor, he drew in a deep breath and slowly, serenely, exhaled.

Three hundred … two hundred … one hundred.

As far as the rockets processing units could determine, Greg's Shrike was a mote against the *Shan-chey's* bloated outline. As the first group of rockets entered the dish, Greg's finger tightened on the trigger. Two Baryon Missiles jetted out, detonating amid that first swarm. The dish forced energy from the blast away from the Shrike, consuming more of the Hadron rockets. Greg launched another pair of Baryon Missiles, then keyed his radio. *"Shan-chey,* now!"

The shuttle lit off its engines and jetted forward. The Nomad throttled the Shrike up, pushing it before the *Shan-chey* like a plow. The Hadron Rockets altered course, many of them falling into the second fireball. Others shot past, unable to course-correct enough to pull out of Haxad Four's gravity well. They exploded harmlessly.

The rest, however, did not. Sparks shot from Greg's command console as his shield indicator went from green to yellow, then red and finally black—that last being the dead monitor's color. The *Shan-chey* kept pushing him forward. He fired the third set of missiles. The combat HUD failed as they exploded in a supernova dead ahead of him.

Then a handful of Hadron Rockets streaked in past the fireball and exploded.

Greg's world went black.

— 7 —

Nick Clark keyed TacOne. "Two and Six; Seven and Eleven, go after the Dulls that have not launched their rockets. Leave the first wave." The little bars on the comms monitor flashed with acknowledgements. He had no expectations that the *Shan-chey* would survive the first wave of rockets, or that any of his pilots would survive the fight. *To change that I have to kill more of them faster.*

He half-laughed. Figuring he was as good as dead freed him of anxiety and fear. He'd have a few regrets, like not seeing Vych again, or Earth, but no guilt. His only failure would be in failing to harvest as many Dulls as humanly possible. *And a couple more.*

Just like the Nomad telling him what engineers and scientists deemed optimal, human pundits had long maintained that space combat would be largely automated and conducted at mind-boggling ranges. Missiles and rockets would have little value since heavy lasers could target and destroy them. That outcome required two things, however: the target having anti-missile defenses *and* the enemy lacking a sufficient quantity of missiles to overwhelm the defenses.

In this case, the *Shan-chey's* anti-missile defenses didn't exist and the Dulls had more than enough rockets. Reality knocked all sorts of combat theories into a cocked hat. This brought a smile to Nick's face because it meant even space combat had a place in it for pilots. Moreover, he was willing to bet that while the Dulls grossly outnumbered his people, his pilots were the best in the system.

And I'm even better.

Nick hauled back on the stick and looped straight toward the *Shan-chey.* The first wave of rockets converged in a series of explosions. Some of the blasts illuminated the shuttle's shields. They collapsed and a couple of rockets exploded near the hull. He couldn't tell if there'd been a breach or not, but there wasn't anything he could do about it if there was.

He rolled up on his port wing, pulled away at ninety-degrees to the shuttle's flight path, then ruddered around so his nose pointed away from the Haxadis ship and the world below. His course took him up past the flight path of the Dulls heading in at the *Shan-chey.* He shifted his shields to cover his top and aft in case any chanced a shot at him, then came over, rolled out and swooped down.

The Dulls had grouped themselves into three flights of four. Nick went after the most forward quartet. He angled in from above and behind, waiting until he was at point-blank range. He left his targeting sensors off until the last second so there would be no warning. With the flick of a thumb he quadded his lasers, then pumped four searing bolts of coherent light into the Dull's bulbous cockpit.

The ship exploded and Nick dove straight through the blast. He hauled back and left on the stick, rolling onto his left wing again, then kicked the right rudder and climbed. The formation he'd hit broke up, with one pilot diving after him, but the formation that had been on the port wing remained intent on the target. Nick came up fast, shifted his armament to the Meson Cannon, and hit the trigger.

Unlike the lasers, which pulsed out short bolts, the Meson Cannon projected a sizzling golden beam that, for a heartbeat, linked the two fighters. It slashed through the port hull and killed that engine. The starboard engine maintained thrust, starting the Dull in a flat spin to the left. Then the tail snapped off and the two halves began a long, slow fall down toward Haxad Four's snowy cap.

Targeting-lock alarms screamed in Nick's cockpit. He hit rudder. The Repeller coils kicked in, skewing the ship's tail around. He rolled, then leveled out for a heartbeat—just long enough for a Dull to drop onto his six. He shunted all power to the aft shields, chopped his throttle back to nothing, then nosed his Shrike down. Red laser bolts flashed against his shields, then the Dull overshot him. Nick pulled back on the stick and stabbed it with a golden spear, then thrust his throttle full forward and rolled to the right.

The Dull exploded and more angry red bolts burned through the space he'd just vacated. Nick laughed aloud. "Ambush isn't turning out the way you thought it would, is it?" He throttled back again, rolling up onto a wing and turning a tight circle, then pointed his nose up and rolled out right. He shifted to quadded lasers. Two bolts hit, one in the engine, one through the cockpit. A fire flashed, blackening the canopy.

One flight down. Not that it really mattered because the other eight Dulls had gotten close enough to begin making attack runs on the *Shan-chey.* Another Shrike rose to engage them. Even as Nick brought his ship around to attack the Dulls, he realized that he'd lost either Greg Allen or Damienne Taine. Someone on the *Unity* would have noted who the first human martyr was in the 301st—a dubious honor which guaranteed immortality would enshrine failure.

A flurry of laser bolts rose from the *Shan-chey's* scattered gunnery pods on. The Dull formations split to give the Haxadissi gunners a harder time. Nick's targeting-lock alarms wailed as he got within range. *They're shooting at everything!* Why they were even there instead of heading back to their homeworld he had no clue, but they were making damned hard to consider them allies.

A voice broke through on TacOne. Nick recognized it as Sun Lee's voice. "Lead, six Dulls inbound. We can't reach them before they launch."

"I've got them, Seven. Hurry in as fast as you can. There will be plenty to kill."

"Roger, Lead."

The first Dull flight had launched from long range as a bit of a gamble. The tactic should have actually worked to kill the shuttle. Why it hadn't, Nick couldn't tell. If the half-dozen incoming Dulls launched from closer range, better gunners than the Haxadissi had aboard would be powerless to prevent the shuttle's destruction.

Nick punched up TacTwo. "The shuttle is still your primary responsibility. I'll take the next wave."

"Roger, Lead."

Taine. Nick shivered. He'd not have guessed Greg Allen would be the 301st's first casualty. *Never thought I'd outlive him. I guess, now, I'll find out for exactly how long.*

* * *

Greg returned to consciousness—or what he assumed to be consciousness—adrift in space. It had to be a delusion; clearly the product of head trauma, because he floated there in his flight suit, with no helmet, no ship, no breathing apparatus. Moreover, he was himself, at least, not physically. He had grown to incredible proportions, such that the Dulls and Shrikes diving and weaving in front of him were small enough that he could have held one in the palm of his hand. The *Shan-chey* could have been an overstuffed duffel-bag.

Greg blinked and as his eyes opened again symbols and lines, circles and numbers underscored and connected all of the ships. It was as if he was adrift in some bizarre simulator, where the Shrike's Combat HUD surrounded him. He knew that couldn't be true since he was in a Shrike. Then reality began to seep into his mind, so he accepted the externalization. His other choice, that instead of being trapped in a cockpit he was really trapped inside his mind, just wasn't a concept he wanted to deal with.

So, here I am. What can I do?

Three icons burned to life in front of him. The gold lightning bolt represented a Meson Cannon. The blue missile clearly was a Baryon Missile—and it had the number two as a subscript by it. That left the sunburst in a circle to represent lasers. The letters S, D and Q hung beneath it, with the D circled and flashing.

Greg stabbed his left finger on the lightning bolt, then dragged it onto the blue egg representing a Dull. A dotted line connected the two symbols. The dots stretched and linked into a single solid line which flashed, then it, and the Dull, vanished.

Greg had no idea what had just happened, if anything had, in fact, happened. He wanted to believe something *had* happened, something *good*; but it all had to be a delusion. Yet even if he were dying, even if this was a cruel game being played by capricious gods to torment him in his last moments, it was a game he'd play to win.

You wanted to know what you could do? Let's see if you can do more.

He tapped the lasers and drew a line from them to another of the Dulls. The dots again solidified, this time into a scarlet line. It pulsed and the target vanished. He tried to link another Dull with the lasers, but the line wouldn't reach, so he willed himself closer, striding among the stars. He connected the two points and the Dull winked out.

The Dulls shifted. A pair broke off and headed in his direction. He watched as lines of dots reached out toward him. Greg dove forward and rolled, as if playing in the ocean. The lines stabbed past him, then he kicked, bringing himself up and over. He dove down again, linked one Dull with the lasers. The red line pulsed, then Greg broke off and rolled to the right, allowing more laser light to flash by.

The sensation of swimming evaporated. Greg imagined himself a bird, a raptor, a peregrine falcon. He came up on a wing-tip, holding there for a second, before a quick beat dropped him a Dull's tail. He gave that Dull a taste of the Meson Cannon, then came up again.

There. A half-dozen Dulls split into pairs as a lone Shrike streaked in to face them. The Shrike fired all eight of its Baryon Missiles, killing two Dulls and scattering the others into evasive maneuvers. The missiles, while fast, did have a limited amount of fuel. If a pilot could evade long enough—and a good pilot in a Dull could break quickly, forcing the missile to shoot past before acquiring a target lock again—the missile would flame out.

The Shrike boiled into the mix and pursued the Dulls aggressively. *Has to be Colonel Clark.* Greg willed himself forward, pressing ahead with all speed. As he approached, the lines and curves became mathematical formulae describing flight paths and velocity. He recognized them for what they were, but his knowledge pushed past that. They were probability equations, pulling together all the data about the Dulls' known performance, what the sensors had gathered concerning their *real* performance, and adding in the tendencies and biases exhibited by the pilots. Ultra-violet sheets curled out, then contracted into ribbons which wove together, finally resolving themselves into solid blue threads as the fighters and pilots pursued Colonel Clark.

Greg spoke, knowing his voice was going out over TacOne. "Tiger Lead, heading 235 point 337, throttle to 57.3 on my mark, then turn to 191 point 024 at full. Do you copy?"

* * *

Hearing Greg Allen's voice, distant and dreamy, completely devoid of emotion, sent a shiver through Nick Clark. He'd have ignored Greg, save for a confident note of sincerity coming through the words, *and* the fact that four Dulls had decided to vape him.

"I copy." Nick brought the Shrike up on its left wing and nosed down, on a course heading toward the *Shan-chey*. Angry red bolts shot past and hissed against his rear shields. "On your mark, Nine."

"Mark."

Nick chopped the throttle back and nosed up while still turning hard to port. Once he hit the new course, he punched the throttle forward. He caught the golden flash of an explosion and two of the Dulls disappeared from his combat HUD.

Had to have been Baryon Missiles, but hitting them that way isn't possible. Still, he couldn't deny what must have happened. *Nor can I dwell on it.*

Nick rolled up and over, then came around and vectored in on one of the last two rocket-packing Dulls. He came in hot, then hit rudder, tracking his nose back along the Dull's flight path. The Dull pilot, feeling pursuit, had reversed his throttle. For a heartbeat—which was all Nick needed—the Dull hung in space.

Nick's quad blast punched through shields and armor, spraying hot metal slag back through the cockpit. Whatever it was flying the thing died fast, then the burning liquid remains got sucked out into space.

Nick located the last Dull on his HUD, but before he could come around, three Shrikes shot past him. One pounced eagerly—he took that to be the Russian in Tiger Eleven; and Sun Lan maintained her position as his wing. The other Shrike headed down toward the Haxadissi shuttle, helping Major Taine drive off the last of the ambushers.

Nick studied his HUD for signs of Greg Allen's Shrike, but sensors picked up nothing matching the power or performance profile of a fighter. "Nomad, backtrack the Baryon Missile trajectory to point of origin. Paint it in gold."

Two parallel lines traced down toward Haxad Four. Nick brought himself around on a course intersecting their starting point. As his Shrike streaked toward it, his sensors picked up an unidentifiable mass with no discernible power reading, but that didn't kill his hope. Survival equipment functioned on its own power supply, heavily shielded to avoid detection, so until he got close enough to be sure, he'd believe Greg Allen still lived.

No dying on me, Allen. It would make your father happy, and that's not on my to-do list. What Greg done to make the shot was, to the best of Nick's knowledge, beyond the ability of any pilot in the 301st—and quite probably any pilot flying. The Baryon Missile had been launched from the outer edge of their range. Greg had launched them in passive mode, using no targeting computers. To avoid warning the targets, the missiles had been programmed to reach a point in space and detonate. No course correction in flight, no pursuit. Hitting the Dulls was the equivalent of a man throwing a pebble to hit another pebble ten kilometers down range.

And he had me lead them right to where they needed to be—but figuring all that out would take hours and need a lot more data than he had available. Wouldn't it.

Before Nick could even begin to consider the implications of what Greg had done, his HUD identified Greg's battered Shrike. He swooped down, flying close enough to identify what was left of the Shrike. Most of the tail had been shot off and the right wing badly mangled, but the cockpit looked intact. On his comms monitor, however, Tiger Nine had greyed out as unresponsive.

Still, as he brought his Shrike up beside Tiger Nine, Nick smiled. His sensors picked up a trace of the survival gear's energy signature. He couldn't see inside because the canopy had darkened as a means of keeping it cool and limiting solar radiation exposure.

Yes. Nick touched the black and white image on his auxiliary monitor. *We're bringing boys back, and that's what's important.*

Nick tapped the *Unity*'s comms tab. "Unity, we need a medical recovery for Tiger Nine. On my position. As fast as you can."

"Confirmed, Tiger Lead. Estimated time of arrival five minutes."

"Understood, Unity." Nick nodded, glancing over at the Shrike's cockpit. "Vych's right, you served well. I think I'm going to need you to serve even better in the future."

— 8 —

Exactly how he managed to contain his fury with the Haxadissi Ambassador's spokesnake Nick wasn't exactly certain. The *Shan-chey* had suffered minor damage during the ambush, and then had grafted itself onto the *Unity*'s hull. The Haxadis ship could have opened a portal between the vessels to allow for a face-to-face meeting, but claimed the damage they'd suffered impaired their ability to do so.

Instead the spokesnake had projected a golden hologram of himself into Nick's office. The image had been bright enough to half-blind Nick, and yet transparent enough to let him look through it at the ruins of Greg Allen's Shrike. Nick focused on the ruined spacefighter and let Vych carry the conversation. They conducted it throughly in political speak which wandered close to the Haxadissi asking for an apology for allowing any damage at all to be done to the *Shan-chey* and yet steering well clear of anything that might be construed as being even vaguely grateful.

Vych handled it all deftly and ended the conversation before Nick's brains geysered up through his skull. He forced himself to smile as the golden serpentine ghost evaporated.

Nick glanced at Vych. "I gotta ask, what did he look like to you? To me he was just a fat guy in a snake suit, sitting on a steaming pile of ..."

"Nicholas!" The Qian shook her head. "I understand your dissatisfaction, but this is a delicate situation."

"Oh, I get that, and I'm still expecting blowback." Nick raked fingers through his hair. "Just tell me one thing, okay? Did they fail to obey the order to return to Haxad Four because they truly didn't understand it, or because the Ambassador was feeling stubborn, or because they just didn't want to take orders from primates like the ones they hunt for sport?"

"I believe, Nicholas, you have drawn a conclusion which will not be shaken no matter what I say to you." Vych strode slowly and effortlessly into the space the hologram had just vacated. Lights played solemnly beneath her flesh and across her face. "The facts really do not matter, as this incident will not exist in any official archive."

Nick stood, frowning. "I don't like *that* either. I get the reasons, but I don't like it." That the attack had come so deep in Qian Commonwealth space—and at the time where the *Shan-chey* would be most vulnerable—exposed a host of problems. The timing suggested that the Ambassador's political rivals had informed the assassins about the journey. *Or political allies decided to sacrifice her to prove the worthlessness of humans.* And while everyone *knew* enemy strikes deep within the Commonwealth were *possible*, they much preferred *potential* problems to *ugly* reality.

He looked up at Vych. "I need the sensor data and reconstruction of the battle so I can figure out what we did wrong and right."

"My superiors will allow me to scrub the data and use it for the basis of a theoretical exercise. Unless we find the remains of Tiger Two's Shrike, we will only be able to infer what he did from long range data. Likewise, of course, we lost the data from Tiger Nine, as his Nomad was unrecoverable."

Nick came around the desk and stared out the window at the battered hulk of Allen's Shrike. "What happened to him?"

Blue and green pinpoints swirled over the forehead of her reflection in the glass. "Shin reports that Captain Allen is in no immediate danger and will recover fully."

He glanced back over his shoulder. "I know there are things you won't tell me, and things you're not supposed to tell me. But you have to remember, I flew with the recovery ship. I landed right beside it, and I was the first one there when Shin cracked the cockpit. I saw his right hand ..."

Nick shivered involuntarily. Allen's forearm had turned an icy blue. It looked as if water had burst all the seams of his glove and had frozen solid over the stick. Only when flighttechs had connected auxiliary power cables to the Shrike, and Shin had attached several sensor patches to Allen's neck, head and chest, did the ice melt and flow back into flaccid simulacrum of an arm and hand.

Vych rested her hand on Nick's shoulder. "I tell you truthfully that I do not know what happened. I know of no other situation with a similar manifestation. We have technicians pouring over what data we have, trying to make sense of it. I will give you answers as soon as I have them."

He turned his back to the flight deck, letting her hand trail down until it rested over his heart. "I've looked at his records. No way could he have made the calculations to deadhead those missiles into the Dulls. And what he did to shield the *Shan-chey* ... I mean, it was pure Gregory Allen to order Major Taine to stay with the shuttle while he went off to engage a dozen Dulls all by himself...."

"Much as you did."

"I knew what I was doing." Nick shook his head. "For Gregory Allen to put himself where he was, when he was, and to do the things he did to deal with that first salvo; that wasn't right. I don't think he was suicidal. I don't get that in him at all, but need to know what was going on. I have to know who I'm dealing with."

Vych smiled broadly, which took an effort since the Qian tended to be closed with their emotions. "Perhaps the accident changed him."

"Maybe. I'll have to keep an eye on him. It's not that I mind what he did; I just want to know who I have flying with me, and what I can trust him to do."

* * *

The first thing Greg Allen noticed upon waking was that his fingers burned as if they'd been frostbitten. He tried to shut the sensation off, but couldn't. He glanced at where his right arm lay hidden under a sheet and commanded his fingers to move. They did, but sluggishly, and the burning increased.

Jiro Yamashita, seated in an uncomfortable chair over by the wall, shifted and stretched. "I wanted to get to you before any of them did."

"Them?"

Jiro looked side to side. "I don't know much of anything about what happened, and I've been told I'll never be able to write up what I do know. Doesn't mean I don't want to know. I need you to tell me what happened out there."

"I haven't been debriefed yet. I don't know what I can and cannot say." Greg eased himself back and up so he could sit against the headboard. "I probably shouldn't be talking to you at all."

"You honestly think that if you knew something they didn't want me to know that they'd have allowed me to be here when you woke up?"

That's an interesting point. Greg shrugged. "I guess they don't think I know anything they don't know."

"So, what happened out there?"

"I really don't think discussing operational details with you is something I should be doing."

Jiro held up his hands. "Okay, let's do it this way. Seven of you go out to guide a shuttle in here. The shuttle gets surprised. One Shrike doesn't come back. The rest are shot up. Word has it that the colonel killed seven, you got six. You're both aces in a day. Major Taine had four. The remaining seven got split amongst the other four."

Greg's stomach tightened. "Who didn't come back?"

"Lieutenant Fields. She got two, but one unloaded two H-rocks into her."

Maddie Fields' smiling face floated before Greg's mind's-eye. Blonde with brown eyes, resident of London, she'd seemed the most enthused about heading out to the stars. *Now she'll be among them forever.* Something in the back of his mind told him that Haxad Four was so far from Earth, that the light that had shined on her Shrike wouldn't reach her home for another three centuries. *Will anyone still remember her when it does?*

Greg ran his good hand over his jaw. "I wonder if they will let us record condolence messages to her family?" Jiro's expression soured, so Greg quickly amended his comment. "I wonder if they'll actually send on the messages they let us record."

"So, what happened out there, Captain?"

"I think you have the story, Mr. Yamashita." Greg shrugged, his mouth sour. "We got jumped and fought our way out of the ambush."

"Yeah, I got that much. And I've seen what's left of your Shrike. How in hell did you get six kills in that thing?"

"I don't know."

"What?"

Greg met his gaze. "I don't know. I was tasked with protecting the shuttle. That's what I did. I don't remember ..."

Jiro stood. "No, you don't get away with that."

"With what?"

"Fog of war. Amnesia. 'It all happened so fast.' Not you." Jiro folded his arms over his chest. "You've always been good for a war story or two, and data backs you up. What happened?"

Greg shook his head. What he remembered of the battle seemed like a dream, and one he was content forgetting. He remembered dropping in front of the *Shan-chey* to shield it, but after he blacked out, or when he came to, that couldn't have been *real.* He wasn't in his Shrike. He wasn't firing lasers or piloting his fighter. He wasn't capable of doing it.

And yet, even as he sought to deny what he remembered, it rang true for him. He realized that when he stared at his arm beneath the sheet, he was expecting to see diagnostic data floating in the air above it. What he'd seen in the latter half of the battle had been unusual and even abnormal, but it had also felt right and welcoming, if not familiar.

And yet to tell him everything, to tell anyone anything about what I saw and thought I did, that would get me grounded, returned to Earth and buried in some asylum; drugged and silenced.

"I'm sorry to disappoint you, Mr. Yamashita, but I have no war stories." He gave the journalist a rueful smile. "I do, however, appreciate your interest in my recovery."

Jiro's eyes narrowed. "Don't think for a moment I'm buying this, Captain Allen. I'm not. This isn't you. I studied you. I know you. A leopard can't change his spots."

"Perhaps that's where you're wrong." Greg's smile grew. "Not about leopard, but about identifying me as one. You see, out here, I'm a tiger. I have no spots to change."

"Really?" Jiro Yamashita arched an eyebrow and studied Greg's face for a moment. "Maybe I'm asking the wrong question, then."

"What would the right one be?"

"Are you any closer to figuring out why you're here?"

Greg glanced down slipping his artificial hand from beneath the sheets. It appeared normal, but wasn't. *Maybe that's what I am, something that appears normal, but isn't. Maybe I'm out here so I have fewer people to hurt when I find out what I truly am.*

Jiro folded arms across his chest. "Pregnant pause there, Captain Allen."

"Just making sure I tell the truth." Greg smiled slowly. "I don't know exactly why I'm here, but part it would appear to be to keep some people alive. For now, that will do me just fine."

For More About the Authors

Aaron Allston: AaronAllston.com

Kevin J. Anderson: WordFire.com

Loren L. Coleman: LorenLColeman.com

B.V. Larson: BVLarson.com

Michael A. Stackpole: Stormwolf.com